"The child will be fully in your charge, Miss Randolph. While I shall provide all that is needed for its care, I will have no personal contact with it. Is that clear?"

Sarah lifted her chin and met Clayton Bainbridge's gaze with her own. "Your *words*… yes. But—"

"There is no *but*, Miss Randolph. Those are the special conditions of your employment. I realize you will require some personal time. The maid Lucy will sit with the child while she naps in the afternoon. And your evenings will be free. Other than that, you will spend all of your time with the child. Do you wish to accept the position?"

Incredible! The man might as well be a marble statue. Had Clayton Bainbridge no feelings? An image of the sweet toddler sleeping upstairs flashed into her head. "Yes, Mr. Bainbridge, I accept the position. I must, sir. Because your *daughter* is a little girl, not an *it*."

Sarah squared her shoulders, whirled away from the look of astonishment on Clayton Bainbridge's face and swept from the room.

Books by Dorothy Clark

Love Inspired Historical

Family of the Heart

Love Inspired

Hosea's Bride
Lessons from the Heart

Steeple Hill

Beauty for Ashes
Joy for Mourning

DOROTHY CLARK

Critically acclaimed, award-winning author Dorothy Clark is a creative person. She lives in a home she designed and helped her husband build (she swings a mean hammer!) with the able assistance of their three children. She also designs and helps her husband build furniture. When she is not thus engaged, she can be found cheering her grandchildren on at various sports events, or furiously taking notes about possible settings for future novels as she and her husband travel throughout the United States and Canada. Dorothy believes in God, love, family and happy endings, which explains why she feels so at home writing her stories for Steeple Hill. Dorothy enjoys hearing from her readers, and may be contacted at dorothyjclark@hotmail.com.

DOROTHY CLARK

Family of the Heart

Steeple
Hill®

Published by Steeple Hill Books™

If you purchased this book without a cover you should be aware
that this book is stolen property. It was reported as "unsold and
destroyed" to the publisher, and neither the author nor the
publisher has received any payment for this "stripped book."

STEEPLE HILL BOOKS

Steeple
Hill®

ISBN-13: 978-0-373-82795-4
ISBN-10:   0-373-82795-4

FAMILY OF THE HEART

Copyright © 2008 by Dorothy Clark

All rights reserved. Except for use in any review, the reproduction
or utilization of this work in whole or in part in any form by any
electronic, mechanical or other means, now known or hereafter
invented, including xerography, photocopying and recording, or in
any information storage or retrieval system, is forbidden without
the written permission of the editorial office, Steeple Hill Books,
233 Broadway, New York, NY 10279 U.S.A.

This is a work of fiction. Names, characters, places and incidents are
either the product of the author's imagination or are used fictitiously, and
any resemblance to actual persons, living or dead, business establishments,
events or locales is entirely coincidental.

This edition published by arrangement with Steeple Hill Books.

® and TM are trademarks of Steeple Hill Books, used under license.
Trademarks indicated with ® are registered in the United States Patent
and Trademark Office, the Canadian Trade Marks Office and in other
countries.

www.SteepleHill.com

Printed in U.S.A.

For thou wilt light my candle: the Lord my God
will enlighten my darkness.
—*Psalms* 18:28

This book is dedicated with boundless gratitude to my extremely talented writer friend and critique partner, Sam Pakan, who read every chapter (though there is not a fistfight or dead body in any of them), encouraged me and prayed for me when "life" happened and interfered with my writing time, and stuck with me through the last two weeks of my writing marathon though he was racing to meet his own book deadline. You sure know how to go the "second mile," cowboy. Thank you.

"Commit thy works unto the Lord, and thy thoughts shall be established."

Your word is truth. Thank You, Jesus.
To You be the glory.

Chapter One

Cincinnati
April, 1838

The hired carriage climbed over the break of the hill and rolled to a stop. Sarah Randolph grabbed for the hold strap as the rig leaned to one side then quickly righted itself when the driver stepped off onto the ground. A moment later the door opened and the driver peered inside. "This is it, miss. This is Stony Point."

Every nerve in her stomach fluttered to life. For one panicked moment Sarah wished she were back at the hotel with Ellen to tend her, but only for a moment. She needed something to do. Something to help her through the pain of Aaron's death. Somewhere to get away from the tormenting memories of him that haunted the streets of Philadelphia. And this position as a nanny answered those needs.

Sarah lifted her chin in renewed determination and climbed from the carriage. A worm of worry wriggled through her as she watched the driver walk around to the back and unbuckle the straps holding her trunk in place. She'd brought only the plainest, most serviceable of her day dresses, but none of her gowns were really appropriate for a nanny. If only there had been time to obtain more suitable attire.

Sarah let out a sigh and closed her mind to the concern. It was of no matter now—her gowns would simply have to do. She glanced down, shook out her long bottle-green velvet skirt, smoothed down the tab-cut leaves at the waist edge of her matching spencer, then lifted her head and appraised the house in front of her. It was well named. The rectangular stone house, with its set-back kitchen ell, sat square in the middle of the point of land that forced the road to curve.

It was an attractive house. Not large, compared to the homes of the elite of Philadelphia, but two stories of generous and pleasing proportion. And, though there was nothing ornate or fancy about the place, it had charm. Shutters, painted the dark green of the pines on the hillside, embraced the home's symmetrically placed multipaned windows and framed its solid wood-plank front door. Ivy spread clinging arms in profuse abandon on the front and climbed the gable end, stretching a few tentacles toward the wood shingles of the roof.

"Ready, miss." The driver, holding her large trunk balanced on one beefy shoulder, appeared beside her.

Sarah stepped back, giving him room to open the gate sandwiched between the two lamp-topped stone pillars that anchored the low stone walls enclosing the home's front yard. She ignored the *maaaa* of one of the sheep grazing on the lawn and followed him up the slate walk. Hope quickened her pulse. Her new life was starting.

Surely tending a toddler would keep her too busy to dwell on the past, to remember the loss of her dream of being Aaron's wife. Surely it would fill the emptiness and make the pain ease. *Oh, if only the pain would ease.*

The driver banged the brass knocker against the plate on the front door, and Sarah straightened her back and curved her lips into a smile. Everything would be better now. Soon, everything would be better.

The solid wood door opened. A stout woman stepped forward and stood centered in the frame. She looked at the driver, noted the trunk he carried and dipped her head toward the left. "Take that o'er t' the side door. Quincy'll let you in." She shifted her gaze. Surprise, then doubt swept over her face. "You *are* the new nanny?"

Sarah felt her smile slip away at the woman's tone. She pasted it firmly back in place and nodded. "Yes. I am—"

"Late! We expected you this morning." The woman stepped aside and waved a pudgy arm toward the interior of the house. "Don't stand there, come in, come in!"

Sarah hesitated a moment, debating the wisdom in pursuing her decision to accept the position. But the challenge was exactly what she needed. And she'd never had a problem getting along with her family's servants. Perhaps the housekeeper was simply feeling the need to establish her authority. She squared her shoulders, climbed the three stone steps and crossed the small stoop. A child's unhappy wails fell on her ears as she entered the small entry.

The woman closed the door and gave a brief nod toward the stairs. "'Tis that we've been sufferin' all day! The little miss is cryin' an' in no mood to be quieted. And Mr. Bainbridge is—" Her words came to an abrupt halt as a door on their left flew open.

"Eldora! Can Lucy not *stop* the child from cry—"

Sarah stiffened as the man in the doorway snapped off his words and swiveled his head her direction. He swept an assessing gaze over her, and his dark-brown brows lowered in a frown. "I was not aware we had a visitor." He made a small, polite bow in her direction. "Forgive me my outburst, Miss…er…"

"Randolph—Miss Sarah Randolph, of Philadelphia."

The man's brows shot skyward. "*You* are the new nanny?" He skimmed another gaze over her. Doubt flashed into his eyes. The frown deepened.

The man's reaction rasped against her tense nerves. Was he going to judge her on appearance only? Did he deem that stylish clothes meant she could not care for a child? Sarah's back stiffened. She gave him a cool nod. "I am. And it sounds as if I am sorely needed." She lifted a meaningful glance toward the top of the stairs. The toddler's cries were gaining in volume.

"Indeed." The man gave her a piercing look. "You seem confident of your abilities."

"And you seem highly dubious of them." Sarah lifted her chin and looked right back. "I would not have written requesting to be considered for the position of nanny were I not competent to handle the child."

The man's eyes darkened. "It will take more than words to convince me of that, Miss Randolph. Competency is a thing that is proven, not—" he winced as a loud wail echoed down the stairs "—declared." His face tightened. "And the first test of yours will begin now. I shall postpone your interview until later this evening. Please see to the child immediately. It's impossible for me to work in this din." Her prospective employer shifted his gaze back to the stout woman. "Mrs. Quincy, show Miss Randolph to the nursery. Immediately!" He stepped back into the room behind him and closed the door.

"This way, Miss Randolph." The hem of the house-keeper's long, gray skirt swished back and forth as she turned and headed toward the stairs.

Can Lucy not stop the child? The man's words were still ringing a warning alarm in her head. Sarah shot a quick glance at the closed door beside her. What sort of man called his daughter *the child?* A tiny frisson of apprehension tingled through her. Perhaps this nanny position would not be as easy as she expected. But she could always go home. She hugged the comfort of that thought close, lifted her long skirts slightly and followed Mrs. Quincy up the stairs.

"Here we are." Mrs. Quincy opened a door at the end of a short hallway.

Sarah stepped forward into a well-furnished, sunny nursery. At least, that was her initial impression. She hadn't time for more with her attention centered on the squalling, squirming toddler trying to twist free of the grip of the young maid sitting in a rocking chair. The maid rocked furiously, jiggling the toddler up and down and making soothing noises.

Sarah froze. Mrs. Quincy stepped forward and looked at her in demand. The maid—Lucy was it?—looked at her in relief and stood to her feet. Oh, dear! They expected her to— What? Sarah's stomach flopped. Her first thought was to turn about, run down the stairs and not stop until she reached the hotel where Ellen awaited her instructions. Perhaps they would both be making the journey back to Philadelphia. But the unhappiness apparent in the toddler's cries held her frozen in place. Perhaps if she could get the child's attention… She moved closer and leaned down to place her hand on the toddler's back. "Hello, little one. I'm your new nanny."

The child didn't even look at her, only squalled louder and squirmed harder. What now? An idea popped into her head. An absolutely absurd idea—but she had nothing to lose. Sarah undid the satin ties of her bonnet and tossed it on the rocking chair, opened her mouth and let out a wail that made both Mrs. Quincy and Lucy jump. The toddler stopped squirming and crying and stared up at her out of big blue eyes. *It worked!*

"There now, that's better." Sarah spoke softly, but firmly. She lifted the startled toddler out of Lucy's arms and started toward the window in the wall on the opposite side of the room. She had no idea what next to do, but movement seemed a good idea. She glanced at the child in her arms and burst out laughing. The little girl was staring at her as if she didn't know what to think of her. That, too, seemed a good thing. "And do you have a name, little one?"

"Nora. Nora Blessing Bainbridge." Mrs. Quincy's answer was followed by the click of the door opening and closing.

Sarah glanced over her shoulder. The room was empty. She looked back at the toddler. "Well, Nora Blessing Bainbridge, it seems you and I are on our own." The child's lips quivered, pulled down at the corners. She placed her tiny hands against Sarah's chest and pushed. "Except for that squirrel. Look!"

Sarah quickly turned Nora so she faced outward, holding her so Nora's small back rested against her chest. "See?" She pointed at a large gray squirrel sitting on a branch of the tree outside the window, nibbling on some sort of bud. The distraction worked. The toddler's tensed muscles relaxed. She stared at the squirrel, caught a broken breath, then another, stuck her thumb in her mouth and began sucking. Her little legs, dangling over Sarah's supporting arm, stilled their kicking.

Thank goodness for the squirrel! Sarah swayed side to side, humming softly, ignoring the child except for an occasional downward glance. After a few minutes, Nora's eyelids drooped, opened, drooped again. A moment later her little head dropped forward until her chin rested on her chest.

Sarah looked down and smiled. Nora had lost her battle against sleep. The toddler's light-brown eyelashes rested on her round rosy cheeks and her little mouth was relaxed, no longer sucking at the tiny thumb. She looked adorable…asleep. Now, if only she could keep her that way until she could collect herself.

Sarah continued to sway and hum as she turned and scanned the room. A cherrywood crib with turned spindles and a white, crocheted canopy stood against the far wall. She carried Nora over, laid her on the blanket-covered down mattress and pulled the woven coverlet over her. She held her breath and stood poised, waiting… Little Nora blinked her eyes, sucked on her thumb and slept on.

Sarah let out a long sigh of relief and glanced around the room. Time to familiarize herself. She stripped off her gloves and tossed them on the rocker with her bonnet, tiptoed to a large, handsomely carved wardrobe and pulled open the double doors. Small dresses, aprons and coats with matching bonnets hung in colorful array on the right side. Little shoes and slippers marched beneath and, on the left, undergarments filled drawers. She noted the fine workmanship on Nora's clothes, shut the wardrobe doors and looked around the room. Shelves, full of books, toys and stuffed animals, filled the alcove formed by the stone fireplace. An exquisitely detailed dollhouse sat beneath a window. A child-size table, set for a tea party, its matching chairs holding the attending dolls, sat in front of the shelves.

Sarah smiled at the evidence of the father's love for his daughter. Obviously, that twinge of warning she had felt on meeting the man was wrong. She had simply misinterpreted his perturbation over Nora's unhappy cries. Thankfully, she had been able to quiet the child. She skirted the chair on the hearth and opened a door onto a dressing room. Sight of the pipe traveling along the stone wall to the wash basin and tub brought a rush of relief. Running water! She had been prepared to give up that luxury. It was wonderful to know that sacrifice wouldn't be required.

She glanced back to check on Nora, moved to another door and peeked inside. A cool draft flowed out of the dark room. Sarah shivered and stepped back, hesitant to enter the gloomy space. There was enough darkness in her life. She pulled the door closed—froze—opened it again. Yes. That was *her* trunk sitting on the rug of braided rags on the wide plank floor.

So this dismal place was to be her bedroom. Disappointment morphed into the barely controlled despair that was always with her. Why had she been so foolish as to think taking this position as nanny would help her over her grief? She should go home where she had every luxury, where she was cosseted and pampered, and…and *wretched*.

Unwanted memories impelled Sarah into the room. Her gaze skittered from the stone fireplace centered on the interior paneled wall, to a writing desk and chair, to the four-poster bed situated between two shuttered windows.

She rushed forward, threw open the shutters and tugged up the bottom sashes. Light and warmth flooded into the room. The scent of lilacs floated in on a gentle breeze.

The horrid tightness in her throat and chest eased. Sarah lifted her face to the waning sunshine and took a deep breath. The tears that had been so close to flowing receded. Another battle won.

The victory gave her courage. Sarah marched to her trunk, unfastened the hasp and lifted the lid. She needed to change out of her travel outfit before Nora's father summoned her. A sigh escaped. How she longed for Ellen. The woman had been her confidante as well as her personal maid since she outgrew her own nanny. She looked down at the trunk's contents, and the victory she had won dissolved. She touched the cool silk fabric of the top dress and tears flooded her eyes. The gown had been designed for her to wear on her honeymoon. She should be aboard ship with Aaron and halfway around the world right now. A sob caught in her throat.

Sarah wrenched her thoughts from what should have been, wiped the tears from her face and lifted out the top dress. She shook out the blue and white silk gown, held it up and gave it a critical once-over, focusing all her attention on choosing an appropriate gown. Were the four flounces that decorated the bottom of the skirt too fancy? Would the gold, watered taffeta with the rolled silk ribbon trim be a better choice? What did one wear to an interview with an employer?

Clayton Bainbridge stared at Sarah Randolph. She was unlike any nanny he had ever seen. Her gown was the equal of those his wife had owned—and there was certainly nothing subservient in her manner. Indeed, her demeanor was more that of a guest than of a woman being interviewed for a position. It had him a little out of kilter. As did her latest revelation. He frowned down at her. "So you are telling me you have no actual experience as a nanny."

"That is correct. However, as I wrote in my letter, I have abundant experience in caring for children." She smiled up at him. "My aunt has an orphanage and I often helped with the babies and small children. She is my reference." She handed him a sealed letter.

"I see." Clayton scowled at the letter, tapped it against his palm. *He would have to start the search for a nanny for the child all over again!* He tossed the unopened letter on the table beside him. "I'm afraid you have made a long journey in vain, Miss Randolph. A reference from a family member is unacceptable."

"Laina Allen may be my aunt, Mr. Bainbridge, but I assure you, she is a woman of great integrity. She is highly respected in Philadelphia—as are all members of my family. You can trust her word."

Sarah Randolph's stiff posture and the gold sparks in her brown eyes belied the coolness of her voice. Clayton hesitated, then yielded to an inner prompting, picked up the letter and broke the seal. Silence, invaded only by the crackle of the fire that had been started to ward off the chill of the evening air, settled around them as he read.

"Your aunt recommends you highly as one skilled in caring for toddlers and young children." Clayton folded the letter, slipped it in his jacket pocket and fastened his gaze on Sarah. She looked regal, with her erect posture, lifted chin and light-brown hair swept high on the crown of her head. And wealthy. That gold gown she wore would cost more than his month's wages. Why had she applied for the post of nanny?

Clayton frowned, continued his assessment. It was certain Sarah Randolph had never done a day's work. Her hands were soft and white, the nails long and neatly shaped. And her face was the face of a pampered woman. He drifted his gaze over the small lifted chin, narrow nose and shapely high cheekbones to the brown eyes under delicately arched light-brown brows. He stiffened. There was a challenge in those eyes. And something else. Pain. He recognized it easily. He should. He saw it his own eyes every morning when he shaved.

Clayton averted his gaze. Sarah Randolph was hurting, vulnerable, despite the bravado of that lifted chin. But she had courage. That was apparent. She was not yielding to her pain. She seemed to be a fighter. Perhaps she was suitable for the post in spite of her delicate, pampered appearance. He cleared his throat. "I believe you aptly demonstrated the skill of which your aunt speaks by quickly silencing the child's cries on your arrival. Because of that, Miss Randolph, the position is yours—should you still wish it after learning of your duties and responsibilities. They exceed the normal ones." He turned and walked to the hearth, giving her time to absorb that information.

The silence settled around them again.

Sarah stared at Clayton Bainbridge's back. He'd done it again. He'd referred to Nora as "the child." And what did "They exceed the normal duties" mean? Her stomach quivered, tightened.

"Should you stay, Miss Randolph, the child will be fully in your charge. While I shall provide all that is needed for its care, I will have no personal contact with it. Is that clear?"

Shock held her mute.

He pivoted to face her. "Do you understand?"

Sarah found her voice hiding behind a huge lump of anger in her throat. She lifted her chin and met his gaze full with her own. "Your *words*...yes. But—"

"There is no *but,* Miss Randolph. Those are the special conditions of your employment. I realize you will require some personal time, and *that* need will be met by having Lucy sit with the child while she naps in the afternoon. And, of course, your evenings will be free. Other than that, you will spend all of your time with the child. Your wages will, of course, reflect the added responsibility. Do you wish to accept the position?"

Incredible! Sarah clasped her hands in her lap to keep from reaching out and pinching Clayton Bainbridge to find out if he was flesh and blood. The man might as well be a marble statue. His face was expressionless, his voice void of emotion. Had he no feelings? An image of the toddler sleeping upstairs flashed into her head. "Yes, Mr. Randolph, I accept the position." She fought the anger that had brought her to her feet, lost the battle and gave voice to the words clamoring to be spoken. "I must, sir. Because your *daughter* is a little girl, not an *it.*"

Sarah squared her shoulders, whirled away from the look of astonishment on Clayton Bainbridge's face and swept from the room.

Chapter Two

He would dismiss her first thing in the morning! Clayton stormed into his bedroom, removed his jacket and threw it onto the chair beside the window. His fingers worked at the buttons on his waistcoat as his long strides ate up the distance to the highboy on the other side of the room.

Your daughter is a little girl, not an it!

And he had felt sorry for her. Ha! His sympathy had certainly been misplaced. How dare that woman offer him such a rebuke! Clayton grabbed the silver fob dangling from his waistcoat pocket, jerked his watch free, dropped it into one of the small drawers, pivoted and paced back toward the window.

And for her to walk out of the room and leave him standing there like…like some servant! He shrugged out of the vest and yanked his cravat free. And what did he do? Nothing! Shock had kept him frozen in place. By the time he'd made his feet move, she had disappeared up the stairs. Well, he was not shocked now. And in the morning he would tell Miss Sarah Randolph she was completely unsuited for the nanny position, give her a stipend for her

time and have Quincy arrange for her transportation back
to Philadelphia.

Because she spoke the truth?

The voice in his head stayed his hand, cooled his anger.
Clayton frowned. He refused to consider that question.
What did Miss Sarah Randolph know of his truth?
Nothing. And, truth or not, she had overstepped her place
in speaking it.

Clayton tossed the vest and cravat on top of his jacket
and sat in the chair to remove his shoes. Finding another
nanny took so much *time*. And meanwhile chaos would
again reign in the household. For some reason Lucy was
unable to keep the child from crying all day. And the first
nanny had not been that successful at it, either. But at least
she had known her place.

Clayton scowled, tugged a shoe off, dropped it to the
floor and wiggled his freed toes, weighing the situation in
the light of that last thought. Perhaps he should give Sarah
Randolph another chance. Perhaps that outburst was only
because she didn't yet fully realize what her position was.
Her erect posture and lifted chin as she faced him down,
proved she wasn't accustomed to servitude. No, Sarah
Randolph was a lady. Every inch of her. A *beautiful* lady.
So why was she here?

Clayton rested his elbows on his knees and stared down
at the floor. The anomaly was intriguing. It was obvious
Miss Randolph was not impoverished. And it could not be
a case of familial division—she had spoken well of her
family, and they of her. At least in the letter. Of course
there was the matter of her temper.

A vision of Sarah's face, brown eyes flashing, burst into
his head. She *was* spirited. And beautiful. Clayton's face
tightened. He grabbed the shoe he had removed, tugged it

back on and lunged out of the chair. Bed could wait. Right
now he would go to his study and work on his progress
report of the needed repairs on the canal locks here in Cincinnati. And on the estimated repairs required on the rest
of the southern section of the Miami Canal. He was due
to report to the commissioners next week. And the plans
had to be perfected, as well. An hour or two spent staring
at blueprints would drive away that unwelcome image.

Sarah looked toward the foot of the bed. Her trunk sat
there…waiting. She did not dare pack the few items she
had taken out for fear of waking little Nora. It would have
to wait until morning—or until an angry fist pounded on
her door and Mr. Bainbridge told her she was dismissed.
She sighed and looked around the bedroom. She had held
her post as nanny for what…a few hours? Well, it was her
own fault. She should have controlled her temper. But—

No buts! It was too late for buts. Too late to take back
her outburst. And too late to leave this house tonight. Sarah
removed her silk gown, hung it in the cupboard beside the
fireplace and tugged the soft comfort of an embroidered
cotton nightgown over her head. She pushed her feet into
her warm, fur-trimmed slippers and shoved her arms into
the sleeves of her quilted cotton dressing gown.

What had caused her to act in such an unaccustomed
way? She had gained nothing by giving vent to her outrage
over Clayton Bainbridge's callus attitude toward his
daughter. Except for the momentary satisfaction of that
look of utter astonishment on his face. Her lips curved at
the memory of his widened deep-blue eyes and raised,
thick, dark-brown brows, the flare of the nostrils on his
long, masculine nose. That had been a gratifying moment.
Of course, an instant later anger had replaced the aston-

ishment. His brows had lowered, his eyes had darkened and the full lower lip of his mouth had thinned to match the top one. And that square jaw of his! Gracious! It had firmed to the appearance of granite. No, her outburst had done nothing to help little Nora. Or herself.

Sarah caught her breath at a sudden onrush of memories, fastened the ties at the neck of her dressing gown and hurried into the nursery. The oil lamp she had left burning with its wick turned low warmed the moon-light pouring in the windows to a soft gold. Tears welled into her eyes as she straightened the coverlet that had become twisted when Nora turned over. She had thought by now she and Aaron might be expecting a child of their own. The tears overflowed. She brushed them away, smoothed a silky golden curl off the toddler's cheek and, unable to stop herself, bent and kissed the soft smooth skin. Nora stirred, her little lips worked as she sucked on her thumb, went still again.

Sarah's heart melted. She resisted the urge to lift the little girl into her arms and cradle her close to her pain-fully tight chest. The hem of her dressing gown whispered against the wide planks of the floor as she walked back to her own room. What was *wrong* with Clayton Bainbridge? How could he not want anything to do with his own child? How could he not love her?

Sarah glanced at her trunk, halted in the doorway. Would whoever took over this position of nanny love little Nora? Would she give her the affection every child deserved? Or would she simply take care of her physical needs and keep her quiet so Mr. Clayton Bainbridge was not disturbed? Oh, why had she ever challenged the man's cold, detached attitude toward his child? She should have kept quiet—for Nora's sake. The little girl needed her.

And *she* needed this post.

Sarah blinked back another rush of tears and walked to her bed. She removed her dressing gown, stepped out of her slippers and slid beneath the covers, fighting the impulse to bury her face in the pillow and sob away the hurt inside. Crying wouldn't stop the aching. It never did. But everyone said time would bring healing.

If only it were possible to hurry time.

Sarah breathed out slowly, reached over and turned down the wick of the lamp on her bedside table. She couldn't bring herself to snuff out the flame. She could do nothing about the darkness inside her, but she could keep the darkness of night at bay. She rested back against the pillow, pulled the covers up to her chin and stared up at the tester overhead, willing time to pass.

Birdsong coaxed her from her exhausted slumber. Sarah opened her eyes and came awake with a start. She shoved to a sitting position, blinked to clear her vision and gazed around the strange room. Where was she?

Her open trunk provided the answer. The moment she saw it, the events of yesterday came pouring back. She sighed and swung her legs over the side of the bed, searching for the floor with her bare feet. Her toes touched fur and she pushed her feet into the warm softness of her slippers and gave another sigh. She wasn't accustomed to rising with the dawn, but she had better get ready to face the day. Mr. Bainbridge was most likely an early riser. Even when he wasn't angry.

She tiptoed to the door of the nursery, glanced in to make sure Nora was still sleeping and yawned her way to the dressing room to perform her morning toilette. How was she to manage without Ellen?

* * *

Soft stirrings emanated from the nursery.

Sarah gathered her long hair into a pile at the crown of her head the way Ellen had shown her, wrapped the wide silk ribbon that matched her gown around the thick mass and tied it into a bow. When she removed her hands, a few of her soft curls cascaded down the back of her head to the nape of her neck. She frowned and reached to retie the ribbon.

The stirrings grew louder.

She had run out of time. Her hair would have to do. Sarah took another look in the mirror to make sure her efforts would hold and hurried from the dressing room into the nursery, smiling at sight of the toddler who was sitting in the middle of the crib, her cheeks rosy with warmth, her blue eyes still heavy with sleep.

"Good morning, Nora. I'm Nanny Sarah—" *at least until I'm summoned downstairs for dismissal* "—do you remember me?"

"'Quirrel."

Sarah's smile widened. "That's right. We watched the squirrel together yesterday. Aren't you clever to remember." She moved closer to the crib and held out her arms. "Are you ready to get up and have some breakfast?" She held her breath, waiting.

Nora stared up at her. "Cookie." She scrambled to her feet and held up her arms.

"Cookie?" Sarah laughed and scooped her up. "I'm afraid cookies are not acceptable breakfast fare for little girls. Would a biscuit with some lovely strawberry jam suit?"

Nora's golden curls bounced as she bobbed her head. "Me like jam!"

"Yes, I thought you might." Sarah looked around for a bellpull. There was none. She hurried to her bedroom, glanced around, frowned. Where was— The truth burst upon her, rooted her in place. Servants did not have bell-pulls. And in this house she was a servant. She tightened her grip on Nora and sank to the edge of the bed, absorbing the ramifications of that truth. Perhaps it was just as well she would be going home. She had no idea what to do. Someone had to prepare Nora's breakfast. But without a bellpull how did she summon—

"Bisit."

Sarah looked into her charge's big blue eyes and sighed. "Biscuit?… Yes. You shall have your biscuit and jam, Nora." She took a deep breath, made her decision. She would take Nora to the kitchen—wherever that was—and have cook prepare breakfast for both of them. "But first I must get you washed and brushed and ready for the day."

Nora squirmed. "Go potty."

"Oh. Of course. Wait a moment." Sarah tightened her arms around the toddler, rose and hurried toward the dressing room.

"Good morning." Sarah smiled as Mrs. Quincy spun around from the iron cooking stove and gaped at her. The woman's flushed face registered surprise, then censure.

"You're not to be using the main stairs." The house-keeper tossed the piece of wood she was holding into the stove, replaced the iron plate and hung the tool she'd used to lift the lid on a hook on the wall. Her long skirts swished as she moved around a large center table and pulled open a door. "These back stairs are the ones you're to use."

Sarah glanced at the narrow stairway with the pie-wedge-shaped winding steps.

"Remember that in future." Mrs. Quincy closed the door, went back to the stove, picked up a spoon and swirled it through the contents in a large iron pot. "Is there somethin' you needed?"

"Yes." Sarah's stomach clenched at the smell of apples and cinnamon that wafted her way. She ignored the reminder that she had been too nervous to eat supper yesterday and carried Nora toward the table. "I am unfamiliar with the way you run the house, and I wondered if you would be so good as to tell me where and when Nora's meals—and mine—are served."

Mrs. Quincy put down the spoon, picked up a griddle covered with slices of bacon and placed it on the stove. "Miss Thompson came down, give me orders for what she wanted for herself and the child and went back upstairs. Lucy toted and fetched their trays."

Sarah winced at the cold, offended note in the housekeeper's voice. Miss Thompson must have been overbearing in flaunting her elevated position as nanny to the daughter of the house. No wonder Mrs. Quincy was less than welcoming. "I see. Well, I do not wish to be an intrusion in your kitchen, Mrs. Quincy. Miss Nora and I will partake of whatever fare is being offered." She gave a delicate sniff. "Breakfast smells wonderful." She paused, rushed ahead, braving the woman's ire. "However, I do wonder if it might include a biscuit with jam for Miss Nora? I promised her one this morning." She offered an apologetic smile. "I shan't make rash promises about meals to her again."

The starch went out of Mrs. Quincy's spine. She nodded, broke an egg onto the griddle beside the sizzling bacon, tossed away the shell and reached for another. "I've biscuits made. And there's strawberry jam in the pantry.

I'll put one on the child's tray. And on yours as well." She grated pepper onto the eggs, added salt. "Lucy will bring them up directly."

"Thank you, Mrs. Quincy." Sarah glanced toward the door that opened on the winder stairs. She didn't feel safe climbing them with Nora in her arms. She waited until the housekeeper was busy turning the bacon and eggs and walked back the way she had come through the butler's pantry and into the dining room.

"Bisit-jam." Nora's lower lip pushed out in a trembling pout. She twisted around and stretched her pudgy little arm back toward the kitchen.

"Yes, sweetie. You shall have your biscuit. But first we have to go back upstairs."

"Bisit! Jam!"

"In a moment, Nora."

The toddler stiffened and let out an irate howl.

Sarah took a firmer hold on the rigid little body and howled louder. Nora stopped yelling and gaped at her. Clearly, the child did not know what to think of an adult who yelled back. How long would that ploy work? Judging from the storm cloud gathering on the small face, Nora was not going to give up easily. The little mouth opened. Sarah shifted her grasp, lifted the toddler into the air and whirled across the dining room. By the time she reached the doorway they were both laughing.

"That is much better." Sarah stepped through the dining-room doorway into the hall and came to an abrupt halt. It appeared her concern over breakfast was in vain. Clayton Bainbridge was striding down the hall toward her, and she had no doubt she would be dismissed as soon as he saw her. Lucy would be the one caring for Nora today. She squared her shoulders as best she could with Nora in her arms and curved her lips into a polite smile. "Good morning."

Clayton Bainbridge stopped in midstride and lifted his gaze from the paper he held. Surprise flickered across his face, was quickly replaced by displeasure. He gave a curt nod in acknowledgment of her greeting. His gaze locked on hers, didn't even flicker toward the toddler she held. "Did I hear yelling, Miss Randolph?"

His tone made her go as rigid as Nora had only moments ago. "Yes, Mr. Bainbridge, you did. Nora and I were playing." That was true. There was no need to tell him the yelling occurred first. Or that the play was to prevent it from happening again.

"I see. In the future, please confine your 'play' to the nursery." His scowl deepened. "There are back stairs directly to the kitchen, Miss Randolph. It is unnecessary for you to bring the child into this part of the house." He gestured behind her. "If you go through the dining room to the kitchen, Mrs. Quincy will show you the stairs' location."

He was completely ignoring his daughter! Sarah resisted the urge to lift little Nora up into Clayton Bainbridge's line of sight where he could not dismiss her. "She has already done so." She matched his cool tone. "But the steps are narrow and winding, and I feel they are unsafe to use when I am carrying your daughter." *And how can you object to that, Mr. Bainbridge?* "Now, if you will excuse us, our breakfast trays are waiting."

Sarah sailed by Clayton to the forbidden staircase and began to ascend, defiance in her every step. What had she to lose? He could not dismiss her twice.

Clayton stared after Sarah Randolph. The woman had an unpleasant and inappropriate autocratic manner. But he would not tolerate her presence much longer. He would dismiss her as soon as she had given the child her breakfast. He pivoted, strode to the dining room, took his seat, glanced at the paper in his hand. A moment later he threw the paper on the table and stormed into the kitchen. The heels of his boots clacked against the stones of the floor as he marched over and yanked open the door enclosing the back stairs. The narrow, wedge-shaped steps wound upward in a tight spiral. His anger burst like a puffball under a foot. Sarah Randolph was right. The winder stairs were unsafe for a woman burdened with a child.

"Was there something you needed, sir?"

Clayton turned to face Mrs. Quincy. She looked a bit undone by his unusual appearance in the kitchen. "Only my breakfast, Eldora." He closed the door on the happy little giggle floating down the stairway. "And to tell you Miss Randolph will be using the main stairs." He turned his back on her startled face and returned to the dining room, feeling irritated, yet, beneath it all, cheered by his sudden decision to keep Miss Randolph on as the child's nanny. There was not a hint of crying from upstairs, and it had been a long time since he had been able to read his paper and enjoy his breakfast in silence.

Chapter Three

Lucy sat in the rocker and pulled the linen she had brought to mend onto her lap. Sarah gave the young maid a grateful smile and tiptoed from the bedroom. Her time was now her own until Nora awoke from her nap—and she had caught only the briefest glimpse of Cincinnati when she arrived.

She hurried down the stairs, crossed the entry hall to the front door and stepped out onto the stoop. The afternoon sun warmed the flower-scented air. She took an appreciative sniff. *Lilacs.* She loved their fragrance. And what a beautiful view. She descended the front steps, hurried down the slate walk toward the gate and swept her gaze down the flat, dusty ribbon of road toward town.

Clayton stared down at the paper spread out on his desk. The blueprint had turned into a drawing with no meaning. The sight of Sarah Randolph holding the child had seared itself into his brain and had his thoughts twisting and turning over the same useless ground.

He put down his calipers, shoved his chair back and

rose to his feet. What sort of man was he to betray a deathbed promise to his mentor and friend, and endanger, through his weakness, the life of the very person he had promised to marry and care for and keep safe? Andrew had trusted him with his daughter's life, and now, because of him, because of one night, Deborah was dead.

Clayton balled his hand and slammed the side of his fist against the window frame so hard the panes rattled. He would give anything if he could take back that night of weakness. He had even volunteered his life in Deborah's stead, but God had not accepted his offer. Instead God had given him a living, breathing symbol of his human failings—his guilt.

A splash of yellow outside the window caught his eye. Clayton looked to his left. The new nanny moved into view, walking toward the front gate. There was a healthy vigor in the way she moved. If only Deborah could have enjoyed such health. If only she had not had a weak heart…

Clayton's face drew taut. He stared out the window, fighting the tide of emotions sight of the child had brought to the fore. Sarah Randolph seemed an excellent nanny. He had not once been disturbed by the child's crying since she arrived, and he was reluctant to let her go. But he would if she did not obey his dictates. He would not tolerate the child in his presence. He needed to make that abundantly clear. And he would. Right now.

He crossed to his desk, grabbed his suit coat from the back of the chair and shrugged into it as he headed out the door.

Sarah rested her hands on the top of the gate and studied the scene below. Cincinnati, fronted by the wide, sparkling blue water of the Ohio River, sat within the caress of forested hills that formed an amphitheater around its clustered buildings. For a moment she watched the busy parade of ships and boats plying the Ohio River waters, but the sight reminded her of Aaron and all she wanted to forget. She drew her gaze up the sloped bank away from the waterfront warehouses, factories and ships massed along the river's shore. People the size of ants bustled around the business establishments, shops and inns that greeted disembarking passengers and crews. Farther inland, churches, scattered here and there among the other shops and homes that lined the connecting streets, announced their presence with gleaming spires. Throughout the town, an occasional tree arched its green branches over a street, or stood sentinel by a home dotted with brilliant splashes of color in window boxes or around doorways. Smoke rose from the chimneys of several larger buildings.

A sudden longing to go and explore the town came over her. Visiting the familiar shops in Philadelphia had become a bitter experience, but there was nothing in Cincinnati to make her remember. No one in the town knew her. Or of—

"What do you think of our city?"

Sarah started and glanced over her shoulder. Clayton Bainbridge was striding down the walk toward her. She braced herself for what was to come and turned back to the vista spread out before her. "I think it is beautiful. I like the way it nestles among these hills with the river streaming by. And it certainly looks industrious."

"It is that." Clayton stopped beside her, staring down at the town. "And it will become even more so when the northern section of the Miami Canal is finished."

She glanced up at him. "Forgive my ignorance, but what is the Miami Canal? And how does it affect Cincinnati?"

A warmth and excitement swept over his face that completely transformed his countenance. Sarah fought to keep her own face from reflecting her surprise. Clayton Bainbridge was a very handsome man when he wasn't scowling. She shifted her attention back to his words.

"—is a man-made waterway that, when finished, will connect Cincinnati to Lake Erie. It is already in use from here to Dayton." He lifted his hands shoulder-width apart and slashed them down at a slant toward each other. "Cincinnati is like a huge funnel that takes in the farm produce of Ohio for shipment downriver. And that will only increase when the canal is finished." A frown knit his dark brows together. "That is why it is vital that I make an inspection trip over the entire southern section soon to check on weak or damaged areas. But first I must oversee repairs to the locks here at Cincinnati."

"Locks?"

Clayton shifted his gaze to her and she immediately became aware of the breeze riffling the curls resting against her temples and flowing down her back. She should have taken the time to fetch her bonnet. She would have to guard against her impulsiveness—it was such an unflattering trait. Sarah held back a frown of her own, reached up and tucked a loosened strand of her hair back where it belonged.

"Yes, locks. There are a series of them on the canal that lift or lower boats to the needed level. Unfortunately, the contractor who won the bid on the locks here at Cincinnati scanted on materials and construction practices to make it a profitable venture. Hence the locks were unequal to the demand placed on them and must now be either repaired or strengthened."

"And that is your responsibility?"

He nodded. "I am the engineer in charge, yes."

"Of the repairs over the entire southern section of the canal?

"Yes."

"That must be daunting."

"It could be, were I not educated and trained to handle the work."

Sarah's cheeks warmed. "Of course. I meant no—" His lifted hand stopped her apology. She looked down at the city.

"I understood your meaning, Miss Randolph. And I wish you to understand mine." His gaze captured hers. "If you recall, during your interview, I told you I do not wish to have any personal contact with the child. Not *any*. I will overlook the incident in the hallway this morning, but I do not want it repeated. See that it is not."

Sarah's budding respect for Clayton Bainbridge plummeted. She drew breath to speak, glanced up and bit back the retort teetering on her tongue. His face had a cold, closed look, but there was something in his eyes she couldn't identify. Something that held her silent.

"I also wanted to tell you I have given Quincy orders to drive you to town whenever you wish."

He was not going to dimiss her? "That is most kind of you."

"It is a necessity." He glanced at the road that led into the city below. "The grade of the hill is mild, but it is, nonetheless, a hill. Now, if you will excuse me, I must get back to my work." He gave her a polite nod and started back toward the house.

Sarah watched him for a moment then pushed open the gate, stepped out into the road and, holding her long skirts above the dusty surface, walked to the carriage entrance and followed the graveled way out beyond the kitchen ell. A stone carriage house snuggled against the rising hill at the end of the way. A gravel walk led off to her left and she turned and followed the path, walking along fenced-in kitchen gardens to another gate set in pillars.

She stopped, gazing in delight at the small formal garden on the other side of the gate. Trimmed lawns cozied up to boxwood hedges lining a brick walk that led from a large back porch to form a circle around a birdbath, sundial and pergola surrounded by blooming flowers. Lilacs and other shrubs, their feet buried in lush green ivy, threw splashes of color against the high stone walls that defined the garden area. Daffodils and other spring flowers bloomed among the ivy. It was a perfect place for little Nora to play in and explore.

Sarah lifted the latch, stepped through the gate and let it swing shut behind her. Birds drinking and bathing or feeding on the ground fluttered up to rest on the spreading branches of the bushes. For a moment silence fell, then the birds started their twittering again. Sarah smiled and moved slowly toward the porch. What a lovely place to sit and read or have an afternoon tea. All of Stony Point was lovely. Though it was much smaller than her home.

Home.

Her pleasure in exploring Stony Point dissolved. Sarah blinked away a rush of tears, lifted her long skirts and climbed the porch steps. She glanced at the table and chairs on her left, walked to a wood bench with padded cushions and sat staring off into the distance. When would the pain of Aaron's death go away? A year? Two? When would she be able to face going home again?

* * *

Sarah moved around the nursery straightening a doll's dress here, adjusting the position of a stuffed animal on a chair there—anything to keep busy. The afternoon had been a challenging time with the toddler, who seemed to think she should have a cookie every few minutes. It had left her no time to think or feel. But Nora was now in bed for the night, the demands of caring for the toddler were over for today, and the night was hers. The dark, idle time that had become her enemy.

Sarah looked around, stepped to the shelves and rearranged the few picture books, fixing her thoughts firmly on the present. Why hadn't Clayton Bainbridge dismissed her? He had certainly been angry with her. The scowl that sprang so readily to his face testified to that. Aaron had never—

No! She would *not* think about Aaron. Sarah spun away from the shelf and searched the room for something else to do. There was nothing. Everything was tidied and in its proper place. She had unpacked and her own bedroom was in order. And she wasn't ready to write her mother and father and tell them she had been accepted in this position as a nanny in Cincinnati. They thought she was still visiting Judith in Pittsburgh. And when they learned what she'd done… Oh, they would be so *worried.* And she didn't want to cause them more distress. They were already concerned for her.

Sarah blinked away a rush of tears, walked to the windows and closed the shutters on the deepening shadow of the coming night. How she hated the dark! She shivered and started toward her bedroom, listening to the light pad of her footsteps, the soft rustle of her long skirts. The quietness, the solitude pressed in on her. She stopped, fought for the breath being squeezed from her lungs by a familiar cold hand. She couldn't do it. She couldn't face the long night with nothing to do, with no weapon with which to hold off the memories. She cast a glance at the sleeping toddler, hurried to the door and slipped out into the hall. There must be a library, or study, or someplace in this house where she could find a book to read.

Sarah hurried to the stairs, lifted the front of her skirts and started down. Light shone out of an open door on the left side of the small entrance hall below. She paused. The room was only a few feet from the bottom of the stairs, and she had a strong intuition it was Clayton Bainbridge's study. Would he hear her? She had no doubt it would anger him to find her snooping about his house in search of reading material. Of course, if she asked his permission there was no need for such clandestine measures.

Sarah descended the last few steps and marched over to rap on the frame of the open door. "Excuse me for inter-rupting, but—" She stopped, scanned the empty room. It was Clayton Bainbridge's study all right. Blueprints littered a table. Papers with mathematical equations on them covered his desk with some sort of reference book open beside them. More books were stacked helter-skelter on the thick beam that formed the mantel on the stone fire-place. Her hands itched to straighten them. Instead, she turned back to the hall. The drawing room, where she had been interviewed, was on the opposite side, door open, lamps aglow, inviting one in to its comfort—unless one was a servant, of course.

Sarah shook her head, turned and walked down the hall toward the rear of the house, retracing the way she had taken that morning. What a strange position she had placed herself in. Whoever had heard of a wealthy, socially elite servant? Perhaps if she wrote of it in an amusing vein to her parents, they would be less concerned with her decision to accept this post. Surely they would understand she had to get away from all the reminders of her loss.

She halted, glanced at the dining room, now dark and uninviting. But candlelight poured through an open door on her left, tempted her into the yet unexplored room. She paused just inside the door, ready to apologize for intruding and make a hasty retreat. But this room, too, was empty.

She relaxed and looked around, admiring the room's slate-green plastered walls, the deep mustard color of the woodwork and window shutters. An old, one-drawer table holding a flaming candle in a large pewter candlestick and a family Bible snuggled into the recess created by the fireplace. A framed needlepoint sampler hung on the wall above the table. Two tapestry-covered chairs sided a settee with a candlestand at one end. She moved to her right, stepped around a tea table and entered a large alcove lined with shelves of books. In its center stood a pedestal game table with a game of Draughts displayed on its surface.

Sarah smiled, slid one of the pieces forward on the board, moved it back to its starting place. How Mary and James loved to challenge and bait each other while playing Draughts—while doing anything. Her younger sister and brother were fiercely competitive. Who was mediating their clashes of wills now that she was gone from home?

A sound of footsteps startled her from her reverie. The door in the outside wall swung inward, exposing the night. The candlelight flickered wildly in a gust of wind that carried a strong scent of rain. The breath froze in her lungs. Sarah stared at the dark gap of the open door, pressed her hand to the base of her throat and took a step back toward the safety of the hall.

Clayton Bainbridge stepped out of the darkness, halting her flight. Surprise flitted across his face. He gave her a small nod. "Good evening."

Sarah stood in place, acutely aware of her pulse pounding beneath her hand, the tightness spreading through her chest. She inclined her head.

"Sorry if I gave you a start, I did not realize you were in here." Clayton pulled the door closed, faced her. "It seems we are in for a bit of weather. The wind is coming up fast."

The sighing moan of wind seeking entrance at the windowpanes accompanied by a distant rumble of thunder testified to the truth of his prediction. Sarah darted her gaze toward the window, fought back a shudder. She would have to hurry. Get back to her room before the storm broke upon them.

"Were you looking for me? Is there a problem?"

She jerked her attention back to Clayton Bainbridge. "No. No problem. I…I was searching for something to read." She lowered her hand, squared her shoulders. "I hope you do not mind?"

"Not at all." Clayton's gaze shifted to the books. "Were you looking for anything in particular?"

"No." Lightning lit the sky in the distance. Sarah winced and turned her back to the windows, focusing on the books in front of her. "I only wanted something to read until I can fall asleep." *Little chance of that now.* She edged in the direction of the door.

Clayton strode up beside her, reached out and pulled a book off the shelf. "The music of Robert Burns's poetry always works for me." His thumb slid back and forth over the black leather cover then stilled.

She was trapped. Sarah watched him, held fear at bay

by trying to identify the myriad emotions that shadowed his eyes. Sadness…anger…loneliness…and something— He lifted his head, looked at her. She flicked her gaze back to the books. Warmth crawled into her cheeks. Had she been fast enough? Or had he caught her staring at him?

"Do you like poetry, Miss Randolph?"

She nodded. "Yes, I do." The wind moaned louder, raindrops spattered against the windows at the far end of the room. The warmth drained from her cheeks. The tightness in her chest increased. If only he would move out of her way!

"Do you enjoy Burns? Or perhaps you prefer Blake or Wordsworth?"

"I have no preference. I like them all." Lightning flashed, throwing light against the walls. There was a loud, sharp crack. Sarah flinched and bit down on her lower lip to stop the scream that rose in her throat.

"But not thunderstorms?"

She glanced up at Clayton. He was studying her. And she knew exactly how she looked—face pale, mouth taut, eyes wide and fearful. No point in trying to deny it. "No. Not thunderstorms. Not anymore." There was a brilliant flash, a sizzle and crack, the burst of thunder. "Excuse me."

Sarah pushed her way between Clayton and the game table, rushed into the hallway and sagged against the wall, struggling to catch a breath. She could still hear the thunder, but its rumble was muffled by the walls, and there were no windows to show the lightning. If only she could get to her room! But her legs were trembling so hard she was afraid to move away from the support of the wall. If she could *breathe*—

"Are you all right, Miss Randolph?"

He had followed her! Sarah nodded, gathered her meager strength and pushed away from the wall. Her knees gave way. Clayton Bainbridge's quick grip on her elbow kept her from falling. She turned her face away from his perusal. "Thank you." She struggled for breath to speak. Panted out words. "If you will…excuse me, I need to…go upstairs. Nora may wake and be…frightened by the storm."

"In a moment. You are in no condition to climb stairs." He half carried her the few steps to a Windsor chair. "You are very pale." His eyes darkened. His face drew taut. "Rest here while I get you some brandy. A swallow always helped my wife when she had one of her spells." He turned toward the drawing room.

"No, please. That isn't necessary." Sarah pushed to her feet, forced her trembling legs to support her. "Thank you for your kindness, but I need to go upstairs to Nora." *And to hide from the storm.*

Thunder boomed. Sarah winced and rushed to the stairs. She heard him come to stand at the bottom, felt his gaze on her as she climbed. He must think her insane to react so fearfully to a simple thunderstorm. Would he judge her unsafe to care for his child because of it?

The sound of rain pelting the roof and throwing itself in a suicidal frenzy against the shuttered windows of the nursery drove the worry from her mind. "Sufficient unto the day are the troubles thereof…" Tomorrow would take care of itself. She had the night to get through.

Sarah tucked the covers more snugly around the peacefully slumbering Nora and ran tiptoe to the dressing room to prepare for bed. Prayers formed in her mind in automatic response to every howl of the wind, every flash of lightning and clap of thunder, but she left them unspoken.

She had learned not to waste her time uttering cries for mercy to a God who did not hear or did not care. It would profit her more to hide beneath her covers and wait for the tempest to pass.

She shivered her way to bed, slid beneath the coverlet and pulled the pillow over her head to block out the sights and sounds of the foul weather, but it was too late. The storm had brought back all the memories, and she was powerless to stop the terrifying images that flashed one after the other across the window of her mind.

Lightning flashed. Thunder cracked, rumbled away. Clayton pushed away from his desk and crossed to the window. Rain coursed down the small panes of glass in torrents, making the barely visible trunks of the trees in the yard look liquid and flowing. He had not seen a storm this bad in years. He frowned and rubbed at the tense muscles at the back of his neck. Hopefully it would pass over soon. If not, the weak wall they were working to re-inforce at the lock might not hold. And if it collapsed it would put them weeks behind the time he had scheduled for the repairs.

Clayton shook his head and turned from the window. There was no sense in worrying—or praying. He knew that from all those wasted prayers he uttered when he found out Deborah was expecting his child. What would be, would be. And he could do nothing until morning. He might better spend his time sleeping because, one way or another, tomorrow was going to be a hard day. He snuffed out the lamps, left his study and headed for the stairs. The sight of his hand on the banister evoked the memory of Sarah Randolph's white-knuckled grip as she had climbed. She had trembled so beneath his hand, he had expected her strength to give out after a few steps, had worried she might fall. But she had made it to the top. And to the nursery. He had listened to make sure.

Clayton cast a quick glance down the hallway to the nursery door. All was quiet. He entered his bedroom and crossed to the dressing room to prepare for bed. What could have happened to make Sarah Randolph so terrified of a storm? Something had. When he noticed her pale face and asked if she liked thunderstorms she had answered, Not anymore. Yes, something frightening had definitely happened to Miss Sarah Randolph during a thunderstorm. But what?

Clayton puzzled over the question, created possible scenarios to answer it while he listened to the sounds of the storm's fury. It was better than dwelling on the possible damage the weak locks were sustaining.

Chapter Four

"Tompkins, start those men digging a runoff ditch five feet back from the top of the bank, then follow me." Clayton slipped and slid his way down the muddy slope and turned left to inspect the lock under repair. One quick look was enough. He squinted up through the driving rain at his foreman and cupped his hands around his mouth. "Tompkins, get some men and timbers down here! We need to shore up this wall."

His foreman waved a hand to indicate he had heard him above the howling wind and ran off to do as ordered.

Clayton swiped the back of his arm across his eyes to clear away the raindrops, tugged his hat lower and sloshed his way across the bottom of the lock to check the other side. The pouring rain sluiced down the fifteen-foot-high wall to add depth to the water swirling around his ankles. He turned and slogged along the length of the wall, checking for cracks or weak spots, but the gravel and clay loam they'd used to reinforce it was holding up well beneath the deluge.

Lightning rent the dark, roiling sky and sizzled to earth

with a snap that hurt his ears. Thunder crashed and rolled. Sarah Randolph's pale, frightened face flashed into his head. He frowned, irritated by the break in his concentration, but could not stop himself from wondering how she was handling the storm. Perhaps it was only at night—

"Look out below!"

Clayton pivoted, squinted through the rain to see a heavy timber come tumbling down the wall on the other side. Men at the edge were poised to drop another. He cupped his mouth. "Stop! Hold that beam!"

His voice was lost in another loud clap of thunder. The two men holding the beam upright at the top of the lock wall gave a mighty shove and leaped aside. The beam tumbled down end-over-end, hit one of the horizontal beams of the form for the new stone wall and knocked it askew. Clayton broke into a run, shouting and waving his arms, trying to catch the attention of someone on the opposite bank before the carelessness of the unskilled laborers caused the unfinished wall to collapse.

Water splashed over the top of his boots, soaked his pant legs and socks as he ran. Rain pelted his upturned face, coursed down his neck and wet his shirt. Lightning flashed. Another beam came tumbling down the wall. No one was paying him any attention.

He ran faster, angling toward the bank where he could climb in safety. His hands and feet slipped and slid as he scaled the slope, adding the offense of mud to his sodden clothes. He heard a loud crash and rumble, stopped climbing and looked to his left. There was a gaping hole where a section of the newly placed, but unsecured, stones of the wall under repair had collapsed.

Clayton glanced up, saw the men who had pushed the last beam over the wall waving other men forward and pointing down at the damage it had caused. He sucked a long breath of cold, damp air into his laboring lungs and resumed his climb, wishing, not for the first time, he had personal fortune enough to hire ten men knowledgeable about engineering work and skilled in the performance of it.

"What a good girl you are, Nora." Sarah smiled approval. "You ate all of your lunch."

"Soup."

"Yes, you liked the soup, didn't you?"

Nora's answering nod set her golden curls bouncing. "Cookie?"

Sarah shook her head, wet a cloth and washed the toddler's face and hands. "No cookie today. You had pudding for dessert."

"Cookie!"

Sarah looked at the toddler's determined expression. It seemed a battle of wills was about to ensue. At least the sound of the storm would cover Nora's squalls. She lifted her charge into her arms. "No cookie. It is time for your nap."

Nora let out an irate wail. Sarah lifted the yelling, kicking toddler into her arms and walked to the rocker on the hearth.

"Cookie!" Nora howled the word, pushed and twisted, trying to free herself.

"No cookie. Not today." Sarah tightened her grip enough so the child would not hurt herself and began to rock. She hummed softly, ignoring the fighting, crying toddler. Nora's storm was as furious as the one outside, but she lacked the strength to sustain her effort to get her own way. After a few minutes of futile exertion, she gave up the fight, stuck her thumb in her mouth and began to suck.

Sarah watched the tiny eyelids drift closed as the

toddler succumbed to the rhythmic motion, the steady whisper of the wood rockers against the floor. She wiped away Nora's tears, studied the dainty brown brows, the tiny nose and soft contours of her baby face. She was a beautiful child. Spoiled but beautiful. Why did Clayton Bainbridge refuse to allow her in his presence? Refuse to even acknowledge her by name? Was she not his?

Sarah's pulse quickened. She stared down at Nora, thinking, remembering, drawing a parallel between her childhood and Nora's. Even if Nora *was* Clayton's natural child, it could be that he didn't know how to be a father. Perhaps he only needed to be encouraged in his relationship with his daughter—the way Elizabeth had encouraged her father to love her and Mary.

Her father.

Sarah leaned her head against the chair back and closed her eyes. She had never told anyone, including Mary, that she knew Justin Randolph was not their real father. Justin, his servants, *everyone* thought she had been too young to remember, but the day that man had come to Randolph Court and taken her mother away was indelibly etched in her memory. And she remembered how the servants had gossiped about how Justin Randolph had gone after them and found the man dead and her mother severely injured from a carriage accident.

She had been only three years old, but she vividly recalled Justin bringing her mother back home, and the horrible whispering when she died. She remembered it well because her nanny had taunted her by telling her the man who died was her real father, and that he and her mother were both evil and that's why they had died, that she would die, too, if she wasn't good. She had been so terrified she had decided not to talk for fear she would say something wrong that would make her die. But when Justin Randolph had married Elizabeth, everything had changed.

Sarah opened her eyes and looked down at Nora asleep in her lap. She had never thought it through before, but Elizabeth had changed everything because she had brought love into their house. Elizabeth had taken her and Mary—two orphans forced upon Justin's care by the death of their mother and real father—into her heart. She had loved them and treated them as daughters. And Justin Randolph had followed her example.

Her *example*. Excitement tingled along Sarah's nerves. The situations were entirely different, of course. Elizabeth had married Justin Randolph. And she had no intention of ever marrying. Aaron had been her dream, her love; she would not betray his memory. But still… If she could only bring Nora into Clayton Bainbridge's presence… Resolve replaced the excitement. There had to be a way. And she would find it. Or she would make a way.

Sarah hugged Nora close, kissed her soft baby cheek, put her in the crib and hummed her way to her bedroom. The brilliance of a lightning flash flickered through the small cracks between the window shutters. Thunder boomed. She flinched, started to back out of her room, then squared her shoulders, marched to the writing desk and pulled it into the center of the room, turning it so her back was to the windows. She was ready to write her parents now, and no storm was going to stop her. Determination brought her inspiration. She opened the clothing cupboard, pulled her green-velvet coal-scuttle bonnet off its hook and put it on, letting the wide silk ties dangle free. There was a loud thunderclap.

Sarah flinched, then smiled. It worked. The deep brim shielding her face prevented her from seeing the lightning flashes from the corners of her eyes. Feeling both cowardly and clever, not to mention a little like a horse with blinders on, she seated herself and took up paper and pen.

The afternoon had passed quickly. Too quickly. Sarah picked up the children's picture books she had used to entertain Nora and put them back on the shelf. She would have to make up more simple baby games. Little Nora caught on to them quickly. She was a very bright little girl—with quite a temper.

Sarah glanced at the toddler now asleep in her crib and shook her head. Supper had been a real challenge. Who would think that such a small body could house such a mass of determination. It had taken all of her ingenuity to get Nora to eat her meat and vegetables before her dessert.

Sarah's smile slipped into a frown. She had a suspicion, based on Nora's frequent requests for sweets and her unpleasant behavior when they were not forthcoming, that the former nanny may have used sweets to quiet her. But Nora's bout of bad temper at supper had soon dissipated, her sunny disposition had returned and they had played quietly until her evening bedtime. She really was an adorable child.

Sarah tucked the blankets more closely around the little girl and roamed into her bedroom seeking distraction. She glanced at the desk that was again in its proper place beneath the window on the far wall. Her letter to her parents rested on the cleared surface, folded and addressed, sealed and ready to be posted. Perhaps she would do that tomorrow afternoon if the weather cleared. She had considered giving it to Ellen to carry home with her, but the post would be faster. And she had been thinking of going to town to visit the shops. Of course Nora's hour or two of nap time did not allow for much exploring. Still, she should have time enough to accomplish all she needed to do, including visiting Ellen to send her on her way.

A clap of thunder invaded her thoughts, reminded her the storm was still raging, though awareness of it was never far away. It hovered like a dark cloud in the background, ready to carry forward painful memories at every flash of lightning or howl of the wind. Sarah shivered, adjusted the wick on the oil lamp and smoothed a wrinkle from the lindsey-woolsey coverlet on the bed. This was not working out as she had planned. She had counted on the demands of a toddler keeping her too busy to remember— or to feel the pain of her loss. But with Nora's afternoon nap and early bedtime that hope had proven false. She had too much free time, especially with the storm adding to her unrest. If only…

Sarah lifted her gaze to the door at the right of the fireplace and absently tapped her thumbnail against her lips. Why not? What had she to lose? She opened the door wide, in order to hear Nora if she woke, and started down the winder stairs, longing for a hot cup of tea and some adult company. The storm had lessened in ferocity, but it still had her shaken and overwrought. She opened the door at the bottom, stepped into the kitchen and turned toward the table. Mrs. Quincy looked across the room, staring at her, most likely resenting this uninvited invasion of her domain. "Good evening." She smiled and moved forward into the room.

The older woman nodded, leaned her direction and squinted her eyes. "Are you feeling all right, Miss Randolph? You look a bit under the weather."

Sarah forced a laugh. "An apt description, Mrs. Quincy. I do not care for thunderstorms." She glanced toward the stove, noted the pots steaming there and looked back. "I wondered if I might have some tea? And if you would care to share it with me? I would be glad of the company."

The housekeeper studied her for a long moment, then walked to a cupboard standing against the wall, took out a tin of tea and headed for the stove. "This storm's been a bad one. Guess you're thankful it's about wore itself out." She measured tea into a red and white china teapot and added hot water from the kettle on the stove.

"Yes, I am." Sarah moved closer to the long worktable and changed the subject. "I apologize for making extra work for you. Is there anything I can do to help?"

Mrs. Quincy gave a snort of laughter. "Lands, this ain't work! My feet and I are grateful for the chance to sit down." She placed the teapot on its tray, added some biscuits from a tin box sitting on the cupboard beside the stove and inclined her head toward the shelves hanging on the wall. "You can get two of them cups if you're of a mind to help."

Sarah hastened to do as she was bid. She had been accepted. At least for the moment. No doubt because of Mrs. Quincy's tired feet.

Clayton dismounted in front of the carriage house, opened one of the wide double doors and led Pacer inside, the argument he had been waging with himself on the long, miserable ride home still engaging his mind. It was the storm. The ceaseless tempest coupled with his inherent protective instinct toward women was what had brought the image of Sarah Randolph's pale, frightened face returning to him throughout the day. It had nothing to do with the woman herself. It was only that he had never known anyone so terrified of a thunderstorm. He had been pondering the possible causes of that fear since last night. Most likely it was some long-remembered childhood fright.

A gust of wind drove the rain into his face, splattered the deluge against the building and tried to rip the door from his grasp. He battled the wind for possession, managed to pull the door closed and headed toward Pacer's stall. Sassy nickered softly, welcoming her barn mate home. Pacer tossed his head and snorted, nudged his back.

"Easy, boy, you will have some oats soon enough. But first we have to get you dry."

The door opened. The wind howled through the breach, lifted hay and dust from the plank floor, swirling it through the air to stick to his wet face and clothes. Clayton blinked, blew a bit of straw off his upper lip.

Alfred Quincy wrestled the door closed. "Saw you ride in." He walked over and held out his hand for the reins. "There's hot venison stew waiting for you."

Clayton nodded. Droplets of water clinging to his hat brim broke free and slithered down his cheeks and neck. He swiped them away. "A plate of hot stew is exactly what I need after the cold soaking I have had today." He gave his mount a solid pat on the shoulder. "And Pacer deserves a long rubdown and a double scoop of oats. He earned them today."

"I'll see to it."

Clayton nodded, stepped outside, lowered his head against the wind and pelting rain and ran toward the house. That stew was going to taste good tonight. There had been no time to eat today and his stomach was growling so fiercely he could not tell its rumblings from the distant thunder.

* * *

The kitchen door opened. Cold, damp air gusted across the room. The lamps flickered. Sarah turned, saw the rain-soaked figure standing against the blackness of the stormy night and gasped. The cup she held slipped from her grasp and smashed against the slate floor. The sound of the breaking china brought her back to her senses. "Oh, I…I am sorry." Her voice quavered. She clamped her teeth down on her lower lip and crouched to pick up the pieces of broken cup, grateful for the table that hid her as she struggled to compose herself.

The door closed. The light steadied. Boot heels clacked on the floor. A shadow fell across her. Sarah closed her eyes, wished she were up in her room. She did not want Clayton Bainbridge to see her like this again. She tried to will herself to stop trembling.

"You look…unwell…Miss Randolph. Leave the cup."

Sarah shook her head, opened her eyes. "That would not be fair to Mrs. Quincy. I broke it and I shall clear it away." She cleared the sound of tears from her voice. "And I am not 'unwell.' I am fine." She reached for a jagged piece of cup and stabbed her finger. Blood welled up to form a bright droplet against her flesh. She gathered another piece, started to rise to throw them away, wobbled and resumed her crouch, reaching for another piece of the cup to disguise the unsuccessful effort. "It was only that you startled me."

The shadow covered her. Clayton Bainbridge's hands closed around her upper arms. He lifted her to her feet. She looked up and met his gaze. Her knees quivered. She dropped her gaze to the pieces of china in her hand.

"You have hurt yourself."

His voice was as warm as his hands.

"A mere prick." She firmed her knees, stepped back. He released his grip. She ignored the sudden cold where his hands had been and brushed with her fingertip at the tiny rivulet of blood before it dropped onto her gown. "I apologize for breaking the cup." She glanced up. "I will replace it, of course."

A frown drew his brows down to shadow his eyes. "That is not necessary. It was an accident. And as you pointed out, the fault was mine for startling you." He swiped his hand across the nape of his neck and turned away.

"Nonetheless—"

"*Miss* Randolph—" he turned back, frustration glinting in his eyes "—*must* you be so fractious? My clothes and boots are sodden and mud-caked. I am weary, chilled to the bone and hungry as a bear emerging from hibernation. I have no desire to stand here arguing with you over a broken cup."

The heat of embarrassment chased the chill from her body. Sarah straightened her shoulders. "I was not being fractious, Mr. Bainbridge, only…steadfast. However, you are right, it would be inconsiderate to continue this discussion while you are in discomfort. We can resolve the issue of my replacing the cup tomorrow."

A scowl darkened his face. "No, Miss Randolph, we will not. This discussion is over." He looked down the long table. "Eldora, I shall be down for my supper directly after a hot bath." He crossed to the winder stairs and began to climb.

Sarah's cheeks burned. How dare he speak to her in such a fashion! Let alone dismiss her as if she were a servant! Truth struck. Of course, she *was* a servant.

She fought down the desire to march to the stairs and

demand an apology and watched until her employer disappeared from view. Even in his rain-soaked, muddy clothes Clayton Bainbridge had a presence, an air of authority about him. He was a strong, determined man and getting him to accept and love his daughter suddenly seemed a daunting task. But she had more than a little determination herself *and* a strong, worthwhile purpose. The little girl upstairs deserved her father's love and attention.

"Are you still wanting tea, Miss Randolph?"

Sarah jerked out of her thoughts and glanced at the housekeeper. "I am indeed, Mrs. Quincy. And please, call me Sarah." She threw the broken cup in a basket holding bits of trash, walked to the shelves and took down another. Tea with the housekeeper had taken on a new importance. It might help her bring father and daughter together if she knew why Clayton Bainbridge held himself indifferent toward Nora, and servants always knew every household secret.

The storm had finally ceased. Sarah opened the window sash and stood listening to the quiet sounds of the night. Moisture dripped from the leaves of the trees, the drops from the higher branches hitting the leaves on those below before sliding off in a sibilant whisper to fall to the ground. There were muted rustlings of grasses and flowers disturbed by the passage of small, nocturnal animals. Somewhere an owl hooted, another answered. But concentrate as she would on the sounds, she could not blot out her tumbling thoughts, could not stop the images that were flashing, one after the other, into her head.

She shivered and wrapped her arms around herself, more for comfort than for warmth. The cold was inside. If only she had not gone downstairs for tea. The sight of

Clayton Bainbridge's rain-drenched figure against the darkness had whisked her back to the night Aaron had died.

Sarah gave a quick shake of her head to dislodge the memories—to no avail. She closed the shutters, adjusted the slats to let the cool night air flow into the bedroom and hurried to the nightstand. The gold embossed letters on the black leather cover of the book resting there glowed softly in the candlelight. *Robert Burns.* She slid into bed, took the poetry volume into her hands and let it fall open where it would. All she wanted was words to read to chase the pictures from her head. She pulled the lamp closer and looked down at the page.

"Oppress'd with grief, oppress'd with care,

A burden more than I can bear,"

Sarah slapped the book shut, tossed it aside and slipped from bed. She didn't need to read about grief, she was *living* grief! She rushed, barefoot, into the nursery, ran to the crib and scooped Nora into her arms. The toddler blinked her eyes and yawned. "Nanny?"

"Yes, Nora, it's Nanny Sarah. Close your eyes and go back to sleep."

Sarah walked to the rocker, sat and wiped away the tears blurring her vision. She covered Nora's small bare feet with part of the skirt of her long nightgown, took hold of one little hand and began to hum a lullaby. Quietness settled over her as she rocked, her tense nerves calmed. She kissed Nora's warm, baby-smooth forehead, touched a strand of silky golden curl, then leaned back and closed her eyes. She had been unsuccessful in her attempt to get Mrs. Quincy to talk about Clayton Bainbridge or his wife over tea. Maybe tomorrow.

The thought of him brought the memory of Clayton

Bainbridge helping her to her feet. The feel of his hands, so warm, so strong yet gentle on her arms. The way his eyes had looked as he gazed down at her.

Sarah opened her eyes and stared down at the child in her arms, disquieted and troubled. Clayton Bainbridge had made her feel…what? She searched for the right word for the unfamiliar emotion that had made her want to turn and run from him, then frowned and gave up. What did it matter? It was of no importance. It had been only a momentary aberration caused by her fear of the storm that had quickly disappeared when Clayton Bainbridge had returned to his customary, unpleasant anger.

Chapter Five

What a beautiful day! The only reminders of the thunderstorm were the areas of damp, dark earth beneath the bushes where the sun's rays hadn't yet reached, and the colorful memory of flowers that littered the ground. Sarah sighed and crossed the back porch to the stairs. The storm had stripped the beauty from every branch and stalk in the enclosed garden. Not one flower was left intact. Still, the storm was over and the horrible constriction in her chest had eased. She took a deep breath of the clean fresh air and helped Nora down the steps to the brick pathway.

"Well, Nora, what shall we do first?" She reached down and straightened the pinafore that protected the toddler's yellow dress. "Do you want to go sit in the pergola and watch the birds take their baths?"

"Birds!" Nora's lace-trimmed sunbonnet slipped awry at her emphatic nod. Sarah laughed, adjusted the bonnet and took hold of her charge's tiny hand. Hoofs crunched against gravel. She looked toward the carriage house, saw Clayton Bainbridge mount his horse and start down the path toward them. She smiled as he neared. "Good morning, Mr. Bainbridge."

"Miss Randolph." Clayton gave her a brief nod, touched his fingers to the brim of his hat and rode on.

Not so much as a glance at his daughter. Sarah stared after him, anger flashing. But as she watched him ride toward the road, her anger dissipated, vanquished by an odd sort of sadness. It was almost as if she could feel his unhappiness, his loneliness.

"'Quirrel!"

Nora's tiny hand pulled from her grasp. Sarah brushed the strange sensation aside and watched Nora run, as fast as her little legs would carry her, toward the squirrel that was scampering along the railing of the pergola. Her anger sparked anew. If Mr. Clayton Bainbridge was lonely, he had no one but himself to blame. She would not waste sympathy on a man who wouldn't even look at his own daughter. But despite her adamant avowal, a remnant of that odd, sad feeling lingered. And irritation at his abrupt departure. She stepped to the gate and looked down the empty gravel path. "You could have stopped a moment to bid us good morning, Mr. Bainbridge."

"What's that, miss?"

Sarah started, turned to see Mr. Quincy emerge from the shadow at the far end of the carriage house. He was pushing a wheelbarrow. Her stomach flopped. Thank goodness he had not heard her clearly. She shook her head. "Nothing, Mr. Quincy." Her nose identified the rotted stable leavings in the wheelbarrow when he drew near. "Is that for here in the garden?"

"Yep." He glanced over the shoulder-high wall and a smile deepened the lines radiating from the corners of his piercing blue eyes, poked dimples in the leathery skin covering the hollows of his cheeks. "'Pears like the little miss is enjoyin' this fine day." He dropped the back legs of the wheelbarrow to the ground and straightened. "I'll come back later and spread this mongst the flowers an' such. I don't want to ruin Miss Nora's playtime. Young'uns need to be outside where they can learn about God's creations, not be—" He clamped his lips shut, gave her a brief nod and turned away.

Not be—what? Sarah took a breath. "A moment, Mr. Quincy."

"Yes, miss?"

The set look on his face told her he had said more than he intended—and did not mean to compound the error. The question hovering on her lips died. She would get no information from him. "Do you know when Mr. Bainbridge will return?"

"Not till supper, miss. Leastwise, he had Mrs. Quincy fix him a box lunch, so he must be figurin' on a long day."

"I see. Then—" Sarah spun at a sudden squeal from Nora.

"'Quirrel, all gone." Nora's lower lip pouted out, trembled.

"'Pears like you've got a problem." Mr. Quincy chuckled and walked away.

"It will be all right, Nora." Sarah hurried down the path and scooped the little girl into her arms for a hug. "You frightened the squirrel when you yelled." She walked to the pergola, sat on the wooden bench and settled Nora on her lap. "Shh." She laid her finger across her lips and softened her voice to a whisper. "If we sit still and are very quiet, the squirrel will come back."

The admonition worked until the disturbed birds returned to their bathing and feeding.

"Bird." Nora pointed and squirmed to get down. Sarah

helped her off her lap, then sat watching as Nora ran from one bird to another, squealing with delight when they fluttered into the air only to land a few feet away and resume their feeding.

The toddler's laughter brought a smile to her own lips. One that disappeared in a small gasp when Nora stumbled and tumbled facedown onto the grass. She rushed to the railing, waited. Nora pushed to her hands and knees, got her feet under her and ran after another bird, her sunbonnet now flopping against her back, her blond curls bobbing free.

Sarah relaxed. It seemed the only damage done by the fall was the smear of green on the pristine white pinafore and that bit of torn lace dangling from the bottom of Nora's pantalettes. The laundress would not be happy. But what did any of that matter in the face of the child's happiness?

Sarah frowned and returned to her seat. *Young'uns need to be outside where they can learn about God's creations, not be—* Kept quiet in the nursery all day? Is that what the former nanny had done to Nora? Of course, the woman was probably following orders. But still, how could she treat Nora like that? It was unnatural to keep a child hidden away like…like some unwanted possession. Did the child's happiness count for nothing?

Sarah's thoughts leaped backward, focused on the cruel woman her mother had hired to care for her when she was Nora's age. Nanny Brown had cared nothing for her happiness. The woman had made her life a misery. And her mother and father had not cared about her happiness, either. They had left her behind with Justin Randolph when they ran off. How could parents disregard the needs of their children?

Sarah took a deep breath and wrapped her arms around

her waist. She had struggled for so long after her mother abandoned her to overcome the horrid, empty feeling of being forsaken and unloved. She could not let Nora feel that way. And the little girl *would* if something did not happen to change Clayton Bainbridge's cold, callus treatment of her. Because, though he provided for Nora's every physical need, he had abandoned her in his heart. Why? He seemed considerate of others. What caused him to treat his child this way? There had to be a reason.

Sarah pushed the question aside to concentrate her attention on Nora. The toddler was no longer chasing the birds but had squatted on the brick path and was poking at something on the ground. She rose and hurried down the steps to discover what had captured the little girl's attention. "Oh. You found a worm."

"Worm." Nora's tiny finger poked at the pink, squiggling worm trying to escape.

Sarah bit back an admonition to not touch the thing, and squatted down. "Be careful, Nora. You will hurt the worm. Do it like this." She squelched her repugnance, took hold of Nora's hand and gently touched the tip of the child's tiny finger to the worm. It wiggled. Nora giggled and touched it again.

"Here are the biscuits you asked for, Miss Randolph."

"Bisit!" Nora pushed to her feet and ran toward the house.

Mrs. Quincy stepped onto the porch, holding a tray. The door banged closed behind her.

Sarah caught up to Nora, lifted into her arms and carried her up the steps. "Bless you for the interruption, Mrs. Quincy." She settled Nora on a chair and gave the stout woman a grateful smile. "She found a worm."

The housekeeper nodded. "At least 'tis better than a

bumblebee. Worms don't sting." She set the tray on the table.

"Gracious! I forgot about bees." Sarah wiped Nora's small hands with the bottom of the grass-stained pinafore then folded them together. "Close your eyes, Nora."

The toddler's lips pulled down. "Bisit."

"You shall have your biscuit after we ask the blessing." Nora let out a screech. Sarah folded her own hands and waited. The child's acts of rebellion were getting shorter. The toddler stopped yelling, stared up at her, then closed her eyes. Sarah bowed her head. "Dear gracious, heavenly Father, we thank Thee for this food. Amen." She handed Nora a biscuit and glanced up. There was a distinct look of approval in Mrs. Quincy's eyes. What had brought about her change of attitude?

"I brought lemonade for you, Miss Randolph. Mrs. Bainbridge liked to sip lemonade while she rested here on the porch. But if it's not to your liking I could bring you some tea."

"Lemonade is fine, Mrs. Quincy. Have you time to join me?"

The housekeeper shot a yearning glance at the padded bench and shook her head. "There's cleaning to oversee, and the baking to be done. Another time, mayhap." She turned toward the door.

"Of course." Sarah took a breath and seized her opportunity. "You said Mrs. Bainbridge *rested* here on the porch. And Mr. Bainbridge mentioned she had 'spells.' Was she unwell?"

The stout woman stopped, nodded. "'Twas some sort of weakness in her heart stole her breath from her if she moved about. Oft times till she swooned." She looked down at Nora and her voice took on a reflective tone. "She was too frail for childbearin'. She died shortly after this one was born. Nora has the look of her."

Sarah studied Nora's delicate features. "Mrs. Bainbridge must have been a beautiful woman. It's a pity Nora will never know her."

"She was beautiful…an' spoiled. An' the little one was followin' along after her, till now." Mrs. Quincy looked up, blinked and gave a little shake of her head. "But 'tis not my place to speak of such things. Don't know why I'm standin' here wastin' time when there's work to be done." She hurried across the porch. "I'll send Lucy to fetch the tray." The door banged shut behind her.

"Bisit?"

"No, Nora. No more biscuits." Sarah gave her a sip of lemonade and lifted her off the chair. "Come with me. I am going to teach you to do a somersault." She helped her down the steps onto the grass, knelt down and placed one hand on the toddler's tummy, the other on her upper back. "All right, we are ready. Now bend waaaay over…"

"Here we are, miss."

Sarah glanced at the building on her right, noted the Post Office sign above the large multipaned window and climbed from the buggy. "Thank you for bringing me along to town, Mr. Quincy. I shan't delay your return home. I will meet you here in one hour." She watched him drive off down the street, shook out the three braid-trimmed tiers of the long skirt of her rose-colored silk dress, checked the time on the locket watch pinned to her bodice and crossed the sidewalk to the door. A gentleman passing by hastened to open it for her.

Sarah smiled her thanks, entered, then paused inside the door waiting for her eyes to adjust to the dimmer light after the brightness of the afternoon sunshine.

"—mark my words, Edith dear, this sickness going around will increase because of the foul weather during that storm—" The two women approaching the door broke off their conversation to give her a polite nod as they passed.

Sarah returned the politeness.

"May I help you, miss?"

She looked toward the sound of the voice. "I should like to post a letter." She pulled the folded and sealed missive from her reticule and walked to the table where a man stood sorting a large bag of letters into small piles.

He took the letter into his ink-stained hand and squinted down at the address. "Randolph Court, Philadelphia." He moved to a high desk standing at right angles to the table, glanced at her. "That will be twenty-five cents. You going to pay?"

Sarah shook her head. "No, Father will pay." She watched him write the charge, date and Cincinnati on the top corner of the folded letter. Her stomach tightened in protest. Her parents thought she was still in Pittsburgh. Well, there was no help for it. And any fears the city name engendered would be allayed when they read the letter. "I expect a reply. Will you please direct it to Stony Point? My name is Sarah Randolph."

"Of course, Miss Randolph." The man pulled a ledger from a shelf below the desk surface and jotted down the information. "How long will you be visiting at Stony Point?"

"Oh, no. You misunderstood. I am not visiting. I am the new nanny." The man's mouth gaped open. Sarah gave him another smile and turned; her silk dress rustled softly as she headed for the exit. A man, who had just entered, doffed his hat, made her a small bow and held the door open. She inclined her head in acknowledgment of the politeness and stepped through the portal into the afternoon sunshine.

One chore completed. And she had a little less than an hour to accomplish the others. Sarah moved into the shadow cast by a large brick building, walked to the corner, turned left and made her way up Main Street, scanning the storefronts. She had spotted what seemed a suitable establishment along the way to the post office. Where…? Ah, there it was. Mrs. Westerfield, Milliner & Mantuamaker and dealer in Millinery and Lace Goods and Embroidery. She moved closer and read the smaller print of the sign.

Keeps constant on hand a splendid stock of Leghorn, Tuscan & Straw Bonnets and Florence Braid, artificial flowers, Paris ribbons, plain & figured silks, satins & etc. suitable for bonnets and dresses which she is prepared to manufacture in the most fashionable style.

Sarah checked her reflection in the window. The flowers adorning her silk hat trembled slightly in the warm breeze. She adjusted the tilt of the hat, smoothed the lace at her throat and entered. A cluster of women examining trimmings displayed in a glass case, and two women seated on a settee studying a book of patterns, glanced up at the discreet tinkle of the small bell on the door. The women looked at her with varying degrees of curiosity, gave small, polite nods and returned to their business.

"If you will excuse me a moment, ladies." The woman behind the glass case smiled and came forward. "Welcome to Mrs. Westerfield's salon. May I help you?"

"I would like to speak with Mrs. Westerfield please."

"Certainly. I will be a moment. If you would care to

have a seat?" The woman gestured toward a grouping of chairs, walked to a door at the back, gave a light tap and disappeared into another room.

Sarah strolled over to look at a display of paintings on the wall. Bits of conversation from the women at the counter drifted her way as she studied the drawings of the latest fashions.

"—heard that Rose Southernby has taken to her bed?"

"Oh, I do like this red silk braid!"

"Did you say Rose is ill?"

"Yes. Dr. Lambert has been making daily calls. She is not at all well, and— The red silk braid is a little…bright, Charlotte. Perhaps the gold…"

"You were saying, Gladys?"

"I beg your pardon? Oh. Yes. I heard the Southernby children are stricken also."

Children. Sarah moved a step closer to the women.

"I'm becoming frightened by all this sickness!"

"I share your fear, Isobel. I have ordered the servants to open our country home. It is early, I know, but I am not going to stay in this city and—"

"Mrs. Westerfield awaits you, miss."

Sarah walked to the back of the room and stepped through the door the woman held for her. A tall woman in a beautiful day dress of ecru pongee with a crossover shawl collar banded in white stood behind a desk. She swept an assessing gaze over Sarah's hat and dress, smiled and came forward. "That will be all, Jeanne."

The door closed. Sarah waited.

"I am Mrs. Westerfield. You wished to see me?"

"Yes. I have recently come to Cincinnati and I am interviewing dressmakers as I find myself in immediate need of a few gowns."

A faint flush appeared on Mrs. Westerfield's cheeks. "I assure you, Miss…"

"Randolph."

"—Miss Randolph, I make the finest, most stylish gowns in Cincinnati. If you will permit me to show you a few of my recent designs." Mrs. Westerfield turned and led the way toward a settee.

Sarah smiled and seated herself, looked with interest at the sketches the dressmaker handed her. "And was your gown made by you or a seamstress in your employ, Mrs. Westerfield?" She eyed the excellent workmanship of the woman's day dress.

"I designed my frock, and Miss Bernard, my highly skilled head seamstress, crafted the dress. I would not wear the work of another, Miss Randolph."

"Nor will I." Sarah handed Mrs. Westerfield three sketches. "These are the gowns I have chosen. Please have Miss Bernard make them in your highest quality fabrics, one in ecru, one in brown, and one in dark blue. But I do not want the lavish adornments, only simple trims suitable for a nanny. I want them commissioned immediately and delivered to Stony Point when they are completed."

"I shall select the fabrics and trim myself, Miss Randolph." Mrs. Westerfield smiled. "And please forgive my confusion. I thought the gowns you have ordered were for you. Miss Bernard will begin work on them as soon as the nanny comes in for a fitting."

"You have made no error, Mrs. Westerfield. The gowns *are* for me. I am the new nanny at Stony Point." Sarah ignored the look of astonishment that flashed over the dressmaker's face and rose to her feet. "I have another appointment, so if you will direct me to Miss Bernard for my fitting…"

* * *

Only fifteen minutes left. Sarah hurried into the Franklin House, nodded to the desk clerk and rushed up the stairs to her room. "Ellen?"

"Miss Sarah! Oh, Miss Sarah, I've been so worried about you what with the storm an' all!" Her maid set aside what she called "busy work," bustled over, pulled her into a strong hug, then stepped back and studied her face. "Are you all right, child?"

Sarah blinked a rush of tears from her eyes and nodded. "I am fine, Ellen. But I have missed you." She gave a little laugh. "I have a new appreciation for how hard you work. You have always made everything look so easy. Whenever I needed anything I simply called for you. Now…" She laughed again, gave a helpless little shrug.

"Miss Sarah—"

"Don't scold, Ellen. There is no time. I must meet Mr. Quincy in a few minutes to—"

"You're going *back?* You're going to *continue* being a nanny?" Ellen's eyes clouded. "I thought you'd come to your senses." She shook her head. "Your mother and father are not going to be happy about this. They—"

Sarah placed her hand on the older woman's arm, halting her words. "There is no time for a lecture, Ellen. I only have time to say goodbye, and I do not want to waste it in useless debate."

The maid studied her for a moment, drew herself up straight. "You're sending me back to Randolph Court?"

Tears surged into Sarah's eyes at the hurt in Ellen's voice. She forced a smile. "I have no choice, Ellen. I shall miss you dreadfully. But whoever has heard of a nanny with her own lady's maid?" Her voice caught. She took a breath. "This little girl needs me, Ellen. And right now I need her."

"And when I'm not here and the nightmare comes?"

"I will imagine you hugging me and pampering me with warm blankets and hot tea. Now—" Sarah cleared her throat and swept her hand through the air toward the trunks stacked against the wall. "Take my clothes with you. I have commissioned new gowns suitable for a nanny." She glanced down at her watch, reached into her reticule and pulled out a small packet of money and a folded letter. "This will cover the expense of your journey and answer any questions that might be asked of you. Now I must go. Safe journey, Ellen. Oh, I shall miss you so." She gave the older woman a quick hug and hurried toward the door, blinking back tears.

"And I'll miss you, Miss Sarah. May the Lord bless you and watch over you."

The soft-spoken words—the last words Ellen spoke to her every night—followed her down the hall.

Now she was truly alone.

Clayton put down his pen, stretched his arms out and to the back and rolled his shoulders to get rid of the kinks caused by the hours spent drawing on the blueprint. He had worked longer than he intended, but it was of no consequence. No one waited for him to finish. All he faced was an empty house and another lonely night.

He shoved back from his desk, rubbed at his tired eyes and snuffed the lamps. The silence of the late night closed around him. Moonlight poured in the windows. Candlelight painted a yellow stripe under the door. Time to go to bed.

He reached for the jacket he had hung on the back of his chair, paused and glanced toward the door at the sound of soft footfalls. A shadow blocked out the gold of the candlelight, passed on. Eldora? No—she was heavy on her feet. And sound asleep by this time.

Clayton slipped on his jacket, tugged his waistcoat back in place and opened the door. There was no one in sight. He stepped across the hall and looked into the drawing room. Sarah Randolph was standing in the center of the room and something in the slope of her shoulders and the tilt of her head spoke to him of deep sorrow. He stepped back to go his way and give her privacy. But his movement must have caught her attention for she glanced in his direction. Their gazes connected. For a moment she neither moved nor spoke, then her chin lifted and her shoulders straightened. The melancholy on her face disappeared as quickly as smoke before a strong wind. Except for the shadow that dulled the golden glints that usually sparkled in her brown eyes. The brightness in them now was caused by the glistening moisture of unshed tears.

Clayton stood frozen in the doorway, wanting to leave but knowing a hasty exit would reveal he had seen her moment of vulnerability. And he knew, too well, how important it was to cover that inner vulnerability with a facade of normalcy to protect your heart and save your pride. He moved into the room, pretended he did not see her tears, did not recognize her sadness. "Did you wish to speak to me?"

"No, I—" She blinked rapidly, turned away. "I was feeling restless, unable to settle for the night. I hope I did not disturb you."

"Not at all. I was finished with my work." He sought for an innocuous subject, something that would give her time to compose herself. "Is there a problem with your room? Are you uncomfortable or—"

"No, the room is quite satisfactory. I—" She took a

breath, turned back to face him and gave a rueful little smile. "The truth is, I posted a letter to my parents today, and I have become a little homesick. We are very close. Especially since—" Her voice broke. She hurried to the fireplace and looked up at the two portraits that hung side by side above the mantel beam. "What a lovely lady. And the gentleman…" She glanced at him, looked back at the picture. "You have the look of him."

A distraction so he would not question her about what she had left unsaid or comment on her tears? Clayton nodded, went along with the change of subject. "Not surprising. That is my grandfather and grandmother, Ezekiel and Rose Bainbridge. They built this place back when this area was the frontier. It served them well. The neighbors used to fort up here when there was an Indian raid."

Her eyes widened. "Truly?"

Clayton smiled at her awed tone. He had captured her attention. Perhaps he could do a little distracting of his own, give her something to think about that would hold her sorrow at bay through the long night hours. He knew the anguish of troubled, sleepless nights. "Truly. Stone doesn't burn, and most of the other homes were made of log back then. Have you noticed the deep gashes in the front door? They are from Indian tomahawks."

"Tomahawks." She looked toward the entrance hall. "I cannot imagine…"

But clearly she did. Clayton strode to a window, reached behind the drapes and pulled the solid wood shutters that were folded up against the deep walls of the window well into view. He pointed to the small square holes in them. "These holes were for their rifles. If they had enough warning, they opened the windows—if not, they broke the glass out. Grandma hated that because it took so long to get the glass to replace the broken panes and the flies and mosquitoes always found the holes."

He folded the shutters back and indicated a large chest that sat against the wall beside the window. "My father used to stand on that chest so he could load my grandfather's long rifles during battles. He used to tell me the stories of those battles when I was young. It is one of my fondest memories. That, and my mother singing me to sleep at night."

He moved to the fireplace, ran his finger over the hole where a cartridge had buried itself in the heavy beam. "There are many reminders of those days in this house. And a story behind every one of them." A smile tugged at his lips. He gave it free rein. "I inherited my grandparents' stories and memories along with their house."

"How lovely for you. I never knew my grandparents." *Or my parents, either.* She looked up at him. "And your parents?"

His smile faded. "They died in a smallpox epidemic at Fort Belle Fontaine when I was four years old. My grandparents raised me."

"Oh." Compassion warmed her eyes. "I'm sorry you lost your parents. But how fortunate that you survived."

"I was here." Clayton looked away. The vision of Sarah Randolph standing beside him with the candlelight highlighting her delicate features and playing with the golden strands of her light-brown hair was disconcerting. "It was a new posting and my parents decided to leave me here until they discovered what sort of living quarters were assigned them. I was to join them when they were settled in."

"But they died. And your drea—your plans to join them died with them."

"Yes." His wife's face flashed before him. The acrid

taste of bitterness spread through his mouth, tainted his words. "It happens that way sometimes."

"Yes. Yes, it does."

The words were little more than a whisper, but something in her voice… Clayton looked back. A fresh spate of unshed tears glimmered in her eyes. She blinked, looked down and smoothed at her skirt.

"The hour is getting late. I believe I shall retire now." She raised her head and smiled. It was the saddest smile he'd ever seen. "Thank you for sharing some of your family history with me, Mr. Bainbridge. It has made Stony Point come alive for me. I shall wonder over every mark I see. Good evening."

Clayton dipped his head in response, clamped his jaws shut and held himself rigidly in place as Sarah Randolph left the room. He did not want to let her go. He wanted to keep her here with him. He wanted to learn what caused that sadness in her eyes and take the sorrow from her. He wanted her company.

Clayton scowled, strode to the front door and stepped outside. Moonlight fell in cool silver radiance from the night sky, chased the darkness into shadows. He walked down the slate path to the gate, stepped out into the road and looked back at the house. Thin strips of golden lamplight showed through the slatted shutters in the front bedroom. He turned and strode off toward the tree-covered hill. Sleep would not come quickly for him tonight. It would not be easy to rid himself of the image of Sarah Randolph's beautiful face smiling that sad smile.

Chapter Six

"*God in heaven, save us!*" *Wind tore the words from her mouth, slapped at her long, sodden skirts, whipped them into a frenzied flapping that knocked her off her feet. A sulfurous yellow split the dark, flickered, streaked downward with a sharp crack. The planking of the deck heaved, shuddered. The ship tilted. She groped for something to cling to, found only emptiness, slid. Lightning flashed, threw flickering light over a gaping hole where the ship's rail had been, over Aaron clinging to the broken end and reaching for her. She stretched out her hand.*

The world exploded. Brilliant light blinded her. Thunder deafened her. She fell through a black void, battered by wind and rain. Frigid water swallowed her, drowned the scream trapped in her throat.

Sarah jerked upright in bed, heart pounding, pulse racing. She wrapped her arms about her ribs and rocked to and fro, shivering, waiting. The terror of the nightmare would pass. It always did. All she had to do was wait. Alone.

Tears surged. Why did Aaron have to die? She had

prayed. She had— No. There was no sense in going over the same old questions. There were no answers. Sarah shoved her feet into her slippers and pulled on her robe. Even its quilted warmth couldn't stop the cold inside. Her teeth chattered. Her body shook. Her fingers trembled so she could not turn up the wick of the oil lamp. If only Ellen were here to bring her some hot tea. Oh, she *hated* the night! The darkness, the solitude, the long hours with nothing to distract her from her thoughts.

The nightmares.

Sarah shuddered, rubbed her upper arms, looked toward the door to the right of the fireplace. A longing, too strong to be denied, welled. She snatched up the lamp, opened the door and started down the narrow winder stairs, her shadow floating on the wall beside her. A step creaked. Another. She paused, listened to hear if Nora woke, then continued down into the kitchen.

The darkness of the large room swallowed the meager light of her lamp. She put it on the center table, removed the globe and lit the candles on the table and in the sconces that hung over the fireplace. The dark withdrew to shadowy corners. Another shudder shook her. She glanced at the hearth, yearned for a fire, but had never started one. Hot tea would have to do.

She rubbed her cold hands together and shivered her way to the big, black iron stove. The weight of the teakettle surprised her. It fell from her shaking hand, clanged against the stove. She gave a guilty start and glanced toward the stair door. All was quiet. Defeated, she put the kettle back in place. The stove was cold. So was she. Cold, and helpless, and inadequate, and lonely. She could not even make tea. Why ever had she sent Ellen home?

Sarah fought the constriction in her chest for breath.

The answer was simple—because it was easy to be brave during a warm, sunny afternoon. But in the darkness when the memories returned and the nightmare came… Tears burned behind her eyes, clogged her throat. She clenched her hands and fought them with all her strength. She was tired of tears. Of grief. She wanted to be happy again. How would she ever be happy again?

Clayton opened his door a crack and listened. Yes, there it was again. The squeak of a step on the winder stairs. Dim light flickered against the wall. A sound of stealthy movement reached him. He tightened his grip on his pistol, eased the door open, pressed into the shadow against the wall of the landing and looked down. A frown drew his brows together. Sarah Randolph was descending the steps, light from the lamp in her hand illuminating the downward spiral, glinting on the silky mass of brown hair loosely re-strained at the nape of her neck and spilling down the back of her quilted robe. The sight of her struck him breathless.

She paused, glanced toward her open door. The terror on her face froze him in place. She blinked tears from her eyes and continued on her way down the stairs.

Clayton rushed into his room, put the pistol away and pulled trousers on over his cotton drawers. What could be wrong? What could have put that look of terror on Sarah Randolph's face? He shoved his arms into his shirtsleeves, fastened a few buttons and tucked the tails into his pants on the way to the door. Barefoot, he started down the stairs, driven by a need to help her. To protect her. From what? How could he help her? Would she even want him intruding into her personal life? He slowed his steps, ap-proached the kitchen door cautiously.

"Was it tea you was wantin'?"

Eldora. Clayton stopped, stood undecided. The sight of his half-fastened shirt and bare feet determined his path. He turned and made his way back up the stairs to his room. The unexpected sight of Sarah Randolph on the stairs had given him a jolt that left him shaken. He was better off staying as distant from her as possible.

He left his door open a narrow slit, finished buttoning his shirt and pulled on his socks before he stretched out on top of his bed—in case. Eldora would call him if he was needed.

A clanking sound, a soft murmur of feminine voices from downstairs filtered in through his slightly open door. Moonlight flowed through his windows, a haunting silver radiance. Clayton frowned. There was something about moonlight that made him lonelier. He folded his hands on his chest and stared at the ceiling overhead, ignoring the ache in his heart, dreading, *hoping,* that his housekeeper would call him.

"Was it tea you was wantin'?"

Mrs. Quincy! Sarah's throat constricted. She couldn't speak to answer the woman's question. She compressed her lips to hold back the rising sobs and nodded.

The housekeeper waddled forward, the hem of the blue robe she wore swishing back and forth around her slippered feet dusting her path. She neared, squinted up at her from beneath the mobcap covering her gray hair and gave a brief nod. "Havin' a bad night, are y'? Well, there's no problem a good hot cup of tea can't make better." She removed the tool from the wall, lifted a front plate from the stove, set it aside and nodded toward a box on the floor. "Hand me some of that kindlin'."

The shock of the enjoinder stabbed through her emotions. Sarah stared. At the woman's second nod, she came to herself, bent and gathered a handful from the box.

The housekeeper crumpled newspaper, stuffed it in the stove and placed the kindling on top. She reached up and turned a knob protruding from the side of the chimney pipe. "Now light this spill from that candle and set this a burnin' whilst I fill this kettle."

Obviously, she was not going to be coddled. Sarah quashed a twinge of offense at not being pampered when she was so upset, took the long, slender piece of wood and hastened to obey. In a moment the kindling was blazing. The warmth felt wonderful on her icy hands.

Mrs. Quincy returned with the filled kettle, glanced at the fire. "You've got that goin' proper. Now add a few of them sticks o' wood. An' lay 'em in easylike. You don't want sparks to fly up and singe your hair." She waddled away to the cupboard.

Sarah did as she was bid. The wood caught. The fire blazed.

The housekeeper returned with a tin of tea in her hand, nodded approval, lifted the iron plate back in place and set the water over to heat. She reached up and fiddled with the knob on the chimney pipe again. "We'll need cups 'n' saucers."

Sarah moved to the shelves on the wall and took down two cups and two saucers, surprised to find her hands were no longer shaking. She took an experimental breath, then another—the pressure in her chest had eased. The activity had made her feel better than being babied ever had. She looked toward the housekeeper who was spooning tea into a china pot. "Thank you for asking me to help, Mrs. Quincy."

The housekeeper nodded, put the cover back on the tin of tea and gave it a sharp rap with the heel of her hand to seal it. "Most times when I'm feelin' plagued by somethin' it helps to keep busy. Keeps me from stewin' on the trouble." She pointed toward a cupboard with pierced tin doors. "Sugar's in the brown crock. I'll fetch some cream."

"Do you want to talk about what's botherin' you?"

Sarah weighed the offer, shook her head. "No. Thank you, but…I want to forget."

Mrs. Quincy nodded, stirred a spoonful of sugar into her tea. "I know how that can be." She reached for a piece of the bread and jam she'd prepared for them. "Mind if I ask how you come to be a nanny? I mean, you could sell one of them gowns of yours for more than a year's pay, so…"

"It is not for the money. It is—" Sarah blinked, looked down at the cup in her hand. "I lost someone I—" she swallowed hard, cleared her throat "—someone I shared a dream with." Tears streamed down her cheeks. She put down her cup and wiped them away. "That dream is gone and I need something to do. I need a purpose. Something to give—" She bit down on her lip, shook her head and picked up her cup. Her hands were trembling again. She put the cup down before she spilled the tea—waited for the commiseration, the comfort Ellen always gave her.

"Whatever your reason, 'tis a blessing for little Miss Nora you're here."

Once again shock pierced through her emotions. Where was the sympathy? Sarah lifted her head, looked across the table at the housekeeper. "Truly?"

"Truly." Mrs. Quincy picked up the plate of bread and jam, offered it to her. "That little one wasn't never out of that room till you come. An' she cried all the time."

"How *awful* for Nora." Sarah shook her head at the offer of bread. Mrs. Quincy held the plate in front of her. She met the housekeeper's steady gaze, took a piece of bread. Still that steady gaze. She took a bite. Mrs. Quincy put the plate down.

"'Twas that, but she's laughin' and playin' like a young'un should now. An' that's thanks to you. You're a blessin' for her, all right. I wasn't sure that would be the way of it when you come—bein' late an' all. I figured you was another one like that uppish Miss Thompson, thinkin' only of her own self." Mrs. Quincy's gaze again steadied on her. Her lips curved in a rueful little smile. "I reckon I wasn't too welcomin'."

Amusement bubbled. Sarah's lips twitched. "You were so stern I almost turned away and ran back to Ellen." Curiosity flared in the housekeeper's eyes. "Ellen's my lady's maid." The amusement fled. Sarah sipped her tea, watched Mrs. Quincy's expression change to that of someone who had received an answer to something they'd been wondering about.

"Well, I'm glad I didn't scare you off. It's nice havin' another woman around the place."

Another shock. "One as helpless as I am?"

The housekeeper chuckled. "You're learnin'. You made the fire and helped set up our tea, didn't you?"

"Yes. I did." A warmth of satisfaction spread through her. Sarah smiled and took another bite of her bread and jam. It suddenly tasted wonderful.

"Tomorrow's Sunday. I was wonderin' if you'd like to go along to church with Mr. Quincy and me?"

Bitterness surged. The bread turned sour in her mouth. Sarah reached for her tea to wash away the rancid taste.

The housekeeper fixed another look on her. "Lucy goes to her church later on, so she can stay with the child."

That robbed her of the excuse that had readily formed on her lips. Sarah searched for another. Nothing suggested itself to her. She looked into Mrs. Quincy's eyes and gave up. The woman would see straight through any subterfuge and she didn't want to tell her the truth. Sarah sighed. After the housekeeper's kindness tonight, she couldn't simply refuse her invitation. "Thank you, Mrs. Quincy. I shall be pleased to accompany you. What time must I be ready?"

Mr. Quincy handed the reins to a young lad, moved up the steps and opened the door. Sarah glanced at the sign fastened to the white clapboard building—Fourth Street Chapel. Reverend William Herr—and followed Mrs. Quincy inside. Curious looks trailed their progress down the aisle. Sarah smiled and nodded a polite greeting to those who caught her gaze.

Quincy opened the door of the pew on his right.

A middle-aged man looked her way, smiled, bowed his head.

Quincy frowned and stepped back so they could take their seats. "At his age Granville should know church is not the place for tryin' to get a leg up on the rest of the young bucks in the city."

The warmth of a blush crawled into Sarah's cheeks at the muttered remark. She gathered the skirt of her gold, watered-taffeta gown, moved to the far end of the pew and seated herself, feigning interest in the stained-glass window beside her in an attempt to ignore the stares aimed her way. Mr. Quincy followed his wife inside and closed the door.

"Can't abide Sherman Granville. Thinks every woman he sees will tumble all over their own feet runnin' to him just 'cause he owns half the county!"

"Hush, Alfred. You're in church."

"Don't make it any less true."

"Amen."

The whisper came from the pew behind them. Sarah snuck a peek from the corner of her eye as Alfred Quincy chuckled low and swiveled his head around. "Mornin', John."

A distinguished-looking gentleman with gray hair smiled. "Good morning, Quincy…Mrs. Quincy—" he glanced her way "—miss."

A man entered from a side door, stepped to the pulpit on the platform and bowed his head. "Almighty God, Thou who thunderest from heaven, yet speaketh in the tenderest, softest voice to Your servant's hearts. Speak to us this day, O God. Touch our hearts, our minds, our spirits with Your words, that we may be renewed in that which is Your will and purpose. Amen."

An organ sounded.

"Christ our Savior, Lord of all…"

Sarah glanced up at the man in the pulpit as he boomed out the first words of the hymn. The congregation joined in. She closed her heart and her mind to the meaning of the words and sang along. When they finished the last chorus, the organ music faded away and there was a general rustle as everyone settled in their seats.

Reverend William Herr cleared his throat. "Today I take my text from Psalms Eighteen, verse six. 'In my distress I called upon the Lord, and cried unto my God.'"

Sarah stiffened.

"'He heard my voice out of His temple, and my cry came before Him, even into His ears.'"

And He did not answer me. Aaron died. Anger pushed hot blood through her veins. Sarah gripped her gloved hands together on her lap and forced herself to remain seated when what she wanted was to rise, storm down the aisle and out the door and never, ever set foot in a church again. She blocked out the reverend's voice by surreptitiously glancing at the people within her view and trying to guess what their lives were like. To the men she assigned occupations, to the women a marital status.

A fist slammed against the pulpit. Sarah jumped, looked up at Reverend William Herr.

"Are you one who gets angry and walks away because God does not answer as you want him to? How prideful! How arrogant!" His voice roared at the congregation. "Were you there when God hung the stars?"

No. But I was there when He sent the lightning that killed Aaron! That exploded the deck beneath him and threw him into the raging ocean that claimed him forever! Anger lifted her chin, glared out of her eyes. The words crowded into her throat determined to be expressed—to be spoken and answered. Sarah choked them back, felt the pressure of them in her chest. Tears smarted her eyes. She blinked, willed the tears to stop. Willed the band of tightness around her chest to relax so she could breathe.

Determined not to make a spectacle of herself, she spent the rest of the service questioning why Clayton Bainbridge's servants occupied his family's pew. And why Clayton Bainbridge stayed home.

Chapter Seven

The weight of sadness pressed down upon her. Sarah took a deep breath to rid herself of the heaviness and hurried to her bedroom. A quick glance in the mirror told her she looked as wan and drained as she felt. It was the aftermath of the nightmare, of the upsetting message in church this morning. She needed some fresh air, some exercise to put some color back in her cheeks. She grabbed her straw sailor hat, opened the door wide and made her way down the winder stairs to the kitchen. The housekeeper was at the center worktable, kneading dough. Sarah plunged into her request.

"Mrs. Quincy, I've put Nora down for her nap. She should sleep for at least an hour or two. I know Lucy is at church, but I'm feeling a bit…undone…and I would like to go outside for a stroll. I wondered if you would mind listening for Nora? My door is open so you can hear if she wakes before my return, though I promise I shan't be long."

The housekeeper looked at her. Sarah fixed a smile on her face. Eldora Quincy nodded and went back to kneading the dough.

"Take as long as you wish. I'll bring Miss Nora down and give her some bread and butter should she wake 'n' you're not here."

"Thank you, Mrs. Quincy." Sarah stepped to a glass-fronted cupboard, put on her hat and exited the kitchen with a gay little wave she was far from feeling, and that likely did not fool Eldora Quincy for a moment. She strolled by the front of the kitchen ell on the stone path that led to the gravel carriageway and followed that out to the road.

The city beckoned from below, but she felt no inclination to be among people. She hadn't the energy or desire to put on a false front—this morning at church had been quite enough. She glanced to her left, felt the draw of the tree-covered hill and started up the road.

Clayton bent down, selected a stone and straightened. The pond was before him, still and waiting, its calm surface mirroring the blue of the sky, the brightness of the sun. An aura of serenity permeated the small clearing—the serenity he'd come seeking as he had all his life. But today it irritated him. It only emphasized his turmoil. What was he to do about Sarah Randolph?

Clayton scowled, fingered the stone, got it into the right position and curved his index finger around the back edge. The problem was his attraction to Sarah. He managed all right when he prepared himself to see her, chalked up the twinges as a result of his loneliness. But last night the sight of her on those stairs with her hair down had given him a jolt he was not ready for—and did not want. And his compelling need to go to her, to protect her from whatever caused her terror—that complicated things. What he felt for her was more than mere attraction—it was caring. And that involved the heart.

Clayton whipped his wrist forward and sent the small, flat stone skipping across the smooth face of the pond. Sunlight sparkled on the tiny sprays of water produced each time the stone skimmed the surface and highlighted the ripples that spread out from the point of contact.

Ripples. He knew about ripples. More than he wanted to know. And he had learned the lesson at the cost of Deborah's life. His face drew taut. One moment of weakness. One night of yielding to his wife's pleas and entice-ments…to his own need and— *Ah, Andrew, my friend, I am so sorry! I promised to keep your beloved daughter safe. I failed you.*

Clayton shoved his fingers into his hair and glared out across the water. He had no excuse. He never should have listened when Deborah begged him. When she said she wanted to know, at least once, what it meant to truly be a woman before she died. She told him she had taken pre-cautions against pregnancy, but he knew precautions often failed. But he had given in. And the ripples had started.

Why? He was self-disciplined and strong-willed. Why had he given in to Deborah's appeals? Clayton lowered his hands and shoved them in his pockets. He hunched his shoulders and studied the ground as he walked along the edge of the pond toward the large, flat boulder that had been his fishing dock when he was a young boy. What did the "why" matter? Deborah had become pregnant. The first ripple. A terribly dangerous one.

Clayton clenched his jaw, pulled back his foot and kicked a stone. It arced into the air and splashed down almost dead center of the pond. He stared at the circles spreading out in an ever-widening pattern from the spot where the stone broke the surface, and felt again the despair that had gripped him during her pregnancy. That was the second ripple—Deborah's health. With her weak heart she grew increasing frail. And no matter what he did for her, no matter how he coddled her, he could not make it better. Every time she had one of her spells, he prayed for her. Fervently. To no avail. Her health continued to decline. So did his faith. That was the third ripple—his loss of faith. And the fourth ripple was Deborah's death.

Clayton stared the fact square in the face, ignoring the pain that squeezed his chest, made his heart ache. And then there was the fifth ripple. The one that went on and on. The one it was becoming more and more difficult to ignore. The one he couldn't bear to look at, because all he saw was his guilt. The child.

Clayton leaned his hips against the boulder and glowered at the pebbles and stones littering the ground at his feet. It had been bad enough before, when he heard the child crying all day. But now, since Sarah Randolph had come, he saw the child daily. And the guilt was intensifying. That was the sixth ripple—his guilt, which enclosed all the others. But now there was a seventh ripple—Sarah Randolph. He would have to—

"Oh…*bother!*"

Clayton spun around, stared toward the path that led to the road. Patches of blue fabric showed through the gaps in the bushes. There was a snapping of twigs.

"Ouch!"

Clayton scowled, strode toward the path to warn off the intruder. This was his private sanctuary. He stepped around the bushes and stopped dead in his tracks. His heart slammed against his chest wall. Sarah Randolph stood in the path ahead trying to free a lock of her hair from a branch. He sucked in a breath.

She glanced his way. Surprise widened her eyes, erased

the frown that had lowered her delicately arched brows into a straight line. "Mr. Bainbridge! Thank goodness. I seem to have become hopelessly entangled with this tree." A blush crawled along the crest of her cheekbones. "Would you please help me untangle— Ouch!" She yanked her hand down and stuck her fingertip in her mouth. "This tree has thorns."

An intense desire to take her finger in his hand and kiss the sting away shook him. He scowled and cleared his throat. "That's why it's called a thornapple." He stepped forward, reached for the branch holding her hair prisoner. Their hands brushed. She jerked back.

"Ow!" She grabbed for her hair, and her fingers closed over his, sprang open. Her startled gaze flew to his face, met his gaze and immediately lowered to somewhere in the region of the third button on his shirt.

"Hold still." Clayton moved closer, bent his head to study the entanglement of hair and thorny branch. The delicate scent of lilacs clinging to her hair teased his nose. He closed his mind to the fragrance, to the silky feel of her hair on his fingers, to the faint blush tinging her cheeks. "The branch is green and too thick for me to break without the possibility of my yanking your hair. I shall have to untangle it. It may pull a little."

"I understand. Do what you must."

He made the mistake of looking down. Their gazes met again. The blush on her cheeks increased. The gold flecks in her brown eyes warmed before she again lowered her lashes.

Clayton's mouth went bone-dry. He frowned and focused his thoughts on the job at hand. "It appears you have made everything worse by trying to free yourself." He unwound a few strands that were snarled by a thorn.

"Tip your head back a bit." She complied. He leaned closer, bent his head to see around to the back side of the branch. She caught her breath. Lucky her. He had no breath left.

He worked swiftly, wishing he had brought his knife along so he could cut the branch and end the torture of being so near her. He stopped being careful, broke the last few strands of her hair and stepped back. "That got it. You are free." He stepped around her and picked her hat up off the path, slapped it against his thigh to rid it of any dust or tiny crawling critters and handed it to her.

"Thank you. It— I—" She whirled and started down the path. "Where does this lead?" She broke into the open and gave a little gasp. "Oh, how lovely! What a nice pond." She glanced up as he followed her into the open. "Do you come here often?"

Clayton nodded, moved to put space between them. "It has been a favorite spot of mine since I was a child. It is far enough off the beaten path to be quite solitary. Makes it good for thinking."

She glanced up at him. "Please forgive me, Mr. Bainbridge. I was out exploring. I didn't mean to intrude." She turned back toward the path.

He moved to block her way. "I did not mean to be rude, Miss Randolph. I was only trying to convey the special draw of this place for me." He smiled. "A young boy has a lot of things to puzzle through. Lots of weighty issues to come to grips with. He needs a quiet place to slip off to every now and again, where he can just sit and ponder the way of things. This was my place."

"I believe it still is, Mr. Bainbridge. The questions only become more difficult when we grow up." A shadow of sadness clouded her eyes, quickly dispersed by a bright smile. "And so, good sir, I shall leave you to your pondering. But first—" She gave a small laugh, walked to the edge of the pond and picked up a small, flat stone. With a quick flick of her wrist she sent it skipping out over the water.

He was still staring at the pond in amazement when she brushed off her hands and made her way back to him.

"Five hops. I can do better. James would be ashamed of me." She settled her hat more firmly, tipped her head up and gave him a polite smile. "I must be getting back to Nora. Good afternoon, Mr. Bainbridge. I hope you find the solution to whatever problem you are contemplating." She started off toward the path.

Solution. Clayton stared after Sarah, held back a roar of frustration. A beautiful, intelligent, sad but brave woman imbued with all the social graces who skipped stones! His problem had just become much worse. He blew out a gust of air, sucked in another. The torture was not over yet. Sarah Randolph was not the only one with social graces. His grandparents had raised him to be a gentleman.

"A moment, Miss Randolph. If you will allow me, I would be pleased to escort you home." Clayton fastened a polite expression on his face and strode forward, trying, unsuccessfully, to ignore the sudden bitter taste of jealousy in his mouth. *Who was James?*

Chapter Eight

"*Cincinnati?* I thought Sarah was in Pittsburgh visiting Judith Taylor." Justin Randolph frowned down at his wife. "I'll not have it, Elizabeth! Not after all Sarah has been through. She needs to be here with her family where we can love her and take care of her—help her through her grief over Aaron's death." He shook his head. "It is not like Sarah to act impulsively. I shall leave for Cincinnati tomorrow morning."

"To what purpose, Justin?"

He paused, searched her face. His wife did not ask idle questions. "To bring Sarah home, of course."

"Oh, *poof!*"

Laina. Justin pivoted toward the doorway, frowned at his sister. "Poof? What does that mean, Laina? And why are you eavesdropping on a private conversation?"

"Private?" His sister laughed and waltzed into the room. "I assure you, dearheart, there was no need to eavesdrop. I could hear you roaring about Sarah being in Cincinnati the moment I entered the house." She laid the book she was returning on the table by the settee, hugged Elizabeth, went on tiptoe and kissed his cheek. "Stop glowering, dearheart, it is most unbecoming. And 'poof' means Sarah very much wanted this position as nanny and you should stop being a bear about it and let her be."

Justin glanced at Elizabeth, saw his own bewilderment written on her face and looked back at his sister. "You do not seem surprised by this news, Laina. How do *you* know Sarah 'very much wanted this position'?"

"Because she told me so when she wrote asking me for a reference."

"A reference." Justin lowered his voice to an ominous tone. "And you gave her one?"

"Well, of course I did. Sarah—"

"Without *speaking* to us about it? Laina Allen, sometimes I—" Justin stopped, glanced down at Elizabeth's hand on his arm. A wifely gesture to calm him. It would have worked better if she was not holding the letter. The sight of it exasperated him anew. He scowled at his sister.

"I would have spoken with you about it, Justin, had I thought the matter serious. I thought it was but a whim to provide Sarah diversion from her grief. I certainly did not know she would go through with it, or be accepted in the position. I am as surprised by that news as you." Laina shook her head. "Imagine Sarah a *nanny.* I have no doubt she will be an excellent one. She has a way with children."

"That is *not* the issue, Laina." Justin released a growled litany of concern. "What of Sarah's grief? Her nightmares? Who will comfort her when the memories overwhelm her? When there is a storm?" He blew out a breath, looked at his wife. "Dear heaven, Elizabeth, what will she do without us if there is a *storm?*"

Elizabeth gazed up at him, her eyes awash with tears. "Perhaps, dearest, without us to console her, to ease her every problem, Sarah's need will overcome her bitterness and she will again seek her heavenly Father. Perhaps she will regain her faith. Surely that blessing is worth the heartache and concern having our daughter at so great a distance will cost us."

Justin watched her force her trembling lips into a smile he knew was for his benefit and covered her hand, still resting on his arm, with his own. Her smile steadied, warmed at his touch.

"And perhaps this position of nanny will carry another blessing from the Lord as well." She blinked the tears from her eyes and stepped back. "Try to clear your heart and mind of your anxiety for Sarah, Justin, and listen to this last part of her letter." She glanced at her sister-in-law. "And you, Laina."

Elizabeth unfolded the sheet of paper, scanned down and cleared her throat.

"'And so, Mother and Father, quite by accident I have found a purpose for my life. Little Nora is an adorable toddler. I grow more fond of her every day. She is a precocious child, and has already learned every game suitable for her tender age that I remember. I am forced to invent games to hold her interest. Yet all is not well for her. Her situation is a sad one. For reasons I have yet to discover, Mr. Bainbridge will not allow his daughter in his presence. He will not even acknowledge her by name. And adorable little Nora needs her father's love.

"'Please do not worry about me. Stony Point is a lovely house, and, other than the treatment of his daughter, Clayton Bainbridge is a thoughtful man, careful for my comfort and every inch a proper gentleman. And though he is young and handsome with much to recommend him, there is no danger of romantic involvement. Mr. Bainbridge still grieves for his wife, and, though he is gone, my heart remains loyal to Aaron. And even if that were not so, who can abide a man who will not even *look* at his own child? I am safe here. Your loving daughter, Sarah.'"

Elizabeth looked up at him. Justin stared down into her beautiful, deep-blue eyes and read their silent message. *Remember?* How could he ever forget? He closed the space between them and pulled her into his arms. "Safe? I think not." Memories curved his lips into a slanted grin. "Not if God has another plan."

"Then you will stay home?"

He kissed the top of her head and nodded. "I will stay home."

She smiled up at him, her eyes still overbright with tears. "Oh, Justin…I know it will be worrisome and painful to have Sarah stay in Cincinnati. But I truly think God is answering our prayers. I think He is using that little girl to bring about Sarah's healing."

Justin tightened his arms, drawing her close, still crazy in love with this woman he had married by accident eighteen years ago. "And I think, Elizabeth—if history repeats itself—Sarah and Mr. Clayton Bainbridge may both be in for a wonderful, blessed surprise."

Clayton frowned down at the report he was working on for his meeting with the canal commissioners in Dayton the day after tomorrow. No matter how hard he tried to concentrate it wouldn't come together in a cohesive whole.

The sound of the child's happy giggles and Sarah Randolph's laughter drifting in through the window kept intruding on his thoughts.

He rose from his chair and stretched to relax the muscles in his back. A dull ache had developed across his shoulders, no doubt from the rigid posture he had maintained to keep from looking out the window. A frown creased his brow. It was unsettling how much he wanted to go to the window and watch Sarah Randolph playing with the child in the yard. But his equally strong guilt held him back. If it weren't for him, Deborah would be the one outside his window. It would be her laughter that enticed him.

Clayton tilted his head, scrubbed his hands over the tense muscles at the nape of his neck. If only he could find peace. But how could that be when he had a living, breathing reminder in his life?

Maaaa, maaaa.

"No! Get away! Leave her alone!"

Clayton pivoted at the outcry and stepped to the window to see Sarah Randolph snatch up the child in one arm while trying, with her free hand, to fend off a sheep intent on butting her. He frowned. A woman hampered by long skirts and the weight of a child was no match for an angry, determined sheep. Not even a young one. Where was Quincy? He swept his gaze over the portion of yard visible from his window.

Maaaa, maaaa.

"Go away! I sai— Oh!"

Clayton jerked his gaze back to see Sarah staggering backward, her free arm flailing as she tried to maintain her balance. She lost the battle and sat down on the ground— hard. And no sign of Quincy. *Blast!*

Clayton whirled, slammed out the doors, leaped off the stoop and ran to place himself between Sarah and the child and the rampaging sheep. He barely had time to plant his feet before the animal charged. He balled his hand into a fist and thumped the black nose. The sheep jumped back. Clayton moved to the side, drawing the animal's attention from its intended targets. The sheep lowered its head and leaped toward him. Clayton thumped its nose again, harder, and harder yet, then stepped in front of a tree. The sheep again drew back and lowered its head to butt. Clayton tensed, waited. When the sheep charged, he jumped aside. The sheep's head rammed solidly into the tree. Clayton slipped behind the trunk, scanned the ground behind the tree for a weapon but spotted nothing. He pressed back against the trunk, rubbed the edge of his hand and watched the irate sheep. It looked around, let out a few challenging bleats, made a halfhearted feint at the tree, then, having lost its target, turned away.

Clayton edged out from behind the tree on the other side.

"Bad sheep." The child, lower lip protruding, pointed a tiny, pudgy finger at the now grazing animal.

Clayton's lips twitched. He jerked his gaze away from the child to Sarah Randolph and stepped over to offer his hand. "Are you hurt?"

Sarah shook her head. "Only my dignity. Thank you so much for rescuing us. I'm afraid I was not much protection for Nora. Would you please lift her off me so I can rise?"

Clayton sucked in a breath, everything in him refusing the idea of touching the child. He closed his hands around her small chest, felt his own constrict with an emotion he immediately squelched. He lifted her to one side, released her and again offered his hand to Sarah. This time she accepted his help. Her hand felt soft and warm in his.

"What happened?" Quincy came hurrying across the yard. "Is anyone hurt? I was in the loft and heard Sarah cry out."

"No one is hurt." Clayton helped Sarah to her feet, forced himself to release her hand. He turned his back as she bent to pick up the child and focused his attention and anger on Quincy. "But that is not to say they were not in danger. Get rid of that hoggerel, it is getting too frisky. You should have known that."

He turned and made his way back to the house, furious at the emotions tearing at him, at his inability to stop them. He strode through the still-open door, yanked it closed behind him and went to his study and stuffed the report into his waiting saddlebags. He would finish it when he reached Dayton. It was impossible to work here with Sarah Randolph so close. With her ignoring his orders to keep the child out of his sight.

Clayton scowled, slung the saddlebags over his shoulder, slammed out the door and took the stairs two at a time. The faint sounds of Sarah entering the house with the child followed him as he crossed the upstairs hall to his bedroom to grab the clothes he would need for the next few days. He paused, struck by an idea. Perhaps he could employ Sarah Randolph to take the child back to Philadelphia and care for her there. Yes. That would solve all his problems. He continued into his room, packed his clothes and toiletries and hurried downstairs. He would consider the possibility while he was away.

Sarah roamed around the drawing room feeling restless and at loose ends. Clayton Bainbridge had gone to Dayton and would not return for a few days. He had not even told her he was going away. Not that he owed her an accounting of his movements, but she *was* Nora's nanny. At least he had told Eldora.

Sarah frowned, glanced at the various objects decorating the shelves in the alcove by the fireplace and moved on. It was odd how empty the house felt without Clayton's presence. She stopped in front of the fireplace and looked up at the portraits of his grandparents. Ezekiel Bainbridge was a very handsome man, with a square jaw and a look in his eyes that led one to believe he could well have fought and won battles against hostiles. But there was a tilt at the corners of his mouth that spoke of warmth and good humor. A pity his grandson had not inherited those traits along with Ezekiel's good looks. Most of the time Clayton looked as if he were walking around with a sore tooth.

Sarah shifted her gaze to Rose Bainbridge, studied her refined features. There was a touch of sadness in the woman's eyes, but nothing like the ill humor that darkened her grandson's. If it was not inherited, what had caused his sour disposition? Was it his wife's death? Aaron's death had certainly changed her. The joy had disappeared from her life, sucked down the same vortex of swirling water that had swallowed him. All that was left was pain and grief and darkness. The light in her world had been snuffed as surely as a candle doused by water. Perhaps it was the same for Clayton Bainbridge.

No. No, it was not the same. He had a child. A part of his wife lived on. She had nothing of Aaron but memories and a dead dream.

An overwhelming longing for home and the way things had been before Aaron's death rushed upon her. Tears blinded her eyes, clogged her throat. It could never be. Not ever again. She collapsed onto the sofa and buried her face in her hands, unable to stop the flow of tears.

The wave of anguish passed. Sarah pushed herself erect, wiped the tears from her cheeks, clenched her hands and made her way from the room. She hated crying. Hated the feeling of hopeless— She stopped, arrested by her reflection in the hall mirror, startled by the anger and bitterness that glittered, cold and brittle, behind the glisten of tears in her eyes. She turned away, lifted her skirts slightly and started up the stairs. It seemed she and Clayton Bainbridge had more in common than first appeared. But he had Nora. Pain stabbed sharp and deep. *Why had God taken Aaron?*

Sarah caught her breath and hurried down the hall to prepare for bed—for another lonely night filled with nightmares, startled awakenings and unanswered questions.

Chapter Nine

"Excellent report, Mr. Bainbridge. Work seems to be progressing nicely."

"Thank you, sir." Clayton noted the looks exchanged between the commissioners seated at the table, and a shaft of worry speared through his pleasure in their approval. Something was in the wind. He sat a little straighter.

"So you judge you will be through with the remaining necessary repairs to the Cincinnati locks in three months' time?"

A warning flag waved in his mind's eye. Had he built too much leeway into his report? No, not nearly enough, given the unskilled laborers he had to work with. "Barring emergency situations, yes, sir."

"And the aqueduct you report in emergency condition?"

"I inspected it yesterday on my way here. It's near collapse and must be repaired immediately." Clayton glanced at the other three commissioners seated at the table, including them in his answer and assessing their re-actions. "I'll start a crew of men working on it as soon as I return, though it will stretch workers on the locks too thin—which could add two weeks to my timetable." He took a chance. "Unless you authorize the funds I requested to hire more men."

The head commissioner looked around the table. Clayton's hopes surged at the unanimous nods of affirmation. He held his face impassive as the head commissioner again looked his way.

"Very well, Mr. Bainbridge. We will give you authorization to hire the extra men you need—within reasonable bounds. In return you will complete all the needed repair work on the entire southern section by the end of June."

"Two months! Gentlemen, what you ask is unreasonable—"

"But not undoable, Mr. Bainbridge—given adequate funds and sufficient numbers of workers. Under those conditions, and given your talents and capabilities, we are certain you will manage to accomplish the task."

Clayton took a breath, weighed his words. "I appreciate your faith in me, gentlemen." He shot another assessing glance around the table. "But even under the favorable conditions you outline the undertaking will be a formidable one. The time constraints—"

"Are necessary—and not of our doing." The head commissioner scanned around the hotel dining room and leaned closer. So did the others.

Clayton responded in kind.

"As you know, Mr. Bainbridge, July fourth will mark the tenth anniversary of the opening of the Miami Canal from Cincinnati to Dayton. The governor intends to commemorate that occasion with a special celebration. There will be speeches and public entertainments in Cincinnati on the third. On the fourth, the governor, the mayor and councilmen of Cincinnati, and those of us gathered around this table, along with everyone's families, will board a passenger packet the governor has ordered specially out-fitted for the purpose and travel to Dayton. There will be stops and speeches at the various towns along the way, of course. That is the reason all repairs must be completed by the end of June. The canal must be in excellent condi-tion for the anniversary trip."

"I see." Clayton sucked in a breath, thankful he had added in those two weeks of leeway. By subtracting that time and adding more men he should be able to get the jobs completed on time. "I shall start hiring immediately, sir."

The head commissioner nodded, leaned back against his chair and smiled. "That brings us to our last piece of business, Mr. Bainbridge." His smile disappeared. "We are not pleased with the quality of construction, nor the rate of progress being made on the new, northern section of the canal. The present chief engineer of the project is unequal to the job. Therefore, we are offering you that position— beginning when your repair work on the Miami Canal is finished in June and the celebration trip is over."

Clayton stared, hoped he didn't look as surprised as he felt. "I am flattered, gentlemen. Beyond that I do not know what to say. Knowing the position was filled—I was not expecting such an offer to be tendered, and there is much to be considered. I should like the opportunity to inspect the project before I respond."

"Perfectly understandable." The head engineer smiled. "You needn't give us your answer now, Mr. Bainbridge. We will talk more about it onboard the packet during the anniversary trip. That should give you ample time to make your decision."

"On the anniversary trip?"

"Yes. I thought I had made it clear that you and your

family are expected to come along. It's the governor's way of expressing his gratitude for your excellent work in engineering the repairs and keeping the Miami Canal functioning at optimum capacity."

Family. The word settled like a stone in the pit of his stomach. Clayton forced a smile. "I am flattered by the governor's favorable opinion of my work, and I will be pleased to join you on the celebration trip to Dayton. But as to family…my wife is deceased."

"Yes. We are aware of that. You have our sympathies. But you have a daughter, do you not?"

Clayton nodded, kept a pleasant expression on his face. "I do." He sought an acceptable excuse, offered it with relief. "But the child is not yet three years old—too young to be away from her nanny."

The commissioner frowned. "Then bring the nanny along. There will be ample accommodations, and the governor was adamant about all family members being present." His tone of voice made it clear he would brook no argument. The frown smoothed to his previously friendly expression. "That concludes our business, Mr. Bainbridge. Would you care to join us for a glass of port?"

"Thank you for the kind offer, Commissioner, but I must decline." He forced his lips into a smile. "Time is of the essence, and I intend to retire to my room and go over the needed repairs to discover how many laborers I must hire to accomplish our goal. If you gentlemen will excuse me?" He rose, inclined his head in a polite bow to all present and left the table.

Now what was he to do? *Pray?* Not likely! Clayton flopped down on the bed and stared up at the plaster ceiling. "I wish you were here, Grandma and Grandpa. I could use some advice. I don't know what to do, how to get out of this snare I find myself in. I had thought to be rid of Sarah Randolph and the child. Now I *have* to take that anniversary trip on that packet. I want that job as chief engineer on the northern Erie section of the canal. It will mean a real advancement in my career, and— Ahh!"

Clayton bolted out of bed, strode across the small room and yanked open the window. Sounds of revelry from the hotel's barroom floated up to him on the night air. Too bad he wasn't a drinking man. He could go downstairs, get drunk, then come back up to this room and sleep the night away. As if that would help anything. His problems would still be here when he woke tomorrow morning. At least this way he had a clear head to think things through and come up with a solution. And the first step was to define the problem. To admit it was not only the child anymore. It was Sarah Randolph, as well. She was so beautiful. So vibrant. So warm and caring and spirited. And when she had looked up at him the day her hair got tangled in that limb… And again yesterday, when she put her hand in his…

Clayton gripped the window frame and stared out at the night. Why had a woman like Sarah Randolph come into his life? And why was it impossible for him to be rid of her?

Bitterness rose, acrid and sour in his mouth. He stared up at the ebony sky. Did it amuse God to see him writhing in the pain of his guilt over Deborah's death? Is that why He took her, even though he had offered himself in her stead? Why He allowed the child to live as a daily reminder?

Clayton shoved back from the window, rubbed his hand over the back of his neck. He was without excuse or defense. He had known carrying a child would likely kill Deborah. He stared into the darkness, filled with remorse, helpless to change what was.

He loathed himself. Every time he saw Deborah's child, his shame and guilt grew. And now there was Sarah. Beautiful, warm, spirited Sarah, who stole his breath by simply walking into a room.

Was she a test sent by God? Clayton turned his back on the night, walked over and flopped on the bed. It would take every bit of strength he possessed, but he would not fail this time. He stared up at the ceiling, the pain in his heart swelling. "Do You hear me, God? I will not fail this time."

Sarah scanned the yard, spotted no sheep and, laughing at herself for being a coward, hurried to the front gate. Clayton Bainbridge had been gone four days, and each day left her feeling more restless. A good brisk walk should help.

A quick, longing glance toward the city below brought a sigh. There was so much of Cincinnati she was eager to explore. And she dearly wanted to go to Mrs. Westerfield's and see how her new gowns were progressing—and visit that shop on Fifth Street, the one opposite the Dennison House. N. L. Cole, that was the name. They had such lovely umbrellas and parasols in the window. But after all the talk of sickness she had overheard on her first visit to town, she was afraid to go again for fear of bringing the illness, whatever it was, home to Nora. She could not bear the thought of the toddler becoming ill.

Sarah pushed open the gate, turned her back on the city and started walking along the road, enjoying the fresh air, the response of her body to the demand of the hill. Unlike most of her lady friends and acquaintances, she enjoyed exercise, thanks to James. She had spent countless hours as a child playing outdoor games with her baby brother. A smile curved her lips. How he hated to be called her baby brother, but age gave one some privileges.

Sarah picked up her pace, her mind leaping from James to skipping stones to Clayton Bainbridge's private pond. Where was that trail…? Perhaps around this next bend? Yes! There it was. She started down the narrow path, careful to avoid the thorny branches that had ensnared her the first time. Clayton Bainbridge was not here to rescue her today. Heat stole into her cheeks. She had been so awkward and bumbling that day, so…inept. But Clayton had not said a word about her foolishness. He had simply untangled her, and very gently, too. And when she had looked up at him…

Warmth rushed through her in remembered response to the look in his eyes. Their blue color had deepened to almost black, and there had been tiny lights, almost like flames, flickering in their depths. For that one unguarded moment he had looked…dangerous. Had made her nervous.

Sarah replaced the disturbing thought with the memory of Aaron's quiet, respectful kiss the day she had accepted his proposal of marriage. Clayton Bainbridge was not at all like Aaron Biggs. Aaron had always made her feel safe and comfortable. Cared for. Not…restive and uneasy.

Sarah rounded the curve in the path and stepped out into the small, open space. The pond shimmered in the sunlight, bright and tranquil. The rocks and pebbles along its shore invited her to skip them across the still surface. The large rock beckoned her to sit and rest in the sunshine. She stood staring at the beautiful little glade, at the serene beauty of Clayton Bainbridge's special place, and tears welled into her eyes, made the pond's calm surface quiver, the trees shimmer and blur. She should not have come here.

She whipped around and rushed back up the path to the road, sobs filling her throat. She did not want to see that pond ever again. Nor the path. Or that thornapple tree! She did not want to remember being there with Clayton Bainbridge. She wanted Aaron. And the safe, undisturbing harbor of his love.

Chapter Ten

Eldora Quincy jumped at the quick, sharp raps of the front door knocker and scowled in the direction of the entrance hall. "How's a body supposed to get any work done with someone bangin' to be let in every five minutes!"

"Would you like me to answer the door for you, Eldora?"

"No. You're busy with Nora, Sarah. I'll go." The housekeeper dropped the stalk of rhubarb she was slicing into the bowl, wiped her hands dry on the towel tucked into the waist of her apron and hurried from the kitchen.

"More berries?" Nora held up her dish.

Sarah fixed her with a look.

"Pwease?"

"Good girl." Sarah smiled, sliced a few strawberries into the dish and placed it in front of the toddler. "You must remember to be polite and always say please and…"

"Tank you!" Nora piped the answer, beamed a smile, then stuffed a pudgy little handful of the sliced berries in her mouth. Her cheeks bulged.

Sarah laughed and wiped the red smear from around the toddler's lips before it stained her fair skin. "Small bites, sweetie. It is impolite to stuff your mouth."

"'Twas another man t' be interviewed fer workin' on the canal." Eldora came plodding back to the table. "Seems like all I got done all day is to answer that door. I would never get this rhubarb put up without you lendin' a hand, Sarah."

"I am happy to help, Eldora. I only wish I could do more." Sarah placed the washrag on the table, picked up the knife and resumed slicing berries. "I have been thinking…" She glanced over at the housekeeper. "I know how to manage a household, Mother taught me that. But, as you well know, I am at a loss in the kitchen. Would you be willing to teach me how to cook and bake?"

Eldora stared at her for a moment, then picked up the rhubarb, finished slicing it into the bowl and started on another piece. "I might could do that. You can start by adding them berries you cut up to this rhubarb an' tossin' in a couple handfuls of sugar." She pushed the full bowl across the table. "Then I'll show you about making crust. Mr. Bainbridge's favorite dessert is strawberry and rhubarb pie."

Sarah paused in her slicing and looked up. Eldora turned away from the table, but not before she had seen the woman's smile. She frowned and dumped the berries in with the rhubarb. What was amusing Eldora? Did the housekeeper think because she had been pampered all her life she was incapable of learning to cook?

Determination stiffened her spine. Sarah wiped her hands on the cloth, dried them on the towel and reached for the crock of sugar.

She had baked a pie. And helped Eldora put up the rhubarb. How surprised everyone at home would be when she wrote them about it. Sarah laughed, crossed the porch and walked down the stairs. She was finding it quite satisfying to learn how to do things for herself. But in spite of her baking lesson and the success of her pie, today had been disappointing. She had waited and watched, but no opportunity had presented itself for her to bring Nora into her father's presence. Clayton Bainbridge had been ensconced in his study all day. He was there still, interviewing potential laborers for the canal. And she had kept Nora far from the front of the house. Some of those applicants looked very rough and ill-bred, and she did not want the toddler frightened.

Sarah sighed and plucked a leaf from a bush, shredding it with her thumbnails as she ambled down the path toward the pagoda. A full week she had been disappointed in her purpose. What would her mother do?

She frowned and brushed the bits of leaf from her fingertips. She knew the answer to that question. Her mother would pray. But she had no intention of doing so. Nothing seemed to shake her mother's faith, but her own had been shattered by Aaron's death. She was not interested in communing with a God that turned a deaf ear to her cries. She cast an angry glance upward and caught her breath. Layers of vibrant red streaked across the cerulean sky, each tier outlined by the glittering golden rays of the hidden sun and diminishing in intensity as they touched the wooded hill. Sunset. She had not realized it was so late. She did not want to—

"Breathtaking, isn't it?"

And heartbreaking. Sarah blew out a breath to rid herself of the onrush of bitterness and turned toward the house. Clayton Bainbridge stood on the porch looking at the sky. "Yes, it is." She did not elaborate on her answer.

He was talking about the beauty of the sunset, not her reaction to it—let him think she agreed. She tensed as he descended the steps and came down the path toward her.

"It feels good to be outside, to breathe fresh air after being cooped up in the house all day." He stopped beside her, looked up at the sky and fell silent.

Why didn't he say what he wanted? Surely he wasn't planning to stay out here with her. Sarah went rigid. She did not want to share the sunset with him...or anything else for that matter. It intruded upon her memories of Aaron. She launched a change of subject. "Are your interviews going well?" The question drew Clayton's gaze to her and the expression in his eyes made her stomach tighten. She could not tell what he was thinking. Did he resent her crossing the servant/employer line by asking about his work? She reached for another leaf, began slitting it with her thumbnail.

"They are going well enough. Though they are taking time from my work I can ill afford to lose. I hope to finish them tomorrow, but it will be difficult. I need at least ten more men."

Through her lowered lashes, Sarah watched him lift his hand and rub the nape of his neck, a gesture that brought her father to mind. Justin Randolph did the same thing when he was troubled. Compassion welled, unbidden and unwanted.

"You see, the commissioners have set time constraints. All the repair work is to be completed by July first." Clayton's gaze sought hers. "And without enough laborers..."

There was concern in his voice, worry in his eyes. She tried to ignore the compassion but it was too strong. She tossed the mangled leaf away, brushed off a shred clinging to her skirt. "Perhaps if you explain their timetable is unreasonable they will grant you an extension." Something flickered in his eyes. Astonishment? Not surprising, he probably thought she was simply a mindless piece of social froth. He could not know the education and respect given the women in the Randolph family.

"Unfortunately, that is not possible. July fourth marks the tenth anniversary of the opening of the Miami Canal and the governor is planning a big celebration. Unreasonable or not, the work must be finished by that date. But, I did not come out here to bore you with a discussion of my work, Miss Randolph—except as it concerns you." He paused, looked off into the distance.

Sarah studied his face. He looked…uncomfortable. "I do not understand, Mr. Bainbridge. How does your work concern me?"

Clayton's gaze swung back to her. "The governor's celebration I spoke of—" He looked away again. "There is to be a trip to Dayton aboard a specially outfitted packet boat. I am invited—" he frowned "—nay, *ordered* to go along. The head commissioner made it quite clear that I must do so." He looked straight at her. "The trip will no doubt assure that I receive the position of head engineer for the new northern extension." He paused again.

Why was there such tension in his voice and posture? Sarah hesitated, but he had said it concerned her. "And is this a position you covet?"

He nodded. "Very much. It will mean great advancement in my career."

She studied his taut face. He certainly did not *look* pleased. "Then I offer my felicitations. But, I confess to confusion. I do not grasp how this concerns me."

His face took on that stony look she so disliked. "The governor has requested that those accompanying him on the packet bring their families along. I explained my wife was deceased and protested the child was too young to be away from its nanny, but I was informed there are ample accommodations for that circumstance. You are to come along to tend the child."

"Oh. I see." So that was what was troubling him. He would be forced to acknowledge Nora. Anger surged. But also excitement. It was the perfect opportunity to bring father and daughter together.

"Of course I will give you extra compensation for caring for Nora during the excursion. And also pay for two suitable gowns." He cleared his throat. "You do not look like a nanny—" he waved a hand toward her "—your gowns, I mean."

Sarah glanced down at the full, rosette- and lace-trimmed, long skirt of her rose-colored silk dress. "I know my gowns are inappropriate and give people the wrong impression, Mr. Bainbridge. But I had no time to order suitable ones before I came." She looked up at him. "However, your offer is unnecessary. I have already commissioned several new gowns. They should be ready soon."

"I see. In that case, I shall bid you a good evening, Miss Randolph. I will explain more about the excursion as the time nears." Clayton gave her a small nod and turned back toward the house. She watched him walk away, again feeling that odd connection to him she had experienced that day in the garden. She and Clayton Bainbridge both were plagued by loneliness and painful memories.

Like long walks in the sunset.

Sarah swallowed hard and looked down at her lengthening shadow on the lawn. One shadow. Aaron's taller, broader silhouette was gone forever. She would never know the comfort of his presence beside her again.

A sudden glow of candlelight spilled through the slatted shutters of an upstairs window brightening the dusk. Sarah stared up at it, her throat tight, her heart aching. Her pain seemed unbearable at times, but how much worse must it be for Clayton Bainbridge who had to sleep alone every night in his marriage bed?

Sarah blinked tears from her eyes and clenched her hands. A walk in the garden had lost all appeal. She closed her mind to the fading sunset and headed for the porch.

She would have to board a boat!

Sarah froze. Panic squeezed her lungs. Her stomach roiled, her body shook. She forced her legs to move, made it to the porch before they gave way. She dropped onto the seat of the wooden bench and stared out into the garden, forcing her mind to concentrate on something else in order to gain control before going inside.

Were those high stone walls surrounding the garden built by Clayton's grandfather? She placed herself in that earlier time, and gave her imagination full rein. What would it have been like to suddenly see Indians pouring over those walls? To see painted, half-naked, yelling savages racing toward you with tomahawks raised? Her skin prickled. Her shoulders stiffened. She stared into the deepening shadows of the night, saw movement and edged along the seat toward the door.

A dark shadow swooped down out of the night sky straight for the porch, sent a screech shrilling through the air.

Sarah shot to her feet and stumbled to the door. She jerked it open, leaped inside, slammed it shut and sagged against the wall, listening to the roar of her racing pulse.

"What happened? What is wrong?"

She started, looked up. Clayton Bainbridge was

hurrying toward her from across the library, a scowl on his face and a book in his hand.

"Indians." She meant it to be light, amusing. To distract him from her appearance and the fear she knew was reflected on her face. And it might have worked—if she had not burst into tears.

"Feel better now?"

Sarah nodded, longed for her mother and father, Ellen, the comfort of home. She could not stop shaking.

"Would you like another sip of wine? It always seemed to help Deborah when she was…discomposed."

"No. No more." She gathered her courage and looked up. "I apologize, Mr. Bainbridge. I— It—" She took a breath, swallowed, looked into his eyes and knew she would have to tell him at least part of the truth. "The sunset brought back some painful memories and I tried to suppress them by imagining what it was like during the Indians raids on this place. And then the owl—" She stopped; it sounded so foolish, but it was the best she could do given the state of her tangled emotions. She gave a helpless little wave. "There is no excuse for my actions. But I am sorry."

Clayton nodded, placed the glass in his hand on the table beside the wine decanter. "There are times I think it must be fortunate to be a woman and have the outlet of tears for inner turmoil." He smiled down at her. "Men are not permitted that luxury, though we are allowed to punch a wall—or each other. Or fight Indians."

"Of the 'Owl' tribe?" She tried again to make it sound light, humorous.

"Especially them."

The understanding in his voice brought tears welling.

Sarah blinked them away and gave up all pretense. He was very good at calming a woman. He must have had a lot of practice with his wife. "And have you done so? Punched a wall, I mean—not fought Indians." That must have been too personal. A frown creased his brow, was quickly erased.

"On occasion."

"And did it help?" Her heart beat furiously at her temerity, but something compelled her to ask. She looked into Clayton's eyes, waited. At last he shook his head.

"No." He looked away, looked back and smiled, but the smile never reached his eyes, and she knew he only did so to lighten the tense atmosphere for her. "At least not always. Only when you punch so hard your hand hurts and you forget the other pain."

Sarah gave a light laugh to reward him for his effort. "Then perhaps I shall try it your way should I again have a need of release, Mr. Bainbridge. For tears never work. They merely give you a headache, a stuffy nose and red, puffy eyes—most unattractive." She rose and gave him a genuine smile. "Thank you for your care, *and* for your understanding, Mr. Bainbridge. It is most appreciated. Now I shall bid you a good evening."

"Good evening, Miss Randolph—and rest easy. No harm will come to you in this house." His gaze held hers. "It was built stout and strong to keep out enemies."

Only mortal ones, Mr. Bainbridge. Grief found you. I can read it in your eyes. Sarah smiled, nodded and walked from the room. Some things were best left unspoken.

Chapter Eleven

Sarah made a slow turn in front of the pier glass in the dressing room. The gown was perfect. It was made of lovely, yet sensible, fabric with no flounces or ruffles, its only trim a touch of dark-red roping at the neck, waist and sleeves that enhanced the red in the material's deep-chestnut color. A plain and serviceable dress—exactly what she had requested. And the workmanship was excellent.

Sarah smiled and patted the matching red roping that held her hair in a loose knot on the crown of her head. There would be no more confusion as to her nanny position due to her elegant, unsuitable gowns now. They were stowed away in her trunk. It was a shame she could not pack her painful memories away with them. But the faint crescents of fatigue under her eyes testified to the impossibility of that.

She sighed and went to her bedroom to open the shutters and let in the morning sunshine. She had not slept at all well. But this time it was not only memories of Aaron that had kept her awake. A vision of Clayton Bainbridge's face, his eyes shadowed with pain, had kept her tossing and turning all night. That, and this strange connection she felt to him. A connection that grew stronger with each encounter.

Sarah frowned, moved over to the desk, sat in the chair and slipped on her shoes. She did not *want* these feelings. She did not want to sense Clayton's grief and pain. Did not want to understand it. Or to feel compassion for him. She had enough pain and grief of her own. All she wanted was to feel safe. That is all she had ever wanted since her mother abandoned her. It seemed little enough to ask.

No harm will come to you in this house. It was built stout and strong to keep out enemies.

Oh, if only that were so. But Randolph Court was built of brick, and she had learned that stout walls could not protect one from the worst enemies, the most painful hurts. Nor could wealth, or social position. Death and grief came to all.

Oh, Aaron, I miss you so. Sarah closed her eyes to conjure the face of her dead fiancé, but it was Clayton Bainbridge's countenance that came into view. She snapped her eyes open, rose and hurried toward the nursery, wiping the frown from her face and curving her lips into a smile as Nora stood in her crib and held up her arms.

"Good morning, sweetie."

"Mornin'." Nora yawned, rubbed her eyes. "Me go outside?"

"After we get you cleaned up and have breakfast." Sarah lifted the toddler into her arms, blinked back tears at the rush of love overflowing her as Nora's small, sleep-warm arms tightened around her neck. How was she ever going to give up this child? But she didn't have to think about that now. Nora would not be taken from her in a moment's time. She would be able to prepare herself for this loss. And meantime she had a purpose for her life.

Clayton rose from his desk chair and held out his hand. "Most impressive recommendations, Mr. Wexford. The job is yours."

"Thank you, sir." The man stood and shook hands. "I'll not disappoint you, Mr. Bainbridge." He picked up his hat and moved toward the door. "When and where shall I report for work, sir?"

"Come here to the house at eight tomorrow morning. I want to go over some blueprints with you and familiarize you with the various projects."

"Very good, sir. I shall be here promptly at eight o'clock."

Clayton nodded, faced the group of men gathered outside the door. "There will be no more interviews. The positions have all been filled. Thank you all for coming." He closed the door on the mumbling, disappointed men and turned back to the study, his steps quick and light. A grin split his face. At last! He had finally found an engineer qualified to oversee the repairs. The man could actually *read* a blueprint. He could put Wexford in charge of the minor projects, freeing himself to oversee the difficult jobs. He would have no trouble meeting that July first deadline now.

A muffled, childish giggle, coming from the direction of the back of the house, wiped the grin from his face. Clayton reached to close his study door, paused at the sound of soft, feminine laughter. His exhilaration swelled, pushed at him. He scowled, fought the strengthening urge, the memory of the understanding on Sarah Randolph's face as he had explained his deadline plight last night in the garden.

Another burst of muffled laughter reached him. He tightened his grip on the door latch, glanced around his empty study, then stepped back into the entrance hall and closed the door. What good was this elation if he could share it with no one? Surely there would be a moment when the child was off playing by itself when he could speak to Sarah and tell her of his good fortune. There was no harm in that.

He strode down the hall and into the library, slowing at sight of the open door. No wonder he could hear their laughter. He stepped onto the back porch, spotted Sarah marching, shoulders back, arms pumping, around the trunk of the maple tree at the side of the garden. The child, imitating her posture and giggling, was following close behind. Clayton's face drew taut. This was not a good time. In fact, it was a bad idea altogether. What had he been thinking? He turned to leave, pivoted back at a sudden squeal. The child was running toward the pagoda, chasing after a squirrel.

"Good afternoon, Mr. Bainbridge."

Clayton looked down. His heart thudded. The sun bathed Sarah's upturned face, highlighted her delicate features, the golden strands among her light-brown hair—especially those strands that had worked loose from the restraint of the red cord and now dangled from her temples to rest against her cheeks. Cheeks pink from her exertions playing with the child. Why did the woman not wear a bonnet? He dipped his head in greeting, not trusting his voice. Was that plain gown supposed to hide her beauty? It only enhanced it.

He stood silent, watched her walk to the porch and climb the stairs, all grace and beauty.

"Were you looking for me?"

All my life. The unbidden answer crowded all other thought from his mind. Guilt assailed him. Would he betray Deborah's memory? Bitterness rose, washed through him. Clayton frowned, shook his head. "Someone left the door open. I could hear your laughter all the way to my study. Please make certain the door is closed in the future."

He stepped back through the door, closed it firmly and headed back to his study, his elation replaced by a grim determination to avoid Sarah Randolph from now on.

That had not gone as planned. Sarah glared at the closed door, itching to open it again—to march down the hall to Clayton's study and demand that he come back to the yard and at least *speak* to his daughter. She clenched her hands, turned and hurried down the steps before she gave in to the desire.

"Nora...come with me, sweetie." She held out her hand, and the toddler came running. Sarah took hold of her tiny hand, opened the gate and started down the gravel way toward the carriage house, hoping Quincy would not be offended if they invaded his territory. She needed a change of scenery. She looked around the far side of the building, but spotted no one.

"Hello?"

No answer. Sarah released Nora's hand, tugged one of the wide, plank doors open a crack and peeked inside. Cool, musty air carrying a hint of oiled leather, feed, hay and manure flowed out of the dim interior, tantalizing her and bringing back childhood memories. She and Mary and James had spent many happy hours in their father's stables. And it had been one of Mr. Buffy's favorite places.

Her lips curved at thought of the huge black dog that had been a gift to her from Justin Randolph. It was the day Justin gave her the puppy she first felt he loved her, and she began to talk that very day. Tears filmed her eyes. Mr. Buffy had been her constant companion for seven years. She had been ten years old when he died. Her smile ebbed. That had been her first experience with grief. She had never wanted another dog.

Sarah pushed away the memory, lifted Nora into her arms in case there should be an unfriendly animal of some sort lurking about, pulled the door wider and stepped inside. "Mr. Quincy?" A low nicker was her only answer. She looked toward the far wall. A dark roan with powerful shoulders extended its neck over the stall door, flared sensitive nostrils, snorted and tossed its head. Clayton Bainbridge's mount. The shoulder muscles bunched, a hoof thudded against the floor. The roan tossed its head again, stared at her out of dark-brown eyes separated by a white blaze.

"My, you are a beauty." Sarah kept her voice pitched low and soft. "And I think you know it, too." The roan's ears twitched, pricked forward. Its stable mate nickered. Sarah shifted her gaze to the smaller bay with a white star on its face that occupied the next stall. The carriage horse. What had Quincy called her? Sassy. Yes, that was it. "Yes, you are a beauty, too, Sassy."

She started forward. Nora wiggled, tightened the arm she had wrapped around her neck. Sarah looked at the toddler, who—thumb stuck securely in her little mouth—was staring wide-eyed at the horses. Anger gushed. She kept forgetting the little girl had been kept caged in the nursery before she came. "See the pretty horses, sweetie? They will not hurt you. Shall we go pet them?"

"Horse." Nora pointed at the stalls, stuck her thumb back in her mouth and squirmed closer.

Sarah gave her a reassuring hug and started toward the smaller bay—stopping as she caught movement out of the corner of her eye. Heart pounding, her gaze locked on a grain box that sat on the floor along the side wall, she backed toward the doors. Something small and gray darted out of the empty stall beside Sassy's and ran behind the chest. A rat? She swallowed a scream, stared at the spot where the rat had disappeared and felt behind her for the door.

"Mew." A tiny gray face with green eyes poked out from behind the box, drew back. *"Mew."*

"A kitten!" Sarah laughed and hurried to the grain box, her long skirts sweeping a trail through the dust and bits of hay and straw covering the puncheon floor. She sat Nora down on top of the chest and peered behind it. Four pair of green eyes gleamed up at her. "Oh, Nora, look! There are four baby kittens."

She reached down. Kittens darted from behind the box and scattered every direction.

"Kitty!" Nora squealed, wiggled to the edge of the chest, flopped over onto her stomach and pushed. Sarah made a grab for her and missed. The toddler landed with a thud on the spotless seat of her white ruffled pantalettes, pushed to her feet and chased after the kitten that had run into the empty stall.

"Wait, sweetie! He will scratch you." Sarah rushed inside the cubicle, pulled the door shut and stooped to pick up the tiny, spitting and hissing, furry ball of feline fury crouched beneath the manger.

Clayton frowned at the rap on the door. He had told Eldora to turn away any further applicants. "Yes?"

The door opened. Eldora Quincy stepped into the room. "Not wantin' to bother you, sir, but—" She stopped, glanced toward the window as light flickered through the room and a low rumble sounded in the distance.

Clayton followed her gaze. Raindrops batted at the leaves on the trees, danced on top of the low, stone wall and tapped at the window. "When did it start raining?"

"A bit ago, sir. 'Tis why I come. Miss Randolph and the child…they are still outside."

"Most likely on the back porch." He returned to his work of assigning men to the various repair jobs.

"No, sir, I checked."

"Eldora, Miss Randolph is perfectly capable of caring for the child. She will come in when—" Lightning flashed, thunder growled. The image of Sarah's frightened face during the last storm popped into his head. Clayton frowned, looked up. "The pagoda?" It was a foolish question. He knew the answer before his housekeeper shook her head no. He fought the urge to rise and go search. The child was safe in her care, and Sarah Randolph was not his concern. "Have Quincy look in the stable, perhaps she took refuge there."

"Mr. Quincy went to the farm early this morning."

"Then send Lucy!"

Eldora started at the snap in his voice, gave him a curious look. "Lucy has been home these last two days tendin' her sick family. An' I've food on the stove and in the oven needs watching. 'Tis almost supper time. That child is goin' to get almighty hungry." She turned with a swish of her long, gray skirt and left the room. He could hear her shuffling down the hall toward the kitchen.

How could footsteps convey disgust? Eldora's clearly did. Clayton shoved his chair back and lurched to his feet.

So much for avoiding Sarah Randolph and the child! He peered out the windows, scanned the front and side yards. Lightning flashed. Rain poured down. He snatched an umbrella from the brass stand by the front door and ran down the hall to check the backyard and stable.

Sarah caught her breath at the glint of lightning, brushed at the dust clinging to Nora's frock and plucked bits of hay from the toddler's golden curls. How was she going to get Nora to the house? She had delayed as long as she could, hoping the storm would move on. Instead it was growing more intense. She gave the hem of the long skirt of her gown a vigorous shake. Dust flew. Nora sneezed. "Sorry, sweetie."

Her voice shook. Sarah took a breath to gain some control, pushed at her mussed hair with her trembling hands. Thank goodness Nora was too little to guess she was terrified.

Lightning seared across the darkening sky, threw its light in the window. Thunder cracked. Sarah jerked. The roan snorted, tossed his head and thudded his hoof against the stall floor. The bay shifted position. Clearly, the horses were sensing her fear. She had to leave. Right now.

"Time to go, Nora."

The little girl shook her head, tightened her grip on the ball of fluff in her lap. "Kitty."

"We will come play with the kitty tomorrow. But now we have to go get cleaned up for dinner. Your tummy is getting hungry."

"And my mouf."

"Yes. And your mouth." Sarah settled the toddler's sunbonnet in place, tied the strings and took the purring kitten from her lap. "I do not want you to get wet in the rain so

I am going to run really fast." She lifted Nora into her arms, gathered every bit of courage she possessed, walked to the door, slipped it open and waited. She would go after the next flash of lightning and, hopefully, reach the house before it came again.

Lightning streaked against the darkened sky. "Hold on tight, Nora!" Heart pounding, Sarah bent forward to cover the toddler with her body, leaped outside, kicked the door closed and ran, terror driving her every step.

They were not in the backyard. Clayton lowered the umbrella to block the slanting, wind-driven rain from his face and opened the garden gate. *If they were not in the stable—* He refused the worry trying to squirm its way into his thoughts and broke into a loping run toward the carriage house. Something hard slammed into his chest just below his breastbone.

"Ugh!" The breath burst from his lungs. He dropped the umbrella, grabbed his assailant by the shoulders. Sarah Randolph lifted her head, stared up at him out of eyes wide with fear. Her shoulders trembled beneath his hands. He tightened his grip, felt something squirm between them and glanced down.

The child lifted her bonnet-clad head and giggled. "We runned fast!"

Lightning rent the darkness. Sarah jerked, shuddered.

Clayton picked up the umbrella, slipped his arm about her shoulders and guided her through the gate and up the path.

Light splashed across the glistening brick. He looked up. Mrs. Quincy stood at the top of the steps holding a lantern to light their way. "You all right, Sarah?"

Wisps of wet hair brushed his hand as Sarah looked up and nodded. "Yes. W-we are fine."

A gust of wind tugged at the umbrella, blew the rain beneath the porch roof. The lantern light flickered as the housekeeper stepped back. Sarah went rigid beneath his arm, her steps faltered as they reached the porch. Clayton stole a look at her face, glanced at his housekeeper. "Eldora, take the child."

Sarah stiffened. "I will care for Nora."

"'Tis only till you get into some dry togs, Sarah." The housekeeper sat the lantern on the bench and reached for the toddler. "Well, Miss Nora, what have you been up to?"

Nora leaned into Eldora's arms. "Me play with kitty. See horsy. And we runned fast!"

"Did you, now? That's just fine. Why don't you tell me all about it whilst I give you some supper." Eldora shielded the little girl with her broad body and waddled into the house.

Lightning sizzled, a brilliant yellow spear streaking to earth. Thunder cracked.

Sarah gasped, broke from his grasp and dashed for the door. She made it halfway across the porch before she collapsed in a heap on the floor.

"Sarah!" Clayton threw the umbrella and rushed to her side. She shook her head, pushed feebly at his chest when he reached for her. He ignored her protest, lifted her into his arms and strode to the door. The howling wind blew her hair loose from its restraint, whipped it across his face. The lantern banged against the back of the bench.

Sarah shuddered, tried to speak.

He shook his head, carried her into the library and lowered her to the settee. "Stay here! I have to get the lantern before it breaks and starts a fire." He ran outside, grabbed the lantern and rushed back. Sarah was sitting up, her wet hair spilling over her shoulders, a red cord in her trembling hands. Her face was the color of plaster. She winced and bit down on her lower lip as lightning flashed.

Clayton hurried to the windows and closed the shutters, then walked over and stood in front of her. "Are you all right?"

She nodded and looked up. He had never seen such fright on a person's face. He did not understand it, was helpless to take it from her. Could not even take her in his arms to comfort her. He jammed his hands into his pockets to resist the temptation. "Why did you not *stay* in the carriage house? Surely you knew I would come for you?" His concern made the words come out sharper than he intended. Color rushed into Sarah's face. She rose and faced him, shaking, her shoulders squared, the red cord dangling from one fisted hand.

"And why would I think you would care enough to come for us, Mr. Bainbridge? You will not even *look* at your daughter! And, as you refuse to allow her in your presence, how would you know we were missing? We could have been trapped in that carriage house all night!" Her chin lifted, she looked straight into his eyes, her own wide and shadowed. "I confess, had I been alone, that would have been my choice rather than go out in the storm. But Nora is my charge and I am not so selfish as to put my fear above her needs. Now, if you will excuse me, I must change out of these wet clothes. Good evening, Mr. Bainbridge." She whipped her long skirts to the side, stepped around him and hurried from the room.

Clayton stood silent and watched her leave, every fiber of his being screaming to go after her. He walked to the table by the door, picked up the lantern, opened the side and lowered the wick. The light sputtered and died. Darkness closed around him. He hung the lantern on its peg by the door, turned and walked out into the hall. There was no sound of Sarah's passing, not even her footsteps overhead. Only the storm—and solitude.

He drew his gaze from the stairs, set his mind against the sting of her indictment against him and walked down the hall toward his study. What Sarah had said was true—and the reasons did not matter. Explaining would not change anything. Things were as they had to be.

Chapter Twelve

Sarah hung her wet dress over the edge of the bathtub, grabbed a towel and rubbed at her dripping hair. Rain pounded on the roof, thunder grumbled. She shuddered, dropped the towel, pulled on her new blue gown and willed her trembling fingers to fasten the fabric-covered buttons that paraded from the prim collar to the narrow vee at the waist. How ironic that the dresses had been delivered when she would not be needing them. After her display of cowardice this evening, it was unlikely Clayton Bainbridge would trust her to care for his daughter—even if he did not love the child.

But for him to dismiss her would be unfair. It was *his* fault she had collapsed. Her legs would not have gone all weak and wobbly if he had not told Eldora to take Nora from her. Having to care for the toddler had given her the strength to face her fear. And when that strength was not required, her knees had given way.

Sarah frowned and shook out her long skirt over her petticoat. If she were summoned, what defense could she offer Clayton Bainbridge? She could hardly tell him the truth—that strong emotions struck her in the knees, a silly weakness she had been plagued with since childhood. That would only further undermine his trust of her reliability. Nor did it explain why she had attacked him that way. She should have held her tongue instead of lashing out at him. But the man was so incredibly frustrating! And he had challenged her when she was most vulnerable. The storm—

Lightning glinted between the closed slats of the shutters.

Sarah shivered, tugged her quilted robe on over the dress, pulled it close about her for warmth and crossed to the mirror. Her hair was a tangled mess. She brushed it out, gathered it loosely at the nape of her neck and secured it with the blue ribbon edged in the same demure scallops that graced her gown's collar and hem. Her hair would dry faster falling free, and her hands were trembling too hard to manage her normal hairstyle. She was having enough difficulty tying the ribbon.

A rush of tears blurred her reflection. Would she ever again tie a ribbon in Nora's golden curls? If she were dismissed, who would care for the toddler? Eldora was too busy. And Lucy was home caring for her family—may have herself succumbed to the sickness going around.

The tears overflowed. Sarah wiped them from her cheeks, turned from the mirror and pulled on her shoes, concentrating on the activity as a defense against the thought she did not want to entertain. But it hung there in the dark recesses of her mind, refusing to be denied. What if Lucy came back and brought the sickness to Nora? What if— *No!*

Sarah jolted to her feet. She would not think that. She would *not!* And she would not worry about being dismissed. She still had tonight. And perhaps Clayton would be too busy meeting his deadline for the repairs on the canal to think about replacing her. That would give her until July to prove her competency. Oh! And he needed her for the excursion trip in July.

Sarah grabbed on to the hope, hurried to her bedroom, tossed her robe onto the bed and opened the door to the winder stairs. Light from the kitchen lit the staircase. A smile trembled on her lips. Eldora must have opened the door at the bottom of the staircase to listen for her. And she had thought the housekeeper so harsh and uncaring. She started down the stairs, paused as Nora's baby voice floated up from below. "A horsy is big! Kitties are little. They scratch."

How endearing. Sarah's throat tightened. She cleared away the lump and started down the steep spiral, being quiet so she could hear Nora's conversation with Eldora.

"They do?"

"Uh-huh. See?"

The thought of Nora's pudgy little hand being held out for Eldora's inspection brought the lump came back to her throat. Sarah swallowed hard.

"My, my! That looks serious. Why don't you eat your last bite of peas like a good girl whilst I baste this roast, then I'll fetch my beeswax salve. That will fix you right up."

Sarah wiped away tears. Trust Eldora to have what was needed. If only she had a salve to heal a broken heart. Or an elixir one could take for a paralyzing fear. But no one could cure those ills. Not even time had lessened their grip on her, though loving Nora helped. Caring for the little girl had turned into a blessing.

Sarah caught her breath, tightened her grip on the

railing. She had to keep her nanny post. She simply had to! But what could she do to secure it? Not even an apology could take back her rash words. Oh, she hated storms. And darkness. And fear. Why could she not simply be safe? And why could little Nora not be loved? What sort of God allowed such cruelty?

Her chest tightened, ached. Sarah blew out her breath, hid her trembling hands in the folds of her long skirts, counted to ten and stepped out into the kitchen.

Clayton shoved the last of the blueprints he would need for tomorrow into his leather pouch and crossed to the door. His work was finished and the study was crowding in on him. More accurately, his thoughts were crowding him. Dinner had been a nightmare of forcing food down his throat while trying to ignore the sound of Sarah's voice in the kitchen. And that glimpse he had caught of her carrying the child up the stairs—

Clayton broke off the thought and yanked the door open. He needed to move. His long strides swallowed the length of the hall, made short work of the library. He lit the lantern from a taper in a wall sconce, opened the back door and stepped out on the porch. Rain drummed overhead, ran off the eaves and splashed on the ground. So much for a walk. At least out here he had space around him.

He set the lantern on the table, leaned on the railing and stared out into the stormy darkness trying to empty his memory of the way Sarah Randolph had felt in his arms— of that one fleeting instant of trust he had seen in her eyes when she had looked up at him. He knew, better than anyone, he did not deserve a woman's trust. Deborah had trusted him and his weakness had killed her.

Lightning flickered in the distance. Thunder rumbled in on a gust of wind. Something rustled behind him. Clayton turned. The opened umbrella he had discarded was trapped between the house wall and the table. He picked it up, grabbed the lantern and trotted down the porch steps and strode to the gate, slipped through it onto the gravel way.

Sarah had run into him right here—headfirst. Knocked the wind out of him.

We runned fast!

A smile tugged at his lips. The child was a brave one. Clayton scowled, squelched the frisson of pride that zipped through him. But the fact remained, dogged his footsteps—the child had been not fearful of the storm, only excited by the adventure. And she liked horses. He had always liked horses. Had never feared them.

Enough of that sort of thinking! Clayton leaned into the wind and picked up his pace. He had come outside to forget about tonight's events—not dissect them. He crowded under the stable's overhang, closed the umbrella and opened a door. The hinges squeaked. The roan snorted, neighed a challenge. "Easy, boy, it is only me." There was an answering whicker, low and welcoming.

The tension in his body eased. Clayton grabbed a handful of carrots from the barrel beside the door and crossed to the stalls. Both horses stretched out their necks, nostrils twitching. "Yes, I have carrots. Here, girl." He fed Sassy, stroked her velvety muzzle, patted her neck and moved on while she munched contentedly on her treat.

Pacer thudded his hoof, stretched out his head and bumped him in the chest. "I have not forgotten you, fella." Clayton scratched beneath the roan's throat latch and gave him his carrot.

Silence.

The sound of it surrounded him, emphasized by the drumming rain, the crunch of the horses' chewing. He opened the door and slipped into Pacer's stall, scratched beneath the black mane then slid his hand down over the roan's withers and back. Pacer turned his head, nudged him in the shoulder and went back to his munching.

Pain caught at his chest. *This was the sum of the affection in his life, a nudge from a horse.* Clayton patted the powerful shoulder and stepped back out of the stall. He gave each horse another carrot, walked to the grain box and sat, leaning back against the wall and studying the Wellingtons on his feet. A knot in a log pushed against his shoulder blade. He shifted his position, crossed his arms over his chest and listened to the rain.

And why would I think you would care enough to come for us, Mr. Bainbridge? You will not even look at your daughter! And, as you refuse to allow her in your presence, how would you know we were missing? We could have been trapped in that carriage house all night!

Clayton scowled. Could he find no peace from Sarah Randolph? Must thoughts of her intrude even here? It was his last haven.

Clayton jerked to his feet and paced across the carriage house. He could not escape the woman. Images of her appeared to him everywhere in the house, in the yard, even at his special, private place at the pond. Usually with her chin lifted and eyes snapping as she confronted him with some offense or other on behalf of the child. But there were those other few moments, when her eyes were warm and—

Clayton sucked in a breath and erased the vision by staring at his reflection in the window in front of him. The woman was an annoyance. But she was excellent with the child. And she cared deeply for her—*it*. The way she had faced her fear of the storm to bring the child back to the house proved that. But she was also a temptation he should put out of his life. His attraction to her was growing and he did not want or need that complication. He wanted no part of love. There was too much pain, too much hurt when you let your heart become involved with someone. And he had already proven himself unworthy of a woman's trust.

He pivoted from the window, paced back across the dusty, puncheon floor and picked up the lantern. Trying to avoid her was not working. He had tried that this afternoon and she had ended up in his arms. He had to dismiss her. Be rid of her. It was the only answer. He reached for the door.

Nora is my charge and I am not so selfish as to put my fear above her needs.

The words stabbed deep. Clayton stiffened, tightened his grip on the bar. That was exactly what he was doing— putting his fears above the child's needs. What sort of man was he? Had he no strength of will? No honor? Sarah Randolph stayed.

He shoved the door open, stepped out, slammed it shut, dropped the bar into place and stalked toward the house, oblivious to the rain, the wind, everything but the turmoil inside him.

Wind slapped at her long, sodden skirts, whipped them into a frenzied flapping that knocked her off her feet. The planking of the deck beneath her heaved, shuddered. The ship tilted. She groped for something to cling to, found only emptiness, slid. Lightning flashed, threw flickering light over a gaping hole where the ship's rail had been, over Aaron clinging to the broken end and reaching for her. She stretched out her hand.

The world exploded. Brilliant light blinded her. Thunder deafened her. She fell—

Strong arms clasped her, lifted her, held her tight and secure against a solid chest.

Sarah opened her eyes, stared into the dimly lit room, disoriented…confused. Her heart pounded, her pulse raced, but something was different. She felt strangely calm. Why should that be? Usually the nightmare left her in a state bordering on panic. Perhaps she was finally getting over her fear—the terror that gripped her when she had almost drowned.

Shivers shook her. The calm disappeared. She would never forget the feeling of the icy-cold Atlantic waters closing over her head. Never.

Sarah pushed to a sitting position, slid her legs over the side of the bed and shoved her feet into her slippers. The storm had diminished. She could hear rain tapping at the window, but the pounding on the roof had ceased. She rose and pulled on her robe, watched for a telltale glint of light through the shutter slats, listened for the sound of thunder. There was only the rain. She took a deep breath, walked to the nursery door and peeked in at Nora. The little girl was sound asleep, her thumb in her mouth, her bandaged finger curled on her cheek.

She is so proud of that bandage. Sarah's chest filled. Her future was uncertain, but she would always treasure this time with Nora. She turned back to her bedroom, rolled up the wick on her bedside lamp and carried it to the desk. The letter from her parents Quincy had brought home with him earlier that evening lay on the polished wood. She picked it up and unfolded it, smiling as she caught sight of the salutation.

"Our dearest daughter,"

Sarah sat in the chair, pulled the lamp close and began to read. She knew what it said, had already read it three times, but tonight she needed the reassurance of their love.

The door at the bottom of the winder stairs opened, closed. Sarah lifted her head and listened, but heard no one calling. She rose, picked up her lamp and opened her door. "Did you want me, Eldor—"

She stopped, stared down into Clayton Bainbridge's upturned face. His features hardened. Her stomach flopped. "Forgive me, I heard the door and thought perhaps Eldora wanted me." She stepped back, closed her door and leaned against it, listening to Clayton's footsteps as he climbed the stairs. They paused on the landing. Her heart leaped into her throat. Would he knock? Tell her to pack and leave, that she was no longer wanted in her post in spite of the canal celebration? The door opposite hers on the landing opened, closed.

She released the air trapped in her lungs, crossed to the bed, adjusted the lamp and removed her robe and slippers. It was difficult to tell in the shadowy light from the lamp, but Clayton Bainbridge had looked angry. Was it only the late hour that had saved her from dismissal? She would know tomorrow.

Sarah sighed, slipped beneath the covers and nestled down into her pillows. She closed her eyes, sat bolt upright and stared at the stairway door. That was it! That was the difference in the nightmare. Clayton Bainbridge had kept her from falling in the water—had held her safe in his arms.

Chapter Thirteen

Clayton rode past the railed pens holding the mules and horses resting from yesterday's hard labor, stopped in front of the handler's shed and dismounted. "Unsaddle Pacer and put him in his pen and give him some hay, Murphy. I will be here the rest of the day." He handed over the reins, patted the roan's neck, then grabbed his leather pouch from behind his saddle and hurried toward the work hut. The work at this site would be finished today. Tomorrow afternoon at the latest. And then they would move to the next job.

Clayton glanced around. Workers were already hard at work cleaning up the site. Men were throwing construction debris from the bottom of the canal into skid wagons to be hauled up the high, sloping bank. On the towpath across the ditch, men with scrapers were lining up to smooth the surface. Things were moving apace.

He nodded to the men loading unused timbers onto a wagon to be moved to the aqueduct that was their next work site and quickened his steps. The canal repairs were progressing faster than he dared hope, thanks to his good fortune in hiring John Wexford. The man had proved himself wholly capable of bossing the easier jobs—and of controlling the hot-tempered, quick-fisted workers. He still had to check on Wexford's sites every couple of days, and his accelerated workload—dawn to dusk every day—was exhausting, but that was welcome. He had not had a glimpse of Sarah Randolph or the child in weeks. He left before they rose and came home after they were abed. Of course that would stop after the July first deadline. And then he would have to act.

Clayton frowned, stepped into the temporary, collapsible hut and tossed the pouch on the scarred tabletop. It still seemed the best solution would be to have Sarah take the child home to Philadelphia and care for it there. It would be well cared for—and they would both be out of his life. The only flaw in the plan was Sarah Randolph. She had not taken the nanny position to earn her living, so offering her increased wages to rear the child might not influence her to agree. If he knew why she—

Wild whoops split the air. Clayton pivoted and rushed back outside. Across the canal, the four men guiding the wooden scrapers were each urging their horses to greater speed, fighting for the lead position. In the dirt behind them were crooked grooves and ridges gouged out of the ground by the corners and edges of the wildly tipping scrapers.

Activity around him ceased as the workers stopped to cheer on their favorites in the impromptu race.

"Stop!" Clayton cupped his hands around his mouth. "You men on the far towpath—stop your horses!" His effort was useless, his order lost in the whooping, shouting din. The wild race went on. One of the scrapers slammed into another, sending it careening toward the edge of the bank. The worker hooted and urged his horse to greater speed, passing the worker trying to steady his wobbling scraper and get back in the race.

Fools. They were going to kill someone! Clayton ran to the edge of the canal and dropped over the side. Half running, half sliding, he charged down the sloping bank, hit the base running and sprinted across the canal bottom at an angle to intercept the racers, the workers he passed laughing and exhorting him to run faster. Heart pumping, breath coming in short gasps, he attacked the opposite bank, scrabbling for footing on the sloping ground, losing momentum as he neared the top.

The sound of pounding hoofs broke through the roar of laughing, shouting voices. He looked up, saw a worker rolling head over heels in the dirt, his wild-eyed horse panicked by the uncontrolled, crazily bumping and swaying scraper he pulled, bearing down on him. The scraper tilted, dropped over the edge. Clayton threw himself sideways. He flopped onto his stomach and hugged the ground. The scraper bounced, hit him in the back, grazed his head. Pain stabbed through him. Lights exploded behind his eyelids. The strength left his body, thought dissolved. Everything went dark and silent.

"Kitties are soft." Nora patted the black-and-gray-striped kitten in her lap, bent forward and placed her ear against the fluffy fur. "An' they go rrrrr-rrrrr."

Sarah laughed at the child's imitation. "That is called a purr. It means the kitty is happy." She reached over and removed Nora's bonnet. The ties were proving too much of a temptation for the kitten. One of the swipes of those tiny sharp claws might catch Nora's face instead of the bow beneath her chin.

The gray kitten, stalking imagined prey through the grass, jumped for the ribbon tie dangling in the air as Sarah placed the bonnet on the bench behind her. She laughed and lifted the wiggling kitten into the air, holding it so she could see its face. "I think these fluffy little bundles of energy need names." She looked over at Nora. "What do you think? What shall we call them?"

"Kitty!"

Sarah looked down at Nora's beaming face. How much Clayton Bainbridge was missing. For the past month he had left for work at dawn and came home after sunset. There had been no opportunity to bring father and daughter together. And it would probably continue that way until after that July fourth anniversary celebration. Three more weeks.

She sighed, pulled her attention back to Nora. "That is a good suggestion, but they are all kitties. They each need a special name—one only for them." Confusion clouded the toddler's shining eyes. "It is the same as Mrs. Quincy and I. We are both ladies, but her special name is Eldora, and mine is Sarah. And you are a little girl, but your special name is Nora." She looked back at the squirming kitten. "And I think this kitty's special name should be Wiggles."

Nora giggled. "I like Wiggles."

"So do I." Sarah pulled the kitten close and scratched behind its ears. It arched its back and rubbed against her hand. "And what about your kitty? What do you think its name should be?"

"Happy."

Sarah smiled at the quick response. "That is a very nice name." She glanced toward the other two kittens wrestling each other on the lawn. "And what about those two kitties? What shall we name the black one?"

"Fluffy."

"And the black-and-white one?"

"Bun'le."

"Bundle?"

Nora gave an emphatic nod. "Fluffy bun'les of engerny."

Oh. Of course. "Very clever. Bundle it is." Sarah laughed, leaned over and dropped a kiss on top of Nora's golden curls. The little girl was so intelligent, so eager to learn and to please. She was an absolute delight. Her family would adore the little sweetheart. And so would Clayton Bainbridge if he would—

A sudden screech of metal against metal jangled her nerves. Sarah tilted her head to the side, listening to the bump and creak of a wagon coming slowly up the road toward the house. And a rider with it. The wagon stopped out front, but the horse's hoofbeats grew louder, turned into the gravel way. Clayton Bainbridge must be home.

Sarah set the cat on the grass, rose to her feet, gave her long skirt a quick shake to rid it of any clinging grass or fur and reached for Nora's bonnet.

"Horsy!" Nora flopped over onto her hands and knees, pushed herself erect and ran toward the gate.

"Nora, wait!" Sarah rushed after her, stopped, stared. It was Clayton's horse, but there was a strange man leading him. Where was—

"Sarah."

There was urgency in the call. She jerked her head around toward the porch. "What is it, Eldora?"

"Come in, please. I need you." The housekeeper turned and hurried back into the house.

Sarah glanced from the still-open door to the riderless horse. A sick feeling settled in the pit of her stomach. She turned and scooped Nora into her arms.

"Horse." Nora twisted round and pointed a tiny finger toward Clayton's mount.

The sick feeling worsened. "We will go see the horses later, Nora. Right now we have to go in the house." Sarah rushed up the brick path, climbed the steps and crossed the porch, uneasiness growing with every step. Maybe she was wrong. Yes, she was being foolish, allowing her imagination to run amok. She hurried through the library and into the hallway. "Eldora?"

"She said yer t' come up here, miss."

Sarah looked up. A dusty, dirty man stood at the top of the stairs. One of Clayton's workers? She wasn't wrong. Her heart lurched. Her legs wobbled. *Not now! Please, knees, do not give out on me now.* She shifted Nora onto her hip, took hold of the banister with her free hand and pulled herself upward.

"Would ya like I should carry the young'un up fer ya?" The man started down the stairs.

Nora stuck her thumb in her mouth and burrowed into the hollow of her neck. Sarah met the man's gaze and shook her head. The tightness in her chest made her too winded to speak. She continued to climb, every step making her more terrified of what awaited.

"In there." The man jerked his thumb toward Clayton's bedroom, doffed his dirty cap and clumped down the stairs.

Sarah stared at the gaping opening of Clayton's bedroom door, heard Eldora issuing orders but could not comprehend the words. Did not know who answered. She could not face another death. She could not. She tried to take a breath, gave up and forced her shaking legs to carry her through the doorway. Quincy was bent over a bed, a pile of dirty, bloodstained clothes at his feet. She closed her eyes, swayed, felt movement. *Nora.* She opened her eyes, forced away the light-headedness.

"There you are!" Eldora stepped out of a doorway on her left and waddled toward the bed. She put the large wash bowl she was carrying on the bedside table beside a stack of cloths, turned and fixed her with a look that said she would stand for no foolishness. "I need you to wash Mr. Bainbridge's wounds. Alfred has to care for the horse, and I have bakin' in the oven and food on the stove to tend." She held out her arms. "Give me the child, I'll keep her with me—leastways till Dr. Parker comes. He should be on his way if that man we sent to fetch him found him at home." The housekeeper took Nora into her arms and looked over her shoulder. "Bring them dirty clothes down to the wash room, Alfred, and I'll set 'em to soakin'. That blood'll never come out, elsewise." She padded out the door. Quincy gathered up the clothes and followed her.

Sarah held on to the door frame and fought for strength. *He is not dead, only hurt.* The reassurance did little to help. Clayton Bainbridge was as pale as the sheets on his bed. Except for the blood on his face. She shuddered, focused her attention on the steady rise and fall of the covers over his chest and took a tentative step to test her legs—moved forward with more confidence when her knees supported her. They quivered dangerously when she reached his bed and took a closer look at him. The hair on the left side of his head was matted with dried blood that extended across his temple and covered his eyelid.

Sarah pressed her hand to her churning stomach and glanced back toward the door. Where was that doctor? Anger surged. Eldora should not have left her here alone. She had no experience in caring for sick or injured people! She looked back down at Clayton, took a deep breath.

Eldora said to clean his wounds, but what if she hurt him? She dipped one of the cloths into the bowl, squeezed out the excess water and dabbed at his matted hair. The blood was hard and dry. Her effort ineffective. She dropped the cloth back in the water and dried her hands on another. She had tried.

I'll set 'em to soakin'.

Eldora's words brought her to a halt. Sarah paused, looked back at the bed. If it would work for clothes, why not for hair? She sighed, squeezed out the rag again, laid it on Clayton's matted hair and wet another. It was not as bad with the gory wound hidden beneath the cloth.

The blood on his temple came off with a gentle scrubbing, but she was afraid to rub at his eyelid. She placed another damp cloth over his eye and dried her hands.

Sunshine streamed in the window above the table. Sarah leaned forward and peered out. Directly beneath was the porch roof, and stretched out beyond was the walled garden. So Clayton Bainbridge could see and hear Nora playing outside from here in his room. A smile curled her lips. She would remember that for when he was better. How long would that be?

She straightened, looked over at him so pale and still. How could he get better if no one cared for him? That wound needed cleansing. Her stomach rebelled at the thought.

Sarah took a breath to quell the nausea and picked up the moist cloth. Perhaps if she did only a bit at a time. She moved the first cloth back an inch and began working at the blood at his hairline.

"You'll never get him cleaned up unless you put a little more effort into your work, young lady."

Sarah gasped, spun toward the open door. A short, stout

man, dressed in a black suit and carrying a black leather bag in his hand, gave her a friendly smile. "Didn't mean to startle you. I'm Dr. Parker."

"Thank goodness!"

He chuckled. "Not used to caring for the sick and injured, eh, Miss…"

"Randolph. And you are correct, Doctor. I am a nanny, not a nurse. So, if you will excuse me?" She started toward the door, stopped when he held up his hand.

"I'm afraid not, Miss Randolph. I may have need of you."

Sarah's heart sank. She hoped with her whole being his prediction would prove false. She nodded, watched the doctor walk to the other side of the bed. He set his bag on the edge, leaned down and lifted the cloths away. Her stomach flopped. She took the cloths and dropped them in the bowl.

The doctor's lips puckered in concentration. His forehead furrowed. He reached down, palpated the flesh under Clayton's matted hair.

Sarah's knees threatened to buckle. She grabbed hold of the bedpost.

"Quite a lump there." The lines at the corners of the doctor's mouth deepened. He pulled a pair of glasses from his pocket, perched them on his rather large nose and leaned closer. He tugged at the bloody hair, exposing a long gash—and turned his attention to the eye.

Her stomach roiled. Sarah turned to the water bowl and doused the cloths up and down, scrubbed them between her hands to remove the red stains. Anything was better than watching the doctor work.

"Hmm, nothing wrong with his eye. Blood is all from that cut on his head. Strange things head wounds. Bleed like a stuck pig, but always seem to heal well."

Sarah swallowed, wished the doctor would not mutter aloud. She could have done without the image his words conveyed. She studied the green vine pattern that trailed around the rolled-over edge of the china bowl.

"Too swollen for stitches. Nothing to do but clean him up and wait to see if he comes around."

If. Sarah's legs trembled. She braced herself against the bedside table, dried her hands and again took hold of the carved corner post on the bed. "*If* he comes around?"

The doctor glanced at her, removed his glasses and stuck them back in his pocket. "Yes. Head wounds are chancy things. But we can pray and hope for the best."

Oh, yes, prayer. The usual balm for frightened, hurting people. Anger took the wobble from her knees. Sarah released her grip on the bedpost and folded her hands in front of her. "Is Mr. Bainbridge in pain?"

"No. Not as long as he's unconscious. It may be a different story when he wakes. The man that came to get me said some kind of wagon hit Clay in the back. I won't know if he has any injury from that until he wakes and can tell me if he has pain." He fastened a steady gaze on her. "Meantime, someone will have to stay with him day and night. He may have bouts of restlessness and he cannot be let to thrash around. He could do himself further injury."

There was no one but her! Panic clutched at her. Sarah caught her breath, cleared her throat. "Is there someone who does nursing care you could recommend, Doctor? I will pay—" She stopped as he shook his head.

"Diphtheria is going around the city. It's waning, but I wouldn't recommend you have strangers come into the house, Miss Randolph. It could be dangerous for all of you."

Nora. She could not endanger the little girl and the

others because of her cowardice. Sarah straightened. "Very well, Doctor. What must I do?"

"Not much you can do. Clean Clay up, stay with him and keep him quiet. Cold cloths sometimes help with the swelling." The doctor picked up his bag and walked to the door. "If there's any change for the worse in his condition, send Quincy for me. Otherwise, I'll come by to check on him tomorrow. He comes from strong stock, and he may come around by then."

Sarah listened to the doctor cross the hall—his footsteps fading away down the stairs. Silence fell. She stared down at Clayton Bainbridge so still and white upon the bed. If he died, Nora would have no one—she would be the same as the children that filled her aunt Laina's orphanage in Philadelphia. Tears welled into her eyes. Sarah blinked them away, but more flowed down her cheeks. Fear for the toddler's future seized her, overrode her anger and drove her to her knees. For the first time since the shipwreck, she bowed her head and folded her hands.

"Almighty God, all my life I have been taught by my parents that You are a merciful and loving Father. That You hear and answer the prayers of Your children. Since Aaron's death, I do not believe that to be so." Bitterness rose, closed her throat. She took a breath and choked out words. "But my unbelief cannot change the truth. Mother and Father say the Bible is true—and I know Scripture says that You desire only good for Your children. Therefore, I ask You to have mercy on Clayton Bainbridge. I ask You to heal him, not only in his body but in his heart as well, that Nora may grow up knowing the love of her father." The anger edged back. "She is only a baby, God. She needs him. Spare him for her sake, I pray. Amen."

Sarah opened her eyes and rose, uncertain whether she

had done Nora good or harm. The prayer had somehow come out more of a challenge than a plea. How did her mother always find faith in times of adversity? She found nothing but doubt. A long sigh escaped her. She wrung out a cloth, took a breath and began to wash the blood off Clayton's eye.

Chapter Fourteen

Sarah wiped the last bit of red from Clayton's eyelid. Soaking the dried blood with the warm wet cloths worked. My, he had long eyelashes! And straight, dark brows—with dirt clinging to a few hairs. She scanned his face, leaned closer. And more dirt on his ear and jaw she had not noticed. No doubt because of all that blood.

She shuddered, rinsed the cloth and scrubbed gently at the dried mud, knowing she was only delaying the inevitable but unable to keep from hoping Eldora would return to cleanse the area around his wound. It was cowardly, but she kept putting off the task and hoping.

The bones of his face felt heavy and strong—so different from her own. She wiped the cloth over Clayton's rugged cheekbones, his long nose and square jaw. His shaved whiskers stubbornly resisted the cloth. She frowned and paused in her work to stare down at him. His whiskers did not normally appear in such contrast to his skin.

How would they feel? She touched his cheek. The dark stubble prickled her fingertips. Warmth rushed into her cheeks. She jerked her hand away and reached for a fresh cloth to dry his face. Worry settled its heaviness upon her. Clayton's complexion was dark and robust from working outside. How could a head injury cause such pallor? She uncovered his arms and checked his hands. Dirt was buried under his nails, ground into his fingers, palms and wrists. She soaped the cloth, washed one limp, unresisting hand, tucked it back under the covers and began on the other. Tears welled into her eyes. Clayton's thick wrists, broad palms and long fingers looked so powerful. They had been so strong when he had carried her into the house. And now—

Sarah gulped back a sob and finished washing his hand. It shouldn't be so. Clayton Bainbridge was a young, healthy man. Much younger than Aaron. And Nora needed him. She dropped the cloth into the bowl. "Must You take him, too, God?" She took a deep breath, fighting to steady her voice. "You shan't have him. Nora needs her father and I will fight to keep him for her." Her quavering words hung in the air, unchallenged, unanswered.

Sarah snatched the cloth from the bowl, squeezed it out and attacked the bloody, matted mass of Clayton's hair. She was so angry she did not even flinch when she reached the gaping wound. She snatched up a towel, tucked it around Clayton's head to catch the runoff and dipped cloths and squeezed fresh, clean water over the wound until there was not a bit of dirt, blood or hair left in it. When she finished, she marched to the dressing room, dumped the bowl, filled it with cold water and marched back. She grabbed up a folded clean cloth, dipped and squeezed it and placed it over the wound. There! He was clean and—and—*still.*

"Mr. Bainbridge? This is Sarah Randolph. Can you

hear me?" No response. She leaned over the bed, staring down at him. "Can you move? Open your eyes? Moan? Do *something?*" Sarah clenched her hands into fists to keep from grabbing Clayton's shoulders and shaking him. She whirled away from the bed and stalked about the room, quivering with anger. She was so afraid.

She walked to the door, listened. There was no sign of anyone coming to rescue her. She moved back to the bed, stood looking down at Clayton. He looked peaceful. And handsome. Softer than usual with his habitual frown erased and the tightness around his mouth relaxed. She wanted to slap him.

Laughter bubbled up, burst from her mouth. She crossed her arms over her stomach and sank to the floor, the laughter punctuated by sobs. She could not do this. She could not stay here in this room waiting for Clayton Bainbridge to die.

Her temples hurt. Sarah lifted her hands and rubbed at the pain. She always got a headache when she cried. It was so annoying, she—

Nora!

Sarah struggled to her feet and hurried to the window, drawn by the sound of the toddler's happy giggles. She shielded her eyes against the brightness and looked down into the walled garden. Nora and Quincy were chasing after kittens. She glanced up at the sun hanging low on the horizon. It was time the kittens were put back in the carriage house and Nora was— *What was she to do about Nora?*

Sarah turned from the window and glanced about the room. If she had to spend the night here watching over Clayton, where would she sleep? And what about Nora?

Gracious, what would she do about Nora? The nursery was too far away to hear her call. Oh, if only this headache would stop. She couldn't think straight. She hurried into the dressing room, splashed cold water on her face, then sat on the edge of the tub and held a cold cloth to her forehead. The pain eased, finally subsided to a dull discomfort.

Sarah hung the cloth on a brass bar and fixed her hair. She turned to go into the bedroom, stopped and glanced back at the cloth. How did the doctor know Clayton was not in pain? He could not tell them. What if he had a headache from that lump on his head? She remembered a few bump-related headaches she had when a child. One rather severe one when Mary had accidentally knocked her out of the hayloft. Of course the doctor knew best. Still, what could it hurt?

She grabbed the cloth and strode into the bedroom and laid it across Clayton's forehead. Perhaps the doctor was right and it would not help him, but it made her feel better. Now, for practical matters like sleeping arrangements and Nora's care.

She pursed her lips, pushed back a tress of hair that persisted in tickling her forehead. They would need the necessary toiletries, of course. And Nora would need cloths. And toys…books… What else? She looked at the deepening shadows in the room, glanced at the lamp on Clayton's bedside table. The lamp must be lit. She could not tend Clayton without light. And to sit alone in darkness waiting for— She shuddered, wrapped her arms about herself. That would be unendurable. But if she could not leave, how—

"How is he? Any change?"

Sarah gasped, swung around toward the door and gave

a little laugh. "You startled me, Eldora. I did not hear you come up the stairs. No, there is no change. He has not moved or spoken. But the doctor says someone must stay with him all the time, lest he become restless and injure himself further."

The housekeeper nodded, crossed to a table in front of the fireplace and set down the tray she carried. "Brung your supper. Roast beef and vegetables. There's broth for him if he wakes."

"When." Where had that come from? Sarah smiled to soften the correction. "Mother always says one should not entertain doubt."

"'Tis true." Eldora lifted the candle from the tray, carried it to the bedside table and lit the lamp. Black smoke billowed upward. She adjusted the wick, replaced the globe and shuffled to the bed. Golden candlelight spilled over Clayton's pale face and dark hair. Eldora lifted the cloth covering Clayton's wound and leaned down to examine it.

Sarah braced herself.

The housekeeper straightened. "You made a good job of cleanin' it." She looked her way, nodded commendation. "Got to go feed the others. I'll send Quincy for the tray." She started for the door.

She was not going to offer to spell her. Perhaps she had not thought about Nora. "Eldora, before you go…"

The housekeeper stopped and looked at her.

Sarah took a breath. "I have been thinking about what must be done. Please send Quincy to me when he is free. If I am to stay in this room tonight to watch over Mr. Bainbridge, I will need him to help me with sleeping arrangements. The nursery is too far from this bedroom. I shall have to keep Nora here with me."

The older woman's eyes gleamed, her lips twitched, firmed.

Sarah straightened. "What is it?"

Eldora shook her head, started again for the door. "'Tis nothin' of import. 'Tis only… The way you was speakin', you sounded like you was mistress of the house." She moved into the hall. Mumbled something under her breath.

Sarah, frowned, held back the apology readying on her lips. It sounded as if Eldora had muttered, "Grant it, O Lord." How *dare* she pray such a thing! She hurried after the housekeeper. If Eldora wanted a mistress of the house then she would have one until Clayton Bainbridge awoke!

"Eldora, wait!" Her tone stopped the housekeeper dead in her tracks. Sarah lifted her chin. "I need you to stay with Mr. Bainbridge while I gather a few necessities from my room. I shan't be long." She turned her back on the look of satisfaction spreading across the older woman's face, lifted her long skirts and sailed down the hall allowing her stiff posture and staccato steps to convey her displeasure with Eldora's attitude.

"Nanny!" Nora all but jumped out of Quincy's arms and came running across the bedroom, a big smile on her beaming face.

Sarah scooped her up, receiving a big hug from soft, warm little arms, and giving one in return.

"We catched the kitties. An' I petted the horsies. An'—" Nora's eyes went wide. She stared down at the figure in the bed. "Him sleepin'?"

Sarah took a deep breath. "No, sweetie. Your papa is not feeling well, and I must stay with him." She ignored the shock that flashed in Quincy's eyes when she said "papa"—no doubt Eldora would hear of *that*—and kissed the toddler's cheek. "And you are going to stay here with me. Will you like that?"

Nora nodded, stuck her thumb in her mouth. "Does his tummy hurted?"

"No, he hurt his head." Sarah carried the toddler over to the chair by the window. "Now, you be a good girl and sit here and look at a book while I talk to Quincy."

She handed Nora a picture book and turned to Eldora's husband. "Quincy, I need you to bring Nora's crib mattress to this room and put it on the floor in that corner." She indicated the place with a sweep of her hand. "Then, I want you to bring the rocker from the nursery and place it there—beside the bed. That will be the perfect spot. I shall be able to watch over both of them at once."

Quincy nodded, ducked his head, stepped out the door into the hallway and hurried off toward the nursery. But not fast enough. She caught sight of his smile.

Sarah frowned, walked to the door and stared at Quincy's retreating back. What was he smiling about? There was nothing amusing about this situation—unless he shared the folly of his wife's wishes.

Sarah scowled, glanced back at Clayton in the bed and Nora by the window, suspicion growing that Eldora and Quincy had maneuvered her into this position on purpose. Well, she had no choice. But if they thought this was an indication of a permanent change, they were going to be sorely disappointed. Such a thing was out of the question. Her heart belonged to Aaron. She was only tending Mr. Bainbridge because there was no one else. She didn't even *like* the man. Who could abide a man who wouldn't even acknowledge his own child?

She dismissed the couple's foolishness, shook off her irritation and went back to studying the room. Had she forgotten anything? She had already gathered the toiletries for herself and Nora and placed them in the dressing room. She had brought picture books and a few of Nora's favorite toys. If Quincy would bring the dollhouse it should be enough to keep Nora content for a few days. She glanced at Clayton, lying motionless on the bed. Surely it would not be longer than that.

She walked to the bed, replaced the warmed cloth on his forehead with a fresh, cool one. Lifted the cloth off his wound.

"Nasty gash." Quincy put the mattress and pile of bed linen he carried in the corner and took a closer look.

Sarah placed a cold cloth over the wound. "I wish he would move or open his eyes or something. He is so still I keep looking at the covers over his chest to be sure he is breathing."

"He's a tough one. He'll come around."

"Yes." *One should not entertain doubt.* Sarah sighed, watched Quincy head back to the nursery for the rocker and walked to the corner to make up Nora's bed. It was not easy to believe good would happen. Not when her fiancé had been struck by lightning and lost in the ocean in front of her very eyes. Not when she had almost drowned.

Sarah replaced the cloths again, looked from her patient to Nora, who was sound asleep on her mattress. Clayton was a very handsome man, but she saw little of him in his daughter.

She frowned, picked up the wash bowl and carried it to the dressing room to get fresh water. This was not the time to be dwelling on Clayton's lack of attention or affection for his daughter. That would wait until he recovered from his injuries. She kept her ears tuned for any sound of movement from Clayton or Nora, dumped out the water, refilled the bowl and set it aside.

A quick glance into the mirror set her to amending the neglect to her own appearance. She looked tired. Not surprising. It was the small hours of the morning and she had not yet slept. She was afraid to. What if he woke, moved and harmed himself? It did not seem likely, but she was still afraid to sleep. Cool water would help. She washed her face, applied a dab of cream and tucked a few stray strands of hair back into place.

The light flickered. Sarah leaned down and adjusted the wick of the dressing-room lamp. The stained cloths she had rinsed clean and hung to dry over the edge of the tub caught her eye. She shook her head, a smile tugged at her lips. She must write her parents of her nursing efforts. They would never believe it. She was so squeamish as a child she was unable to look at a simple scratch without feeling ill. Even as an adult she averted her gaze from any sort of wound, no matter how small. Until now.

The smile faded. Sarah carried the bowl back to the bedside table, hoping all the cold cloths would help with the swelling as the doctor said. She yawned and stretched her back then roamed about the room, uncomfortable at being among Clayton's personal belongings. A frown creased her forehead. She did a slow pirouette, looking at the walls, the tops of his tables and desk. That was odd. There was no portrait or miniature of his wife in sight. Her father had—

"Unnnggh."

Sarah whipped around. Clayton was rolling his head from side to side. She gasped and rushed to the bed. "Mr. Bainbridge, you must lie still!"

Get 2 Books FREE!

Steeple Hill Books, publisher of inspirational romance fiction, presents

Love Inspired

HISTORICAL
INSPIRATIONAL HISTORICAL ROMANCE

A new series of historical love stories that promise romance, adventure and faith!

FREE BOOKS!
Get two free books by acclaimed, inspirational authors!

FREE GIFTS!
Get two exciting surprise gifts absolutely free!

2 FREE BOOKS

▲ To get your 2 free books and 2 free gifts, affix this peel-off sticker to the reply card and mail it today!

We'd like to send you two free books to introduce you to the new Love Inspired® Historical series. These books are worth over $10 but are yours to keep absolutely FREE! We'll even send you two wonderful surprise gifts. You can't lose!

Each of your **FREE** books is filled with engaging stories of romance, adventure and faith set in various historical periods from biblical times to World War II.

FREE BONUS GIFTS!

We'll send you two wonderful surprise gifts, worth about $10, *absolutely FREE*, just for giving Love Inspired Historical books a try! Don't miss out —
MAIL THE REPLY CARD TODAY!

GET 2 FREE BOOKS!

HURRY!

Return this card today to get **2 FREE Books** *and 2* **FREE** **Bonus Gifts!**

INSPIRATIONAL HISTORICAL ROMANCE

YES! *Please send me the 2 FREE Love Inspired® Historical books and 2 FREE gifts for which I qualify. I understand that I am under no obligation to purchase anything further, as explained on the back of this card.*

affix free books sticker here

302 IDL ERYT   102 IDL ERX5

FIRST NAME   LAST NAME

ADDRESS

APT.#   CITY

STATE / PROV.   ZIP/POSTAL CODE

Steeple Hill®

Offer limited to one per household and not valid to current subscribers of Love Inspired Historical books.
Your Privacy – Steeple Hill Books is committed to protecting your privacy. Our Privacy Policy is available online at www.SteepleHill.com or upon request from the Steeple Hill Reader Service. From time to time we make our lists of customers available to reputable third parties who may have a product or service of interest to you. If you would prefer for us not to share your name and address, please check here ☐.

® and ™ are trademarks owned and used by the trademark owner and/or its licensee.
© 2008 STEEPLE HILL BOOKS

(LIHR-LA-08)

▼ DETACH AND MAIL CARD TODAY! ▼

Steeple Hill Reader Service — Here's How it Works:

Accepting your 2 free books and 2 free mystery gifts places you under no obligation to buy anything. You may keep the books and gifts and return the shipping statement marked "cancel." If you do not cancel, about a month later we will send you 4 additional books and bill you just $4.24 each in the U.S. or $4.74 each in Canada, plus 25¢ shipping & handling per book and applicable taxes if any.* That's the complete price and – at a savings of at least 15% off the cover price, it's quite a bargain! You may cancel at any time, but if you choose to continue, every month we'll send you 4 more books, which you may either purchase at the discount price or return to us and cancel your subscription.

*Terms and prices subject to change without notice. Sales tax applicable in N.Y. Canadian residents will be charged applicable provincial taxes and GST. Offer not valid in Quebec. All orders subject to approval. Books received may not be as shown. Credit or debit balances in a customer's account(s) may be offset by any other outstanding balance owed by or to the customer. Please allow 4 to 6 weeks for delivery. Offer available while quantities last.

If offer card is missing write to: Steeple Hill Reader Service, 3010 Walden Ave., P.O. Box 1867, Buffalo, NY 14240-1867

BUSINESS REPLY MAIL

FIRST-CLASS MAIL   PERMIT NO. 717   BUFFALO, NY

POSTAGE WILL BE PAID BY ADDRESSEE

STEEPLE HILL READER SERVICE
3010 WALDEN AVE
PO BOX 1867
BUFFALO NY 14240-9952

NO POSTAGE
NECESSARY
IF MAILED
IN THE
UNITED STATES

He raised his hand, clawing at the cloth over his eyes, trying to lift his head.

"No, you must not move!" Sarah grabbed his hand, pulled it to her chest, pushed gently on his forehead.

He sagged back. Quieted. His arm went limp.

She tucked it back under the covers, replaced the cloth and stood there shaking. Had he been awake? He had not opened his eyes. She stared down at him, hoping he would move, terrified that he might. Oh, if only Eldora were here. But she was sound asleep downstairs.

She stood by the bed until her body screamed at her to move. She took a step, grabbing for the corner post as her numb legs collapsed beneath her.

Tears stung her eyes. Sarah pulled herself straight and made small circles with her ankles, wincing at the pains shooting into her calves. When the pains abated, she took a tentative step, released her grip on the bedpost and moved around the room.

A leather pouch full of papers someone had dropped on the floor beside Clayton's desk drew her attention. She picked it up and carried it to the cupboard by the fireplace. Clayton's clothes hung inside, his shoes and boots on the floor beneath them. Would he ever wear them again?

Sarah caught her breath, set the pouch on the shelf beside his hats where it would be safe from Nora's curiosity and quickly closed the door. The click of the latch was loud in the silence. The horrible silence of an endless night.

Sarah rubbed at her tired eyes, looked longingly at the rocker. She did not dare sit down. She was too tired. She might not wake if he started thrashing around again.

"Deborah—" Clayton rolled his head from side to side.

Sarah raced back to the bed. "Mr. Bainbridge, please lie still. You will hurt yourself."

"—died." Clayton dragged his arm from beneath the covers. His hand flopped against his chest. "My fault— my fault."

"Mr. Bainbridge, please! It's Sarah Randolph. Can you hear me?"

"Baby—" He rolled his head, the cloth crumpled into a wad. "Deborah— No...no—"

What should she do? He did not even know she was here!

His hand lifted slightly, moved toward his head.

Sarah grabbed it, held it in both of hers. He quieted. She fixed the cloth, covered his arm, pulled the rocker close and sat, too exhausted to stay on her feet a moment longer. She had to rest for a minute. Her eyelids slipped down. Her head dropped forward.

Sarah jerked upright, tried to focus. It was no use, she was simply too tired. She uncovered Clayton's hand, clasped hold of it, propped her arm on the bed so it could not fall off and rested her head against the rocker back. She should have thought of this earlier. She could sleep now. If he moved he would wake her. She sighed and closed her eyes.

Clayton opened his eyes, stared at the ceiling in the dim, yellow light. He had fallen asleep with the lamp on. He turned his head. Pain exploded behind his eyes, throbbed in his temples. His stomach churned. He took a couple of deep breaths, eased his head back to the former position. It helped. The pain was not quite as severe.

What was wrong with him?

There was a soft rustle on his left, something moved beneath his hand. Careful not to move his head, he shifted his gaze that direction. Sarah Randolph was asleep in a chair beside his bed. His heart lurched. *Why*— A jolt of apprehension set his pulse pounding, his head throbbing harder. He must be ill. He moved his hand slightly, felt a response. She was holding his hand. He must be very ill. He should ask. He opened his mouth, took a breath, then let it out slowly. She looked so tired, was sleeping so soundly. He would wait…ask…tomorrow…

He curled his fingers ever so slowly until her hand was snug in his grip and closed his eyes.

Chapter Fifteen

Clayton woke to birdsong and to pearl-gray light filtering through dew-kissed windowpanes. Dawn. His usual time to rise. But not today. His head throbbed. And beyond that pain was a discomfort, a weakness in his body. Something was wrong with him. Memory rushed back. Or maybe it was a dream. It had to be. Why would Sarah Randolph be sleeping in a chair beside his bed? He took a slow, deep breath, focused on his left hand, became aware of the soft, warm flesh it encased. It was no dream. Last night was real.

So what was wrong with him?

Clayton frowned, dredged through his memory but found no answer. Could illness cause such a thing? Could you be so sick you could not remember becoming ill? Fear brought a tightness to his chest. He fought down the temptation to seek comfort by tightening his grip around Sarah's hand. He had no right. No one knew that better than he. But he could not make himself release her hand—told himself it was only that he did not want to wake her. An excuse he could live with.

Perhaps he was trying too hard. Perhaps he would remember if he relaxed and let his mind drift.

Clayton forced down the fear, closed his eyes against the strengthening light and listened to the gentle sounds of morning's awakening. Nothing came to him but a growing certainty that he was creating a painful memory for the empty years ahead. His face tightened. He opened his eyes and slowly uncurled his fingers.

Sarah Randolph gasped. Her hand jerked free of his grasp. She surged to her feet, leaned over him and stared down into his eyes. "You are awake!"

The soft gladness in her voice, the sight of her relieved, happy smile brought a longing that stole his breath, constricted his throat. If only—

"You *are* awake?" Worry shadowed her eyes. "Can you hear me?"

"Yes." He forgot and nodded. The pain swelled, burst into splinters and speared him behind the eyes. "Ugh!" His stomach churned.

"You must not move, Mr. Bainbridge. *Please.*" Tears welled into the beautiful brown eyes gazing down at him. "The doctor said if you move you could do yourself more harm. You must lie still."

The stabbing pain in his head held him mute. Clayton closed his eyes, gritted his teeth and fought a swirling darkness.

Fabric rustled, water splashed.

"If you can hear me—I have a cold cloth for your head, Mr. Bainbridge." Something cold and damp touched his forehead, rested there. "And another for your wound." The pillow beneath the left side of his head depressed slightly, cold touched the hammering pain centered there. He caught his breath, waiting for the spinning to cease, the pounding to subside to its former throb. The darkness deepened. He felt himself sliding in, reached out a hand, felt Sarah's soft hands grasp it just before he sank down to the place of unknowing.

"Hmm, you did a good job cleaning this wound. And the cold cloths seem to have helped with the swelling. It's no larger. Might even have gone down a tad." The doctor replaced the cloth, wrapped his fingers around Clayton's wrist and looked at his watch. He pursed his lips, nodded his head. "Pulse is good and strong."

Sarah folded her hands, stared at the doctor from across Clayton's bed. "And that is a good sign for his recovery?"

"It is favorable, yes." He gave her a tired smile, looked back at his patient. "You say he woke?"

"Yes. Early this morning. For a moment only."

"You are sure he was awake? In head cases like this, the person sometimes open their eyes and talks. Nonsense usually." He took a wooden tube out of his case, placed the flared end on Clayton's chest, leaned down and put his ear against the small end.

"I am quite certain, Doctor. He answered yes when I asked if he could hear me."

"That all he said?"

"This morning, yes. Last night he muttered a few words when he was restless."

"Thrash around, did he? I warned you he might." The doctor put the tube back in his bag. Pulled out a small bottle. "I'll leave this with you. Give him some for pain when he wakes up, if he wants it—but only when he's fully awake." He handed her the bottle, closed his bag. "It makes people sleep and he's already sleeping too much, so half a spoonful should do."

Sarah nodded and put the bottle on the nightstand. "Is there anything else?"

"Keep putting the cold cloths on the wound—they seem to be helping. And continue to keep him quiet. Don't let him thrash around and hurt himself. And wait for him to wake up—if he's going to." He looked at her, frowned. "I think this household must be prepared, Miss Randolph. It is possible Clay will stay this way, even after his wound heals." He fastened the buckle on his bag and walked to the door. "If he does wake, don't feed him anything but a good strong broth till I come by again." He stepped out into the hall.

Sarah stood frozen in place, staring at the empty doorway. How dare he tell her such news and then simply walk away! How dare he say such a thing. "If he does wake." *If.* A horrible little word. She looked down at Clayton lying so still in his bed, and tears sprang into her eyes. He was so young. So vital. His whole life was before him. And what of Nora? Is this all she would ever know of her father—a lifeless form in a bed?

Death and life are in the power of the tongue…

The words of Scripture dropped into her mind—clung there. What did it mean? That she was to pray? Sarah stiffened. She knew better. The power of life and death was in a bolt of lightning, a raging sea—or a wound to the head. Not in prayer.

She turned her back on the bed and walked to the window. She looked down into the walled garden, slid her gaze to the carriage house. Memories of Nora poking a worm, chasing after animals, petting horses and kittens made her heart hurt, her throat tighten. What if the Scripture was true? But how could it be? That day on the ship she had prayed "God save us!" and Aaron had died.

And all things, whatsoever ye shall ask in prayer, believing, ye shall receive.

A quietness came. A knowing. Sarah closed her eyes, faced the truth. Her words had only been an expression of her fear, not a call of faith. She had not believed. She had not expected God to save them. She had not *prayed*. She had only spoken empty words born of her terror and blamed God for not honoring them.

Tears slid from beneath her closed eyelids and coursed down her cheeks. This is what her parents had tried to explain to her—what she had refused to hear. But it was easier to be angry than to be honest. Easier to be haughty than humble. Easier to blame God than to admit Aaron should never had sailed out into the ocean that day. Sarah wrestled with her pride, sank to her knees and choked out words. "Forgive me, Lord. Please forgive me. And help Thou my unbelief."

She stayed there on her knees by the window, waiting, unable to rise though she did not understand why. A pressure built deep inside, grew in intensity. Words formed in her heart, rose to her mouth and poured from her lips. "Almighty God, Thou who hears and answers the prayers of Thy children, have mercy on Clayton Bainbridge, I pray. Restore him to fullness of health and richness of life for Thy glory, O God. For Thy glory. O God, have mercy on Mr. Bainbridge. Have mercy and heal him I pray in the name of Your beloved Son, Jesus. Amen."

Sarah drew a breath—a sweet breath, free of the bitterness she had harbored in her heart all these months. She wiped away the tears, opened her eyes and rose to her feet. She walked to the bed and looked down at Clayton. Nothing had changed—he was pale and still. Yet everything had changed. She knew it. Her fear was gone and in its place was a peace she had never before experienced. She replaced the cloths on his head with fresh, cool ones, crossed to the rocker, took hold of his hand, closed her eyes and yielded to her weariness. She would sleep while Eldora and Quincy cared for Nora.

"An' Wiggles jumped really, really high. Way up on the big box!"

The voice tugged at him. Clayton floated to the surface of the darkness. Struggled against heaviness, tried to summon energy to speak.

"Gracious! He must have been frightened."

Sarah. He fought to open his eyes.

"It was a big, *big* doggie! But Q'incy chaseded it away."

The child. What was the child doing in his room? Clayton stopped fighting the heaviness of his eyelids and listened.

"My! You had a busy day. But no more talking now. It is time for you to go to sleep."

Sleep? It was morning. Or had he slept the day away?

The rocker creaked, began a quiet, rhythmic movement that was peaceful and comforting in the silence. Sarah hummed softly, the sound conjuring a picture of what a family could be. Should be. But never would be. Not for him. Clayton took a long, slow breath and forced himself to think of Deborah.

The rocker stopped. He tried not to pay attention, but his will and his body betrayed him. His ears strained to pick up sounds, his brain to sort and identify them. Dress fabric whispered and soft footfalls sounded. Would Sarah return after she put the child to bed? Or would she leave him to go through the dark night alone?

Clayton frowned, swallowed back the name he wanted

to call out. He reminded himself again he had no right to keep Sarah near—that the very fact that he did not want her to go was proof that she should. He clamped his mouth shut, listened, judged direction and distance by the level of sound and followed Sarah's movements in his mind. Why was she walking toward the corner instead of the door?

"Good night, sweetie. Happy dreams."

The whispered words were followed by soft sounds he couldn't identify yet understood. The sounds of a woman tucking a child into bed. So the child was sleeping in his bedroom. He concentrated on the thought. Wondered at how little anger it provoked. He did not seem to have the energy for anger. No doubt because of the sickness. But he still knew what he wanted—no, what was *right*. What he *wanted* was wrong. He gathered his strength and opened his eyes to golden lamplight. "Miss Randolph?" It came out a raspy squawk.

There was a soft gasp, and then Sarah was beside the bed looking down at him, a smile trembling on her lips. "You are truly awake."

"Yes." It was so hard to frown when he wanted to return her smile. He needed to distance himself from her, did not want to ask her to do anything for him—but his throat and mouth were so dry his words were little more than a croak. "Water…please."

"Yes, of course." She started away, whirled back. "You must not move. It is very important that you lie still."

She disappeared. He heard her running water in the dressing room. A moment later she was back with a glass of water and a spoon in her hands. "You cannot lift your head, Mr. Bainbridge. The doctor said you could do further injury to yourself if you move. I will give you the water from a spoon."

Clayton scowled at the idea, but remembered the pain when he had moved his head and obediently opened his mouth when the spoon touched his lips. Cool water dribbled over his tongue, soothing the parched tissue. Water had never tasted as sweet. He swallowed the entire glassful, one spoonful at a time. "Thank you."

Sarah nodded and put down the glass. "Let me replace these cloths."

Before he could say no, she had lifted the warm cloth from his forehead. She replaced it with a fresh, cool one and repeated the process on the left side of his head. The throbbing ache eased a bit. Clayton took a relieved breath. "Thank you, that eases the pain."

"That pleases me." She smiled down at him. "I was not sure it would help."

He held his heart firm against that smile. "What is wrong with me? Did I take ill?"

"No, you were injured." Her eyes clouded. "You have a wound on your head."

"Injured? How did I—" A flash of a wooden scraper bounding over the earth and arching into the air behind a wild-eyed bay brought a surge of anger. *Those fools with the scrapers!* The throbbing in his head increased. Clayton took a breath, closed his eyes against the pain. "How bad is the wound?" He lifted his hand.

Sarah grabbed it, held it down. "Do not *move*, Mr. Bainbridge." She covered his hand with the blanket. "The doctor said your wound is better. The swelling has gone down a bit. And—" She stopped, cleared her throat. "And I am certain your waking means it is much better."

Her voice sounded different. He opened his eyes. There

were tears shimmering in hers. For him? The injury must be serious. His heart thudded. "How long did I sleep?"

She took a breath, blinked the sheen of tears away. "You have been unconscious, except for a few brief moments, since they brought you home in a wagon." She hesitated. He held her gaze. "That was yesterday afternoon."

"I see." He might as well hear it all. "Any other injuries?" His head pained so fiercely he had not noticed any other specific aches.

She took another breath. "You could have other injuries we are unaware of. One of your laborers told the doctor you were hit in the back by a piece of equipment of some sort, but the doctor did not want to move you to examine you while you were unconscious and unable to tell him what was wrong."

"Umm." The strength he had mustered was draining away. Clayton closed his eyes and garnered the little that remained. Other discomforts were now making themselves known. "I need...Quincy."

"I'm sorry, but I can't leave you to go after him."

The worry in her voice gave him the will to open his eyes. "I'll not...move. Please...get him."

She drew breath to speak, snagged her lower lip beneath her teeth and whirled away. He heard her run lightly across the floor, open the door to the winder stairs and start down at a hurried pace.

Silence settled. His bedroom felt empty, *lonely* without her. How would he ever manage to erase the visions of her presence from it?

Chapter Sixteen

"I shall wait in my bedroom in case you need me, Doctor. It is there—" Sarah waved her hand toward the space beyond Clayton's open door "—across the landing." She glanced at Quincy, standing by Clayton's bed ready to help the doctor, bit back a plea for him to be gentle and left the room. There was no sense in giving him and Eldora fodder for their useless hopes. It was not that she *cared* for Clayton Bainbridge. It was only that she had witnessed the intensity of his pain when he moved his head, and she hated to see anyone suffer.

She left Clayton's door ajar, did the same with her own to better hear if the doctor called for her, then hovered there, close to the door, massaging the tense, tired muscles across her shoulders and listening to the faint sounds of Eldora working in the kitchen while Nora chattered in the background. A smile tugged at her lips. Nora had taken over the household. Eldora gave the toddler her meals in the kitchen, and Quincy took her to the carriage house when his work took him there—which seemed to be quite frequently of late. Her smile widened…faded. Of course,

Clayton Bainbridge still held himself aloof from his daughter. But that would change when his health improved. On that she was determined.

The sound of the doctor's muttering, to Clayton or Quincy or himself, brought a shudder. Sarah moved away from the door, not eager to overhear any of his indelicate, gory comments. She walked to a window, wrapped her arms about herself and looked up at the white clouds dotting the azure sky. That one looked like a rabbit. And that one like a dog. Goodness, how one's mind wandered! She had not played the cloud game since she was a little girl. She would have to teach Nora. She smiled, leaned forward and searched the sky as she had when she was a child. But this time she sought a perfect fluffy-cloud pillow to give to Clayton so it could soothe his aching head.

"Ugh."

The utterance came, muted by distance and walls, but clearly conveying pain. Sarah sucked in a breath, abandoned her childhood game. "Please, Almighty God, help Mr. Bainbridge to bear the pain of the doctor's examination. And please, help them to not injure him further. Please do not let him be harmed in any way, Lord God Almighty, please. I pray this in Your Holy Name. Amen."

How horrid it would be if the doctor did Clayton harm. Such things happened. Sarah blinked sudden moisture from her eyes, chided herself for her cowardice and walked back to open her door a little wider. It was of no benefit to Clayton Bainbridge for her to stand around in her bedroom imagining awful things and suffering for him. She might better put this free time to good use. She took clean clothes from her cupboard and hastened to the dressing room. The doctor said his examination would take some time. If she hurried, she would have time to bathe.

* * *

That was better. The quick but thorough wash had chased away the stiffness from sitting and standing by Clayton's bedside. Sarah wound a towel around her wet hair, donned the chestnut-brown gown and stepped into her kidskin slippers, all the while listening for the doctor's call. There was only silence and an occasional murmur, the voices and words indistinguishable.

A few minutes work brushed the tangles from her hair. Sarah piled it on the crown of her head, secured it with pins and the length of red roping and gave it a last pat. She turned from the mirror and walked into her bedroom, a smile flirting with her lips. She had become quite adept at styling her hair—Ellen would be proud of her. So would her parents.

She halted on her way to the dresser, arrested by a sudden awareness of how much she had changed since coming to Stony Point. She was no longer the pampered and cosseted young woman who had arrived in Cincinnati. The circumstances she had faced—was still facing—challenged her in ways she had never imagined. And she had met those challenges. The old Sarah would have run home to be coddled. Indeed, she had almost done so when faced with Eldora Quincy's sternness on her arrival. Thank goodness she had stayed.

Sarah continued on to the dresser, took a lace-edged linen handkerchief from the top drawer and glanced at her partially open door. How different her life had become. If Ellen were here she would nurse Clayton Bainbridge and care for Nora in her stead. The maid would free her to go to town, to do whatever she chose. And Ellen would indulge and coddle her when the nightmares came. She would certainly never make her build a fire and prepare her own tea. Why, Ellen would be outraged at the very idea. And a short time ago her own attitude had been the same.

Sarah walked to the window and looked out at the wooded hill across the road. She had been resentful of Eldora's lack of sympathy that night after the nightmare. And she had been shocked at being asked to build the fire. But the truth was, helping to make her own tea had given her a satisfaction she had never before experienced. She liked it. And she loved caring for Nora.

Clayton Bainbridge was a different matter. A frown creased her forehead. Nursing him filled her with trepidation. It frightened her. Yet, even though in the beginning she had nursed him against her will, she had come to a place where she would not want Ellen or anyone else to take her place tending him. That strange connection she felt to him had become—

"Miss Randolph?"

Sarah spun about, rushed to the door and looked across the landing at the doctor. "Yes?"

"You may take up your nursing chores again." The doctor disappeared into Clayton's room.

Sarah gathered her skirts into her hands and hurried after him. Clayton was propped up on pillows. His eyes were closed and he was very pale. They had hurt him! She drew breath to speak, blew it out again. It was not her place to know what the doctor had found during his examination. "Have you any new instructions for me, Doctor?"

"No. Continue on the same." Dr. Parker frowned, took his bag into his hand. "There's nothing to be done for Clay's head or back but rest. Keep him quiet." He dipped his head and walked out of the room.

So Clayton's back *was* injured. Was it causing him

pain? Sarah stared down at Clayton. His skin was pasty white, his features pinched. He looked exhausted. Was he sleeping? Or unconscious? Or simply done in by his ordeal? She looked at his hands, limp on the coverlet, and a lump formed in her throat. He should not be like this. He should be at work directing the repairs to the locks on the Miami Canal. Or in his study drawing blueprints of the work yet to be done. He should be lifting his daughter and holding her safe in his strong arms.

Sarah blinked the film of moisture from her eyes, cleared her throat and headed for the dressing room to get cloths and a fresh bowl of water. It was all she could do to help him—to restore him to Nora. Except pray. And she would do that, too. She would pray without ceasing. And she would not allow herself to doubt. Not ever again.

It was like the thick fog that filled the mountain valleys before the morning sun burned its way through. Clayton turned this way and that, searching for a way through the cold darkness, struggling to reach the place of warmth and light. But the darkness closed in on him.

Sarah let go of Clayton's arm, lifted her weight off him and slipped backward until her feet touched the floor. Thank goodness that was over. He had been muttering and thrashing around so insistently, the only way she had been able to stop him was by throwing herself across him.

She shook out her skirts, sighed and pushed back a few strands of hair that had worked loose in her struggle with Clayton. She missed Nora, but it was good that Eldora and Quincy were watching the toddler between her nap and bedtimes. She could never tend to both of them at once.

Sarah refreshed the cloths that had become dislodged,

replaced them on Clayton's head and stood studying his face. He looked gaunt. Of course, that could be the result of the whiskers darkening his cheeks. But most likely it was weight loss. How long could he go without eating? At least he had been taking water when he was awake. She reached out and brushed the tip of her finger over the dark stubble of his beard. Did it annoy him? Or—

"*Oh.*" Heat rushed into her cheeks. Sarah jerked her hand back and looked down into Clayton's dark-blue eyes. His clear, *aware* dark-blue eyes. "You are awake." An inane thing to say. "I mean, *really* awake."

"Yes."

Had he felt her touching his face? The heat in her cheeks increased. She wiped her fingertips against her skirt and cleared her throat. "How do you feel?"

"Thirsty."

"I have water here for you." Sarah lifted the glass from the bedside table and held it to Clayton's lips, her own parting slightly as he drank. "I am sure it is much more satisfying for you without the spoon. Are you more comfortable propped up on the pillows? Does it ease your pain?"

She frowned and clamped her lips together to stop her prattling. She always did that when she was embarrassed. She took a breath and held it. Avoided his eyes. When he finished the water she set the empty glass back on the table. "Is there something more I can do for you?"

"Nothing at the moment. And, yes, being propped up does ease the pain in my head…somewhat. But the cold cloths help the most." He lifted his hand off the coverlet toward his head.

Sarah's stomach flopped. "Do not move!" She grabbed hold of his hand, pulled it against her. Clayton went still.

Had he lost consciousness again? She looked up at his face—met his gaze, and was suddenly acutely aware of their clasped hands—of the breadth and warmth of his palm, the calluses on the pads of the long fingers that were slowly uncurling, releasing their grip on her.

She looked down and yanked her hand free. It felt naked. "The doctor said you could harm yourself if you move."

"Not my arms. Not when I am awake. It is my head and back that are injured and must be kept still."

His voice sounded strained. Was he overtiring himself? Sarah chanced another look at him, relaxed in relief. His eyes now held their normal, cool expression.

Knuckles rapped softly against the hallway door.

Sarah jumped, hurried across the bedroom, grateful for the interruption that would give her a chance to regain her aplomb. "Yes, Doc—" She stared at the young man standing in the hallway, hat in hand. "Oh. I thought you were the doctor returning."

Dark curls tumbled forward as the man dipped his head. "John Wexford, at your service. The housekeeper—"

"Come in, Wexford."

Sarah glanced over her shoulder at Clayton, swallowed the protest she had no right to make and stepped back to allow the man entrance. She started to leave, took another look at Clayton's pale face, noted he had removed the cloths from his head. She left the door and moved to the far window, feigning interest in the view. With a slight turn of her head she could watch Clayton out of the corner of her eye.

"How are you, sir?"

Clayton scowled. "Never mind about me—how is the work progressing?"

"Work is finished at my present site. We will move to the upper lock tomorrow." The man stepped closer to the bed. "Your crew finished work at the lock the day you were injured, and all equipment has been moved to the aqueduct site. I was there today, overseeing the setup and the initial demolition." John Wexford frowned, slapped his hat against his leg. "That job requires close supervision, so I figure to boss your crew until you return. I set Thomas over my crew in my absence. Does that meet with your approval, sir?"

"It is your only option." Clayton's scowl deepened. "Thomas is a good man, but he has limited ability. You shall have to check the site often." Clayton's voice lost strength. The covers moved as he took a deep breath. "Keep the newly hired laborers under your control. And watch Maylor. He is…a fighter…troublemaker. He will try to run over Thomas…and you."

Sarah frowned, willed Mr. Wexford to leave. Could the man not see Clayton's pain and exhaustion—could he not hear it in his voice? She turned from the window, started for the bed.

"Thank you for the warning, sir. I will keep a wary eye on Maylor."

"Good. And do not hesitate to call upon me should a problem arise, Wexford. Otherwise…I shall expect you to…report to me every other day. Good evening."

Finally! Sarah swerved toward the door to show Mr. Wexford out.

"Before I go, sir." She halted; John Wexford's voice held a hint of desperation. "The needed repair work cannot go forward without your blueprints. If you will tell me where to find them…"

"They were…in shack…" Clayton's voice faded. He took a breath. "In…leather pouch…"

"No, sir. They were not found—"

"I believe they are here, Mr. Wexford." Sarah went to the cupboard, opened the door and lifted out the paper-stuffed leather pouch she had placed there. "Are these the blueprints you are seeking?" She stood in front of the cupboard, which was adjacent to the hallway door, and held out the pouch as a lure to draw Mr. Wexford away from Clayton's bed.

The young man strode across the room, took the pouch and scanned the contents. "The very ones." There was relief in his voice.

"How fortunate."

"Yes." John Wexford lifted his head, smiled down at her. "Thank you for your help, Miss…"

There was an interested gleam in his eyes she did not care for. Sarah gave him a cool nod. "I am pleased to help. Good evening, Mr. Wexford." She cast a meaningful glance toward the open door. The gleam dulled. Good. The fact that she had ignored his invitation to tell him her name had not gone unnoticed. Nor had her silent invitation for him to leave.

"Good evening." He tucked the leather pouch under his arm and left the room. A moment later she heard the thud of his boots against the stair treads.

Sarah hurried to the bed. Clayton's eyes were closed, his breathing slow and even. He had fallen asleep. She dipped the cloths he had removed in the cold water, put them back on his head, then sat in the rocker and closed her eyes. She had a few minutes to rest before Eldora brought her dinner.

Silence settled, punctuated only by the sound of Sarah's soft breathing. Clayton opened his eyes, studied her face.

Her beauty stole his breath; her touch, his strength and de-termination. His face drew taut. Deborah's death and the child would always stand between him and any other woman. And Sarah Randolph deserved a better man than he.

Clayton closed his eyes, called back the image of John Wexford's face when Sarah had opened the door, the quick glances the young man had stolen of Sarah while he stood by his bed talking business with him, the softness in his deep voice when he spoke to her. There was no doubt the man was smitten. And John Wexford was a man of good character, with a promising future as an engineer.

Clayton set his mind against the sharp pangs of jealousy, relaxed his clenched jaw, and considered what he could do to foster a relationship between Wexford and Sarah. He would begin by extolling the young man's virtues when Sarah awoke. And by hiding his own feelings for her behind a solid wall of indifference. He would find the strength to do that somehow. For her sake.

Chapter Seventeen

"Me gonna play wiff kitties." Nora wiggled in her chair.

"Not if you do not finish your breakfast, sweetie." Sarah reached over and tapped the edge of the toddler's plate. "Eat your egg so you will be ready to go with Quincy when he comes downstairs." She cast a quick glance toward the open door at the bottom of the winder stairs. What was taking Quincy so long? Was something wrong? She frowned, nibbled at the soft corner of her upper lip. Perhaps she should go—

"That egg not t' your likin'?"

Sarah jerked her attention to Eldora. The housekeeper's expression was far too bland. It made her true thoughts very apparent. Sarah stiffened and picked up her fork. "The egg is fine." She took a bite and swallowed any explanation for her preoccupation along with the food. To offer one would do not one whit of good. The woman was determined to believe what she wanted to believe. It was most frustrating. Neither Eldora nor Quincy would accept the fact that her concern was only for Clayton's health— and for Nora's sake—that she had no personal interest in the man. No matter what she said they merely nodded and smiled at her with that *look* in their eyes.

Sarah took another bite of her egg, looked over at her charge and put down her fork. "You need a good wash, sweetie. The kitties will gobble you up if you go to the carriage house with bacon grease on your hands and egg smeared all around your mouth." She rose and wet a cloth.

Nora obediently lifted her face and held out her hands. "The kitties do this." She licked at her washed hand.

"No, the kitties would do *this*." Sarah bent and nibbled at Nora's pudgy little fingers. The toddler burst into giggles. Sarah smiled, got a towel and dried Nora's face and hands.

"Me see horsy. And me do—" The toddler bounced up and down on her chair.

What did *that* mean? "Eldora?" Sarah looked to the housekeeper for help.

Eldora chuckled and shrugged her round shoulders. "I've no notion what she means." She went back to fixing Clayton's breakfast tray.

Boots pounded against stair treads. Quincy was coming. Sarah looked back at the toddler. Surely Quincy would not allow her to do something that could be dangerous for her. Still, he might have a different idea of what construed danger to a child. She lifted Nora into her arms. "What will you do, sweetie?"

"Me do—" Nora bobbed up and down as best she could in Sarah's tight hold.

Deep male laughter erupted from behind her. "So you want another wheelbarrow ride, do you, missy?"

"So *that* is what she meant!" Sarah laughed and turned to face Quincy. "I could not imagine…" She shook her head and kissed Nora's soft cheek. "You be a good girl for

Mr. and Mrs. Quincy, sweetie. And I will see you at nap time." She gave Nora a last, quick hug and surrendered her to Quincy's arms.

Gracious! Sarah stopped beside the door and stared at Clayton. He was propped up against his pillows, clean-shaven, his hair brushed, and wearing a clean nightshirt. So that is what took Quincy so long. She tightened her grip on the tray and stepped into the room.

Clayton opened his eyes.

Sarah held back a frown. For all the improvement in his grooming, it was clearly evident he was still in pain. She could see it in the shadows in his eyes, the sallow tinge in his face, though his complexion looked more normal. And he *had* lost weight. Without the stubble of beard hiding his features it was obvious his cheekbones were more pro-nounced.

"Good morning." She placed the lap tray across his extended legs.

"Good morning." Clayton looked down. "What is this?"

"Your breakfast."

"Broth?"

Sarah glanced up, caught his frown. "Doctor's orders. You are to have nothing solid to eat until Dr. Parker gives his permission."

"Dr. Parker is not the one who has not eaten for two days."

Sarah let the faulty math stand. Judging from his dis-gusted tone, Clayton would not take correction kindly. She shook out the napkin, spread it over his shirtfront and picked up the spoon. "Shall I feed you?"

Clayton's frown descended into darker regions. "I will feed myself—if I have the strength."

Her lips twitched. She pressed them together and handed him the spoon.

"I amuse you?" He scooped up a spoonful of the broth, swallowed it and scooped up another.

Sarah shook her head and poured him a cup of coffee. "I am not amused…exactly. I am pleased. Mother says, when a man who has been ill starts complaining it is a certain sign he is getting better."

"I see." Clayton gave her a sour look. "I shall endeavor not to improve too much."

The laughter broke free. She couldn't hold it in. "Forgive me. I did not mean—" she took a breath "—it is only…you sound like James."

"James?"

The word was a growl. Sarah stared at Clayton's face. His eyes had darkened to almost black and his lips were taut. He looked as if he could bite the spoon in half. He *was* feeling out of sorts. "Yes, James…my brother. The one who taught me to skip stones."

She studied his face. His mouth had softened, but still. "Is your pain severe? Would you like a cold cloth for your head?"

"When I am finished with my breakfast." He looked down and spooned up the last of his broth. "I ask your pardon, Miss Randolph. I should not have taken my frustration out on you." He tossed his napkin on the tray and looked toward the windows. "I should be working. There is much yet to be done, and instead I am confined to this bed." He put down the spoon and leaned back against the pillows.

She handed him his cup of coffee. "Mr. Wexford is not capable of doing the work with your help and supervision?" He met her gaze and something bitter came into his eyes. He looked away.

"Wexford is very capable—but he is a gentleman."

Sarah removed the tray. Her skirts swished softly as she carried it to the table by the stair door. "You make being a gentleman sound a disadvantage."

"Only when handling the tough men that make up our crews."

She turned back to face him. "You are a gentleman, and you handle them."

"There is a difference. I was raised here in Cincinnati, not in an eastern city." He held her gaze with his. "I am a gentleman with rough edges. Mr. Wexford is more refined than I."

His face had gone taut again. The pain must be increasing. His effort at conversation was taking a toll. "Then you shall have to help Mr. Wexford develop some rough edges, Mr. Bainbridge. But for now, drink your coffee." Sarah swerved toward the dressing room, looked back over her shoulder. "I shall be back presently with a cold cloth for your head."

Clayton scowled and watched Sarah disappear into the dressing room. *Help Wexford develop some rough edges.* She had missed his point about Wexford being an eastern-city-reared gentleman worthy to be considered as a potential husband entirely. And that little speech had cost him.

He sagged back into the pillows and closed his eyes against the bright sunlight pouring in the windows. He would try again to make her look at Wexford with favor. Later. After the throbbing in his head eased…

"And did you have a ride in the wheelbarrow?" Sarah dried Nora's face and hands, brushed the last of the bits of straw out of her hair.

The toddler nodded, beamed up at her. "An' we founded the kitties' mommy. She does—" Nora hunched her little shoulders and imitated a hissing cat.

Sarah laughed and tugged a soft cotton slip over Nora's head. The little girl pushed her small arms through the banded openings, stretched them into the air and yawned. Sarah smiled, sat on the bench Nora was standing on and pulled her onto her lap. The toddler stuck her thumb in her mouth, leaned back and closed her eyes. Sarah dropped a kiss on top of Nora's golden curls and pulled clean stockings on over her small, bare feet.

Knuckles rapped against her partially open door— Quincy's signal that he had finished tending to Clayton's personal needs and she could return to his room. She rose. The rap repeated.

Sarah frowned. Was something wrong? She turned Nora in her arms so the toddler's head rested against her shoulder and hurried into her bedroom. "Yes, Quincy?"

"Wanted to let you know I have errands to run that will keep me busy all afternoon."

Sarah nodded. "Very well. Tell Eldora I shall keep Nora with me." The very opportunity she had been waiting for— praying for. She waited until Quincy had gone down the stairs and into the kitchen, then closed her eyes. "Please let this work, Lord. Please let Clayton Bainbridge accept Nora and learn to love her. Please—"

Do not entertain doubt.

Sarah took a breath and looked toward the ceiling. "Thank You, Lord, for giving me this opportunity to bring Clayton Bainbridge and his daughter together. He *shall* learn to accept and love her, by Your grace. For I pray it in Your Holy Name. Amen."

Sarah carried Nora across the landing and into

Clayton's bedroom. Her gaze met Clayton's as soon as she stepped beyond the door. Surely he could not have heard her whispered words? Heat climbed into her face. She ducked her head to hide her burning cheeks, hurried to the corner and went onto her knees to put Nora down for her nap.

"Keep your right leg straight and *slowly* lift your foot six inches off the bed. Does it hurt?"

Sarah paused on the stairs to hear Clayton's answer to the doctor's question.

"A little."

She breathed out a sigh of relief and hurried up the last two steps.

"Do the same with your left leg."

"Ugh."

Tears sprang to her eyes at Clayton's grunt of pain.

"That one doesn't want to work, eh? Not surprised. That is a bad bruise on your back. Does it hurt if I press here?"

Sarah could hear Clayton's sharp, indrawn breath all the way out on the landing. She clasped her hands. *Please, Almighty God—*

"It's a piece of luck whatever hit you missed your spine."

"It does not feel lucky." The words were choked, breathless.

The doctor chuckled. "Nonetheless, I think you will be good as new if you stay still and let these muscles heal. Of course, that knock to your head will keep you quiet a few more days. Lump's almost gone. Gash is healing well, but there is no way to know what is going on inside your skull."

"Feels like someone is using a sledge to drive spikes behind my eyes."

Sarah's stomach turned over. She took a long breath to squelch a surge of nausea and blinked tears from her eyes.

"You will make it worse if you move around. Now let me fetch that pretty nurse of yours." The doctor's footsteps approached the door.

If Clayton saw her hovering on the landing, listening— Sarah whirled and dashed through her bedroom door.

"Miss Randolph?"

Sarah took a breath, counted to five and opened her door. "Yes, Doctor?"

"You can come back in now." He led the way to Clayton's bed and picked up his bag. "He's to stay in bed until I see him again in a few days."

"A few *days!* See here, Doc, I have responsibilities—"

Dr. Parker clamped his free hand on Clayton's shoulder. "Do as I say, son. If you do yourself harm, you could be in that bed for weeks." He glanced across the bed to her. "He's stubborn as his grandpap. Tie him there if you have to." He slapped his hat on his head and strode to the door.

Sarah glanced at Clayton's scowling face and hurried into the hall after the doctor. "Excuse me, Dr. Parker, but what about his food? Is he to have only broth, or—"

The doctor paused at the top of the stairs and looked back at her. "No, regular food is fine. Keepin' him quiet is the main thing." His lips twitched. "I think you may have a time doing that, Miss Randolph. Good day."

"Good day, Dr. Parker."

Sarah watched him disappear down the stairs, squared her shoulders and marched back into the room prepared for battle. Clayton was sagged against his pillows, his face pale, his eyes closed. She hurried to the dressing room, wet a cloth and rushed back. She leaned down and placed it on his forehead. Her hands brushed his cheeks.

Clayton opened his eyes, looked straight into hers.

Her heart leaped, felt as if it might escape her chest. Sarah covered the spot with her hand, drew back, struggled for breath from lungs that refused to fill. "I—I have to get Nora." She groped for the corner post of the bed, turned and started toward the winder stairs, her need to be away from Clayton Bainbridge lending strength to her weak, shaking knees.

Chapter Eighteen

Sarah tuned out the murmur of the men's voices and cast a longing glance at the door to the hallway. How she would love to go outside for a walk. Of course that was impossible. But it had been so long since she had been alone. Since she had had time to think. That was her problem. She was quite certain of that. She loved Aaron. She did. So why could she not recall his face?

Sarah wrapped her arms around her waist and stared out the window. The sun was sinking behind the hill, throwing its golden light upward to outline the layers of clouds in a last defiant gesture to ward off the coming night. The lengthening shadows below the hill's crest announced it was a losing battle. It would soon be dark. She did not even shiver. She was too busy to have time to worry over the dark of night.

And that must be the reason she could not remember Aaron. She was simply too busy. The activity had chased all thought of him from her mind. Sarah sighed and closed her eyes. He had hazel eyes, with deep wrinkles at the corners from squinting out over the ocean in the sunshine.

And thick, dark brows. And a neatly trimmed beard and mustache streaked with gray. His nose was long and— She frowned, pursed her lips. If she could remember his features one by one, why could she not see his face?

"Miss Randolph."

Sarah lowered her arms and turned. John Wexford stood a few feet from her with his hat in his hand and Clayton's leather pouch slung over his shoulder.

"Forgive me for interrupting your thoughts, Miss Randolph, but I am taking my leave and wanted to wish you a good evening."

"You have arrived at a solution for your emergency, Mr. Wexford?" She looked down and straightened a fold in her skirt to avoid his intent gaze.

"Yes. Mr. Bainbridge has been most helpful."

"How fortunate you have him to call upon." She looked up and gave him a polite smile of dismissal. "I wish you well as you endeavor to carry out Mr. Bainbridge's instructions."

The young man's warm smile faded. He gave her a puzzled look, dipped his head and left the room.

Silence fell. The light outside waned; the shadows in the room deepened. Sarah walked to the table and adjusted the wick on the lamp to give more light.

"An excellent man, John Wexford. Would you not agree, Miss Randolph?"

Sarah darted a glance at the bed. "I am sure he is very capable." She pushed a stray lock of hair into place and moved back to the window, unwilling to risk looking into Clayton Bainbridge's blue eyes again. She wanted to think about hazel eyes that looked at her with adoration, that made her feel comfortable and safe, not…discomposed.

"I was not speaking about work, I meant in a personal

way. Would you not agree he is a very eligible bachelor who will make some fortunate lady an excellent husband?"

"Perhaps." Why did he not leave her alone? Could he not tell she was in no mood to converse? She did not want to think about John Wexford or any other man. She wanted to remember *Aaron*.

"You sound doubtful, Miss Randolph." Clayton's voice was quiet, insistent. "Have you an objection to Mr. Wexford?"

Sarah blew out a breath and pivoted. "I have neither objection nor opinion of Mr. Wexford, Mr. Bainbridge. You are a leader of men, and as such are experienced at judging character. I shall leave any decision as to Mr. Wexford's suitability as a husband to you and whatever lady you are considering as a possible bride for him."

"I was considering *you,* Miss Randolph."

Sarah gasped, went rigid. "You overstep your bounds, Mr. Bainbridge! You are my *employer,* not my father."

"That is true." Clayton stared into her eyes. "But I cannot help but notice Mr. Wexford's interest in you. And, as you are alone without family here in Cincinnati—and under my care as it were—I thought it prudent to offer a bit of guidance as to his recommendation as a possible suitor."

The gall of the man. Sarah clenched her hands. "Well, you may forget prudence, sir. I am *not* a child, nor am I your responsibility." She took a step forward, jutted her chin into the air. "And I am perfectly capable of choosing any possible suitor for myself. Indeed, I did so while residing in my father's house." *Oh, Aaron, why did you have to die? I had my life all arranged.*

Her ire fled. The starch left her spine and shoulders. Sarah blinked her eyes, turned back toward the window and stared at her blurry reflection against the darkness. "As for Mr. Wexford, he may take his interest elsewhere. I do not wish his attentions—or those of any other man."

Clayton stared at Sarah. That sadness he had noticed in the drawing room the night he had told her of his grandparents was on her again. So it had to do with a man. Who had hurt her? He scowled, fisted his hands, then slowly relaxed them. Sarah Randolph's life was not his concern. It was his feeling for her that created a problem.

He lifted his hands and rubbed at his throbbing temples. If only he were not confined to this bed. If only she were not the one caring for him. It was torture to have her so near him every day. And the *nights*—waking and seeing her sleeping in the rocker beside his bed…

Clayton gritted his teeth so hard his jaw cramped. Reminding himself Sarah was a test of his resolve did not help. And his plan to avoid her—An idiot racing a scraper had taken care of that. He threw a dark look toward the ceiling. *You must be amused at how well You destroyed that strategy, God. Were You laughing while I thought up the scheme, and the one to interest her in Wexford as well? That has come to naught, also.*

Clayton closed his eyes, hearing the fabric of Sarah's dress whispering as she moved. Those *gowns*. Their very simplicity enhanced Sarah's beauty, revealed in greater measure the grace of her movements. He tried not to, but the temptation to look at her was too great. He opened his eyes and watched her walk over to the corner, kneel down and straighten the blanket over the child. She would be a wonderful mother. If only—

Clayton veered his gaze to his open door. In the bedroom across the hall, on the far outside wall between the two windows, was where the bed had been. Deborah's bed. The one where she had given birth to the child he was responsible for—the bed she had died in. It was not there now. The bed was gone. As Deborah was gone. As his old bed was gone. He had taken an ax, chopped the beds to pieces and burned them. But the fire could not purge his guilt. The living proof of that was sleeping on a mattress in the corner.

Clayton sucked in a breath, forced himself to remember every detail of that night with Deborah. How he wished he could take back that night. But he could not. And he could not bring Deborah back. He had tried to keep her alive. Had prayed for God's mercy. Had offered himself in Deborah's place. But all his prayers, all his begging had changed nothing. Deborah had died.

Clayton's face tightened. He had to face that guilt every day. Had to endure the burden that grew every time he saw the child. But he did not have to add to the burden. And he would not. He would not allow himself to love Sarah Randolph.

"Deborah...*no*..."

Sarah jolted awake.

"...baby...mustn't..."

"Wake up, Mr. Bainbridge." Sarah caught hold of Clayton's flailing hand, held it in both of hers.

"...dead...no, take me..." He sat bolt upright in bed.

"Oh!" Sarah dropped his hand and grabbed hold of his shoulders. "Wake up!"

"My fault..."

Should she push him down onto the pillows, or would it hurt his back? She tightened her grip. "Mr. Bainbridge! Please wake up! You will hurt yourself."

He opened his eyes.

Sarah stared into Clayton's eyes, saw awareness returning and drew her hands back. "You were having a nightmare." She reached behind him, fluffed his pillows. Why was she blushing? She had done nothing wrong. "There. Can you lower yourself to the pillows, or do you need my help?"

"I will manage."

His voice was gruff, raspy. She nodded and stepped close, ready to do what she could if her help was needed.

Clayton placed his palms on the bed on either side of him, took the weight of his body on his arms and leaned backward. Pain knifed him on the lower left side of his back. He stopped the slow torture and let himself fall into the nest of pillows. "Ummph." He closed his eyes against the pain.

"Are you all right? Can I get you anything?"

"A new head and back would be nice." The words came out a little breathless, not jovial as he had intended.

"I wish I could grant your request. Or at least do something to ease your pain."

There was genuine concern in Sarah's voice. He knew it was unwise, but he opened his eyes and looked at her. "You have done more than I had any right to ask or expect, Miss Randolph. I am not your responsibility. The child is. But I thank you for your kind care. I do not believe I could have stood the pain without your cold cloths easing it somewhat." *Or your presence, which makes everything better. And worse.* Her answering smile stole the breath he had managed to regain.

"But you did not ask me, Mr. Bainbridge. I was ordered by Mrs. Quincy to care for you. And I confess to a great reluctance." She reached out and straightened his coverlet.

"You see, since a little child, I have been sickened by the sight of blood." She glanced up at him. "I am quite over that now."

Her laughter was soft as the soughing of wind through the branches of trees. He would never forget it. Nor would he forget the way the dim lamplight made the golden flecks in her brown eyes shine and emphasized the shadows cast by her long, sooty lashes when she looked down at him.

Clayton drew himself up short. He moved his head to a more comfortable position and tracked her progress around the foot of his bed. "You said I was having a nightmare. Did I...say anything?"

Sarah paused, nodded. "You mumbled something about Deborah." She moved along the other side of his bed, straightening the covers as she went. "And you mentioned a baby." She looked down at him, her eyes warm with sympathy. "Nightmares are horrible things. I hope you do not suffer them often."

It would be so easy draw her close. To taste the sweet softness of her lips... Clayton clenched his hands and shoved them beneath the coverlet on his lap. "No, not often." He looked closer, noted the clouds in her eyes. "You sound as if you have experience with nightmares."

"Some." She looked away.

"From a childhood mishap?"

"No."

Her tone did not invite further questions. Intuition dawned. "From a thunderstorm?"

A shudder shook her. "I do not wish to discuss it."

Clayton gave a careful nod. "As you wish. But should you ever care to do so, I will be ready to listen. Sometimes, talking about a nightmare breaks its power over us and it goes away."

"Yours has not." Sarah offered a challenge in her stare. "Is that because what you say is false? Or because you do not discuss your nightmares, either?"

He should have let the nightmare topic die. His curiosity had him backed into a corner. But he could not lie to her. "I do not discuss it. My nightmare is true." Clayton sucked in air, spoke the words he had never before said aloud. "I made a terrible mistake. There were severe, irreversible consequences. Talking about it cannot make my guilt go away."

Sarah took hold of the bedpost beside her, blinked her eyes. "Forgive me, Mr. Bainbridge. I did not mean to bring the memory of a painful time back to you." She blinked her eyes again. "I know how devastating that can be. My nightmare is also real."

Sleep would not come. She was afraid to let it. Afraid the nightmare would come. Every time her eyelids grew heavy she got up and walked around the room. She remembered Aaron's face now. The way he had looked at his last moment on this earth—the moment before the lightning struck him. It was her last memory of him.

Sarah shuddered, rose from the rocker and pulled the blanket that covered her lap around her shoulders. It was a futile effort. The cold was inside. Nonetheless, she hugged the blanket close and wandered about Clayton's bedroom, wondering again why there were no paintings of his wife, no mementoes of her anywhere.

She strolled to the window and stood looking out into the moonlit night, mentally going through every room in the house searching for something that proclaimed Deborah Bainbridge had lived here. There was nothing. She was familiar with all of the rooms, except Clayton's study. Perhaps that was where Deborah's picture hung. Perhaps Clayton wanted it near him all day. Or perhaps he did not want to be reminded of Deborah.

Clayton had called out his wife's name while he was thrashing about in his bed. Was Deborah Bainbridge Clayton's nightmare? As Aaron was hers?

Sarah lifted the hem of the blanket off the floor and walked over to the corner. Clayton had also said "baby." Was little Nora involved in the nightmare? Was that why Clayton would have nothing to do with his daughter? And if he would not speak about it, how would she ever be able to bring father and daughter together?

Chapter Nineteen

Sarah carried Clayton's breakfast tray to the table by the stairs, came back and tugged the rocker away from the bed.

"What are you doing?"

She braced for battle, looked up at Clayton and launched into her prepared speech. "Quincy must go to the farm today, and Eldora will be putting up preserves. I will have Nora here with me. I thought it best to move the rocker away from the bed so we will not disturb your rest."

There was no display of anger. Clayton went absolutely still. His face had taken on that carved-of-stone look. She leaned down and tugged at the chair.

"Leave the rocker in place. Lucy will watch the child."

His voice was quiet, devoid of all emotion. *The child.* The words grated. As did his attitude. Anger would be better than cold indifference. At least it would show he had some feelings! Sarah lifted her chin. "Lucy is at her home. She has been taken with the sickness that is going around. And *I* am Nora's nanny." She took a firmer grip on the back of the rocker, glanced over her shoulder and backed toward the side wall.

"Stop! Leave the chair."

Sarah jerked to a halt at the barked words, looked up at Clayton. There was no indifference now. The expression on his face—the tightened lips, the pain, anger, *despair* in his eyes held back her defiance on Nora's behalf. That odd connection welled, stronger than ever. A desire to help Clayton, to see him healed. To see whatever caused him such pain erased. The longing rose, as strong as her purpose to give Nora her father.

She clenched her hands, hid them in the folds of her long skirt. Why did she have these feelings? How was she to help Clayton when her own heart was broken? What about *her* pain? Anger filled her eyes with tears. She ducked her head and blinked them away.

"The chair is too heavy for you. Get Quincy to move it."

Clayton sounded resigned. Well, she was *not*. She was grieving Aaron, and she did not have the strength to take on Clayton Bainbridge's burden. Sarah blinked her eyes clear and lifted her head. "Quincy has left for the farm."

Clayton's chest swelled. He blew out air. "Then leave the chair where it is."

"But—"

"Miss Randolph, do you not understand the roles of a servant and an employer? That was an *order.*"

Sarah stared, bit back a retort. He was right. She was only a servant to him. She had forgotten that while caring for his wounds. Evidently he had not. And she had been concerned about him having a wounded heart? She ignored the pang of hurt. It was nothing but wounded pride.

"Very well." She lifted her hands from the chair and took a step back. "If there is nothing you need at the moment, I will go down to the kitchen and bring Nora back." She waited to a count of three, pivoted and sailed across the room. His dirty breakfast tray waited there on the table. She snatched it up and hurried out onto the landing before she gave in to the urge to throw his coffee cup at him, wound or no wound. It was a good thing for Mr. Clayton Bainbridge she was a lady!

Clayton leaned back against his pillows, bereft and hollow. He had accomplished his goal of distancing himself from Sarah. And all because he had been worried she would hurt herself moving that heavy rocker. He should have realized—should have challenged Sarah's pride earlier. Her stiff posture, lifted chin and flashing eyes were proof of a wall he would not be allowed to scale no matter how he longed to reach her heart and claim it for his own. All he had to do was make certain that wall stayed in place—and return to work as soon as possible. The less time he spent in her company the better.

Clayton lifted his hand and gently probed the wound on the back of his head. It was scabbed over and tender to the touch, but there was no eruption of pain, only a dull throbbing. He would not be bedridden if it were not for the injury to his back. He may not be in condition to supervise the work sites, but he would at least be able to care for himself, and work in his study. He would be independent. Sarah Randolph could return to being a nanny instead of his nurse. And he would be able to avoid all contact with her.

Clayton flattened his palms against the mattress, braced himself and lifted his right leg a few inches off the bed. It hurt, but the pain was nothing he could not bear. He shifted his weight slightly, gritted his teeth and tried his left leg. "Ahhugh!" Pain thrust deep into his side, slashed across his lower back, agonizing and intense.

His stomach churned. Cold sweat beaded on his fore-head and upper lip, moistened his palms. Clayton clamped his jaws together and sagged back against his pillows. Pain pulsated in the bruised area above his hip, traveled down his leg. For all his effort had cost him, his leg had not moved. Fear clamped his chest, squeezed his throat. What if he was crippled? That would make it certain he could not have Sarah. Ever.

"Mr. Bainbridge!"

Clayton opened his eyes. Sarah, the child in her arms, stared at him from the open doorway. He closed his eyes again, unwilling to let her see his agony.

"Sit here, sweetie."

The rocker squeaked. The blanket on his left pulled down. She was leaning over him. He kept his eyes closed.

"How can I help you?"

The sound of her soft voice was like balm, the fact that she cared, enough. But he could not tell her. He could never tell her. The wall had to remain firmly in place. Clayton rolled his head side-to-side, heedless of the healing wound, and waited for the pain to ease.

"And what is this?"

Sarah's voice, pitched soft and low—the whispering rhythm of the rocker in the background. Clayton frowned. He must have fallen asleep. He opened his eyes and looked toward the chair. Sarah was sitting with the child on her lap, holding an open book.

"A cow."

His lips twitched. The child was speaking in an ex-aggerated whisper. She must have been warned to be quiet.

"Very good! And what does a cow say?"

"Moooo."

"Yes. Now, what is next?"

The child twisted her head around and looked up at Sarah.

"A butterfwy!"

"Shhhh…" Sarah placed her finger across her lips and glanced his way. Her eyes widened. "You are awake." She rose, still holding the child, and stepped close to his bed. "How do you feel?"

"All right." Lamplight danced among the crests and valleys of the child's golden curls. *Deborah's hair.* He looked away, glanced out the window. The sky was gray. Layers of dark clouds foamed in the distance. "Looks as if we are in for some weather."

"Yes." Sarah took a breath. "Are you hungry? We ate some time ago. But Eldora will fix a tray for you."

Clayton nodded, tried not to notice the child who was staring down at him.

Sarah turned, lifted the picture book off the seat of the rocker and carried Nora to her mattress in the corner. "Now you be a good girl and look at your book, Nora. I have to go get your papa's food, but I will be right back."

Papa. Clayton's stomach knotted. "Take the child with you."

Sarah shook her head. "I have to carry your tray, and Nora cannot climb the stairs." She hurried out of the room. Closed the door behind her.

He was trapped! Clayton glared down at his useless leg.

"Duck…quack, quack."

Paper crackled—a page turning.

"Horsy!"

He pressed back into his pillows, closed his eyes and willed Sarah to hurry. There were soft rustling sounds…

hesitant steps…a bump. He did his best to ignore them. They grew louder, drew nearer. His heart thudded. Ridiculous to be frightened of a child. His blanket moved.

"Me petted your horsy."

Clayton sucked in a breath, opened his eyes. The child was leaning against the bed staring at him, her tiny hands holding on to the covers, her chin level with the mattress. *How did she— The bed steps! If she moved—* Clayton's heart leaped into his mouth. He shot a glance at the closed stair door, looked back at the child. *Better keep her talking.* "You did?"

Her blond curls bobbed with her emphatic nod. "Horsies are *big*." She let go of the covers and spread her little arms as wide as they would go—teetered.

"Careful!" Clayton grabbed hold of her arm. *She was so small.* He cast another look toward the door. Where was Sarah? He looked back. The child was looking up at him. There was something about her blue eyes… He swallowed hard and held out his other hand. "Can you climb up here and tell me about the horses?"

She nodded, slipped her tiny hand in his. His chest tightened. He ignored the sensation, lifted her up onto the bed and sat her down in the center, beside him, where there was no chance she would topple off the edge.

"Horsy go—" She made a sound he interpreted as a snort, dipped her head and pushed it forward.

He recognized Pacer's nudge. "That means he is glad to see you."

"Uh-huh. And kitties, too!" She wiggled into a more comfortable position against his legs. "Kitties go, rrrrr-rrrrr, 'cause they be happy when you petted them. And they gots special names."

"Oh." Rain pattered against the windows. A soft,

soothing sound. He watched it flow together, form small rivulets and run down the panes.

"Uh-huh. They be Happy an' Fluffy an' Wiggles an' Bun'le."

Clayton's brow rose. Four kittens? He had told Quincy to take them to the farm.

"Me gots a special name. Me Nora." She yawned, stuck her thumb in her mouth and looked up at him. Blue eyes full of trust. Her eyes…

Clayton's heart lurched.

The stair door clicked open.

Sarah stepped through the door, leaned against it and pushed back until it clicked closed. She looked over at the bed and almost dropped the tray she carried. "Nora!" She rushed across the room. "How did you get up on your papa's bed?"

"She climbed the bed steps. I thought it prudent to keep her up here where she could not get hurt."

Sarah put down the tray and lifted Nora into her arms. The toddler snuggled close and closed her eyes. "I forgot about the steps, Mr. Bainbridge. I—" His raised hand stopped her apology. She searched his face. He had that stony look again. She could not tell if he was angry with her or— *O Lord, please do not let him blame Nora. It was my fault. I forgot about the steps. O Lord, please, please do not let him be angry with Nora.*

She gave the toddler a hug. "It is bedtime for you, sweetie." She tucked her in, gave her a kiss and hurried back to give Clayton his tray.

"Thank you."

Polite, expressionless. She could read nothing in his voice. She walked to Nora's dollhouse, straightened the furniture. Rain splattered the window beside her. The tree branches outside tossed in a rising wind. Her hands itched to close the shutters and pull the curtains, but it was not her room and she did not dare. She finished her work and turned her back to the window, looked toward the rocker. It faced his bed and the window beside it. There was nowhere for her to hide. Nothing for her to do.

Lightning flickered its white brilliance through the room. Thunder rumbled in the distance, from somewhere over the hill. She went rigid. The storm was coming.

"Would you remove my tray, please?"

Sarah whirled, walked to the bed. She lifted the tray and carried it to the table by the stairs. *The stairs.* There were no windows in the stairwell. Perhaps she could sit—

"And if you would close the shutters, please?"

She glanced his way, read the understanding in his eyes. She forced a smile. "Thank you. You are very kind." She hurried from window to window, focusing on her task, trying not to see the storm outside.

Lightning flared. Thunder cracked. She winced, jerked away from the last window. It was coming closer.

"Come sit down, Miss Randolph."

Sarah glanced at Clayton and walked over to perch on the edge of the rocker, unable to relax—ready to run.

"While you were down in the kitchen fetching my tray, I heard a tale of four kittens."

"Oh?" What did kittens matter?

"I had told Quincy to take them to the farm."

Oh. Had she gotten Quincy in trouble? "I apologize, Mr. Bainbridge. I asked Quincy to allow Nora to play with them. I hope any displeasure you may feel will be directed at me, not Quincy."

Something flickered in Clayton's eyes. "You are very

quick to throw yourself on the sacrificial pyre, Miss Randolph. But you need have no concern for Quincy." A smile played with his lips. "I inherited him along with the property, and Quincy has his own quiet way of running things around here. I am quite certain, should I confront him with the situation, he would remind me that I did not tell him *when* the kittens were to be removed to the farm."

Light flashed through the cracks around the closed shutters. Thunder crashed.

Sarah gasped, jolted to her feet, clasped her trembling hands. How could Nora sleep?

"You see, Quincy worked for my grandparents and he considers it his 'boundin' duty' to ignore any orders I give that fall contrary to what he deems is best for this place. And Eldora—"

She could not listen any longer. Sarah took a breath, faced him. "Mr. Bainbridge, I realize what you are doing. And I thank you for trying, but distraction does not work."

"Nor does hiding." He glanced at the corner, looked up, caught her gaze and held it with his. "There is no place to run to—nowhere to hide from a…nightmare, Miss Randolph. And it seems we must both face ours today." She tensed as he drifted his gaze over her face. "What has made you so frightened of storms?"

Sarah looked away from the concern in his eyes. He had been so understanding of her moments of panic. And she *was* caring for his daughter. She owed him an explanation. She hid her trembling hands in the folds of her skirt and looked up at him. "When you were a child, did you have a dream for your life, Mr. Bainbridge?"

His countenance changed, became guarded. For a moment she thought he would not answer, but he nodded. "I wanted to be a soldier—like my father. But, having listened to stories of Indian attacks all my life, I wanted to be an army engineer so I could build strong forts that would keep other soldiers and their families safe."

There was disappointment in his voice. She forgot her own tale. "What happened to your dream?"

He took a long breath, looked off into the distance. "I became an apprentice to a highly respected engineer who became my mentor and friend—more so after my grand-parents died." The muscle along his jaw twitched. "A short while before I was to leave my position with him to go in the army, he became ill. I delayed my departure and took over his work. His health failed quickly, and I promised, on his deathbed, to give up my dream of being a soldier and instead—" He shook his head. "I am going astray. We were speaking about childhood dreams. Mine did not come to pass." His gaze came back to her. "What was your dream?"

Sarah took a breath, forced out the words. "My father owns a shipping line and I grew up listening to talk of faraway places. My dream was to marry the captain of one of Father's ships and sail with him around the world on—" her voice broke "—on our honeymoon."

"And you found your ship's captain." Clayton's face went still.

She nodded. Lightning glinted. Thunder cracked. She gave a soft cry, hid her face in her hands and whirled away from the bed. Clayton's quick grasp on her arm stopped her from running for the stairwell.

"You have nothing to fear, Miss Randolph." His calm, deep voice washed over her. "You are with me, and—"

"And I was with Aaron also!" She yanked her hands from over her eyes, stared at him. "We were betrothed, and I felt safe with him. But—" She stopped, drew a long quivering breath and sank into the rocker. "We were to have married last Christmas. And to have set sail on our honeymoon voyage shortly after the first of the new year."

"But that did not happen."

How calmly he stated the fact.

"No." She looked down, smoothed a fold from her skirt. "Last October I went to Boston to visit my friend Elaine and engage her in the wedding plans. Father had ordered a new ship built at her father's shipyard. It was near completion. Plans were made for Aaron and his crew to come to Boston and sail the new ship home to Philadelphia." Her throat closed. She rose, walked to the bedside table and poured a glass of water.

"And he did not come?"

The words were gently spoken, but offensive nonetheless. "Of course he came!"

Lightning snapped. A sulfurous light invaded the room.

Sarah shivered, wrapped her arms about herself and hurried away from the window.

"What happened?"

She glanced over her shoulder at him. "Elaine and I were to travel home with him. But Elaine became ill. I had wedding preparations to make that could not await a more opportune time, and so, as it was only a day's sail down the coast and I was expected home, I joined Aaron aboard ship."

Her chest tightened. She could feel her face drawing taut. She turned away from his penetrating gaze. "It was a beautiful day, but as we were boarding a-an elderly sailor on the dock warned Aaron not to sail. He said there was a bad storm brewing." The pressure in her chest increased. That familiar cold hand squeezed her lungs.

"And he was right."

Another calm statement of fact.

She turned to face him, to defend Aaron against any blame. "The storm came out of nowhere. One moment the skies were blue and the sun was shining, and the next moment dark clouds rolled across the sky and shut out the light." Her voice quavered.

She moved forward, took hold of the bedpost and fought for breath. "Aaron tried to head for the open sea and outrun the storm, but the wind tore the sails to shreds. Waves, high as this house, threw the ship around like— like a toy. It plunged toward huge rocks in shallow water and there was nothing he could do. He—he ordered two of the crew to take me to the dinghy."

She stared off into the distance, lost in the horror of that day. "The rain came so thick and fast, breathing was almost like drowning. And the wind—it was impossible to stand. The sailors tried to hold me upright, but the ship was pitching so violently it tossed us about and I was wrenched from their grasp. I…I slid toward the side of the ship. I heard Aaron shout, and then—and then the light-ning—"

A deep shudder shook her. She closed her eyes. "There was a h-horrible crack, and the deck in front of me disap-peared. There was only a black h-hole and I could not stop sliding. And then I saw Aaron." The strength left her legs. She sagged against the bed. "He was clinging to the end of the broken rail and stretching his hand out to me. I…I reached for him but the lightning struck again. Aaron…the deck…everything vanished. I fell into the water. It was so c-cold and dark…"

She opened her eyes, stared down at Clayton's hand gripping hers, felt the strength and warmth of it. How had that happened? Had she reached out to him? She sighed, too emotionally spent to be embarrassed, too needy of his comfort to slip her hand from his, though she should.

"Thank God you were saved, Sarah." His grip tightened on her hand. "Forgive me. I should not have asked you about such a harrowing experience."

"You could not know." She gathered her inner fortitude and slipped her hand from his. Her remaining strength seemed to ebb with the broken contact. She glanced at the rocker, took hold of the corner post and started around the foot of the bed. She needed to sit down, before she collapsed in a weary heap on the floor. "When I awoke, I was in the dinghy. The skirt of my gown had caught on a piece of broken deck floating on the water, and two sailors saw it. They pulled me from the water and were able to get the dinghy over the rocks and into a small cove." Her lips trembled. She sank down into the rocker and closed her eyes. "We three were the only ones who survived. The sailors went on to Philadelphia, and a family who lived in the cove took me in until Father came for me."

Tears slipped from under her eyelids and ran down her cheeks. "The lightning struck Aaron, and the sea he loved claimed him. He, and my dream, died that day. But my heart remains loyal to him. I want no other…"

Clayton lay studying the ceiling over his head. The storm had played itself out. All was quiet, except for an occasional grumble of thunder in the distance.

He glanced at Sarah, asleep in the rocker. Telling him her story had exhausted her. But she had seemed calmer for having unburdened herself to him. He hoped he had helped to chase her nightmare away forever.

Clayton shuddered, cold knots forming in his stomach. It had been such a close thing. If her skirt had not caught

on the jagged edge of that broken-off piece of the ship…
If those sailors had not seen it through the rolling, crashing
waves of the storm-tossed ocean and pulled her into their
dinghy, she would have been lost forever. Swallowed by
the sea along with her fiancé.

His hands flexed. He ached to wake her and tell her he
loved her. But he was destined to remain silent.

…my heart remains loyal to Aaron.

Clayton compressed his lips, held back a bitter laugh.
His struggles to deny his love for Sarah, to distance
himself from her, were all for naught. Even had he yielded
to his feelings for her and tried to win her for his own, it
would have been useless. She loved another, though he
was gone. He had been torturing himself needlessly. He
closed his eyes and waited for sleep to claim him.

Chapter Twenty

Nora dropped her doll, gripped the windowsill and went on tiptoe. "Me go outside?"

Sarah shot a quick glance at Clayton. It was difficult keeping Nora quiet all day. But after yesterday's episode of the toddler's invasion of her father's bed, she dared not take the chance of offending him. "Not now, sweetie. Quincy is busy. Shall we look at a book?"

Nora's lower lip pouted out. She shook her head. "Me go see horsy." Her little chin quivered.

Oh, Nora, please do not cry! Sarah scooped her up into her arms and turned away from the window. "Can you find the horse in the book for me?"

Golden curls swung from side to side. The little lip protruded farther. Sarah's heart sank. Nora was not going to be easily distracted from her goal.

"Go see horsy. An' kitties."

Sarah kissed Nora's cheek. "I cannot take you outside right now, sweetie. Your papa—"

"Is fine."

Sarah turned toward Clayton.

"Take Nora outside, Miss Randolph. She wants to see the animals."

Nora. He had called her by name. Sarah squelched her elation. "But you may need something, and—"

"And if I do, I shall call for you. There is a bell on the table by the bed in the bedroom across the hall—bring it to me. The windows are open. You will be able to hear the bell from the garden."

Was he being considerate of Nora's wants—or did he want to be rid of her? Anger stiffened Sarah's spine. "Very well. I will be a moment. I have to also fetch Nora's bonnet." She turned toward the door.

"There is no need for you to take Nora. You will accomplish your tasks more quickly without her."

Sarah froze, her heart in her throat. *Had she heard him correctly?* She turned back, looked at Clayton.

"She will be safe here on the bed."

His voice was cool, his face impassive. Still... "Of course." Sarah held her own face expressionless, lowered Nora to the bed and forced herself to walk calmly from the room. She crossed the hall at the same sedate pace, entered the other bedroom and closed the door. The click of the latch set her free. She burst into laughter, spread her arms wide and whirled about the room, unable to contain her joy. "Thank You, Lord. Oh, thank You! You heard my prayers. You are giving Nora her father!"

Tears filmed her eyes. Sarah blinked them away and stopped her impromptu dance. She had to hurry back. She looked about the room. A bed, garbed in a woven tester and coverlet, the soft-blue color of the room's plastered inner walls, sat between two windows in the stone wall opposite the door. A brass bell sat beside a lamp on the table by the bed. She picked it up, jumped at its sudden sharp clang, clamped her other hand over it to stop its ringing and left the room.

The bell. He hated that sound. Clayton closed his eyes, fought an onrush of painful memories.

"Does your head hurted?"

"Only a little." He opened his eyes. The child was on her knees, staring up at him. His heart jolted, just as it had last night. He had not been wrong. She had his grandmother's eyes. And mouth. In fact, except for her coloring and curly hair—which were Deborah's—she could be a very young Rose Bainbridge. His heart squeezed, his chest filled. He had always thought of Nora as Deborah's child—when he was forced to think of her at all—but she was part of him. His daughter. Rose's great-granddaughter.

"Me make it better."

Before he realized what she was about, Nora placed her small hands against his chest, stood and kissed his forehead. Emotion rocketed through him, too complex, too mysterious to be defined, and he knew he would never be the same. His life had changed forever. This tiny waif in his arms suddenly owned him, body and soul. He pulled her close, kissed the soft, silky skin of her cheek. She slipped her little arms around his neck, hugged hard, then pushed back and looked at him. "Me make it better?"

Clayton blinked the tears from his eyes and cleared his throat. "Yes, you did. Thank you." *And I promise you, everything is going to be better from now on.*

Nora nodded and plunked down on his lap. "Me gonna go see horsy."

"So I understand. Will you give Pacer and Sassy a carrot for me?"

"Uh-huh. But not the kitties. Me gives kitties milk, an' soup, 'cause they go—" She stuck out her tongue and lapped at the air.

Clayton laughed, filled with sudden paternal delight at her precocity.

"What is so amusing?"

He looked up. Sarah stood in the doorway, smiling at him. His heart constricted. His mouth went dry. He looked away before she could read in his eyes what was hidden in his heart. His gaze fell on the bell in her hand. Deborah's bell.

Everything rushed back. Guilt stabbed his heart, soured his stomach. Clayton shook his head. "Nothing, really. It is only that I am learning what an unending source of information a child can be. For instance—it seems Quincy is feeding the kittens from the kitchen instead of letting the mother cat teach them to be proper barn cats that hunt for their food."

Sarah's smile disappeared. "I found the bell." She walked to the bed. "I will put it right here where you can reach it." She set it on the edge of the bedside table, turned and slipped the bonnet she held over Nora's curls. "Come, Nora, we will go outside and let your papa rest." She lifted the toddler into her arms and left the room.

His arms felt empty, his heart desolate.

Clayton stared down at the bed. This could not go on. Every day ate away at his resolve. He had to get out of this house! He set his mind against the void in his heart and threw back the covers. He gritted his teeth, braced his palms against the mattress and strained to lift his left leg. Daggers pierced his side, searing heat coursed down his leg. The agony was worth it. His foot had come off the bed. Not far. But it had definitely risen off the bed.

Clayton wiped the beads of cold sweat from his brow and sagged back against the pillows to gather his strength for the next try.

The room was barren. The mattress gone from the corner. The rocker and toys returned to the nursery. He had told Quincy to take them away after supper. A mattress on a floor was no place for a child to sleep. And a rocking chair no bed for Sarah. It was the right thing to do. But his heart ached nonetheless. His only connection to Sarah now was the bell.

Clayton stared at the dim area beyond his open door. The landing at the top of the winder stairs, lit only by the light flowing out from his room and Sarah's room on the other side—her door open to hear his call should he need her.

Need her? He was dying inside for want of her in his life. But that would stop now. She would no longer be caring for him day and night. He would see her as little as possible from now on. And when the strength returned to his injured muscles, not at all. Except for that celebration boat ride up the canal on July fourth. But, even on the packet, she would be busy caring for Nora, and he should not find it hard to avoid her company. He would manage some way.

Clayton scowled, picked up the book he was pretending to read and stared at the printing on the pages.

Sarah lifted Nora from the tub, dried her off and pulled the nightgown with tiny embroidered flowers on the smocking over her head. She had rejoiced too soon. Clayton Bainbridge had shoved his daughter out of his life as soon as he was able. Well, she would see about that! She brushed the tangles from the toddler's damp curls and lifted her off the small bench. "All right, sweetie, time for bed."

"Me see Papa?"

"Yes. You will see your papa tomorrow." She carried Nora toward her crib, swerved and headed for the rocker, back now in its customary place on the hearth. She did not want to let go of Nora yet. She would hold her for a little longer. She sat and cuddled the toddler close, hummed softly.

"Wiggles scratcheded me." Nora offered her arm for inspection.

"I know, but he did not mean to hurt you." Sarah kissed the red mark on the pudgy little wrist. "There. All better."

Nora yawned, wiggled closer. "Me made Papa's head better."

Sarah froze in midrock. "What did you do?"

"Me made…Papa's…head better…"

Sarah looked down. Nora's eyes were drooping. No. *Do not sleep yet, Nora.* "You kissed your papa's head?" She held her breath.

Nora's head moved up and down against her breast in a sleepy nod. She stuck her thumb in her mouth. Her eyes closed. Sarah released her breath, stared down at the smudge of brown lashes against round, rosy cheeks, the tiny nose, the soft pink mouth circling the small thumb. *Why, you little sweetheart!* She laughed softly, rested her head back and resumed rocking. She should have known Nora would not need her help to capture her father's heart.

Thought of Clayton brought the worry that had been haunting her leaping over the barrier she had raised against it. Was he all right? She frowned, rose and carried Nora to her crib, tucked her in and lowered the wick in the lamp. Clayton Bainbridge was no longer her concern. And he certainly did not want her fussing over him. He had dismissed her nursing services and rid himself of her presence at the first possible moment. His wishes could not be more clear. And she was thankful to be rid of the responsibility of his care. He meant nothing to her. Her concern for him was merely habit.

My, it was quiet.

Sarah closed the shutters, adjusted the slats to let in the warm night air and looked around the room. Everything had been put back in its place. It was good to have things settled again. She walked into her bedroom, glanced toward the landing. The lamp was burning bright in Clayton's room. He must be reading. He had requested several books from the library earlier.

She went to the cupboard in the fireplace nook and took out a nightgown, her robe and slippers. Should she change into them? What if he needed her during the night? That did not seem likely. He did not wake and thrash around anymore. It had been she that needed him yesterday, during the storm. He was very wise. She had taken his advice and it truly had helped to talk about what had happened to Aaron and to her. Last night was the first time she had slept through the night since that tragic day. And it had nothing to do with Clayton Bainbridge holding her hand. It was the unburdening of her spirit that helped. Still, he had been kind and understanding.

Sarah worried the soft cotton fabric of her nightclothes between her fingers and looked at the door. Perhaps she should go and see if he needed anything before she retired. She tossed the clothes on her bed, walked to the door and stepped out onto the landing. The light in Clayton's room dimmed and went out. She stopped, took another step, listened. Nothing but silence. He had no need of her.

A wave of emotion, a horrible feeling she did not understand, swept over her. She felt…*rudderless*…like one of her father's ships adrift on the ocean without course or direction.

She blinked and dragged in a deep breath. There was something horribly wrong with her tonight—but she would be better tomorrow. Yes. Everything would be better tomorrow. And right now the best thing for her to do was have a good wash and go to bed. She turned and went back into her room.

That was close. Too close! Clayton scowled into the dark. He had turned his lamp down just in time. Sarah moved so softly, if it were not for that squeaky board on the landing he would not have known she was coming until it was too late to feign sleep. And he was not at all sure he would have the strength to tell her he did not need her. He never had been a good liar.

Chapter Twenty-one

"Hmm, the bruise looks better. Still have a hard lump here above your hip bone though."

The doctor's fingers prodded his flesh. "Ugh." Clayton scowled, gritted his teeth.

"Still tender, eh? How's the head?"

"Fine. No pain at all."

"Good, good." Dr. Parker moved toward the foot of the bed. "You say you can lift your foot now?"

"Yes." Clayton braced himself for the test that was coming.

"Lift it up."

He held his breath, lifted his left foot, held it there, muscles quivering, until the doctor nodded.

"Good. You are doing better than I expected."

The doctor gave him an assessing look. Clayton relaxed his clenched jaw, smiled—though he feared it was closer to a grimace.

"Think you can swing your legs over and sit on the edge of the bed?"

"Doc, if it will get me out of this bed, I will do a somersault."

Dr. Parker chuckled, moved up closer to the head of the bed. "All right, then…easy now."

It took everything he had, but Clayton managed to move his legs to the side of the bed and hang them over the edge. He gave the doctor a crooked grin. "Victory."

Dr. Parker grinned back and gave him a clap on the shoulder that almost toppled him from the bed. "You're as tough as your father was, Clay. Now where is that cane your grandpap used when his rheumatism outdid his stubborn?"

Clayton's heart leaped. "In the cupboard by the fireplace—leaning in the back corner."

The doctor nodded, walked to the cupboard and got the cane. "I'll have your word that if I let you out of bed, you will not try it on your own. You only get up when Quincy is about to help you. A fall could do you a lot of harm."

"I understand."

"All right, then. Put your hands on my shoulders, brace your weight on me, and slide forward till your feet touch the floor. Good thing you got them long Bainbridge legs. You could never navigate them bed steps with a cane."

Clayton did as ordered. His leg threatened to collapse under him when he stood, but he willed it to hold.

"Rest a bit, then we will walk to the chair there by the window—one step at a time, and rest in between."

It took four steps with Dr. Parker's help to cover what was normally one stride for him, but he made it.

"Rest a few minutes, son, then we will get you back in—"

"Doc! Doc!" A boy burst in the room, laboring for breath.

"What is it, Willy?"

"It's Pa…he fell out the…haymow. He ain't movin'. Ma said I should…come fetch you back with me."

"Sorry, Clay, I have to go." The doctor picked up his bag, slapped on his hat and hurried for the door. "I'll tell Eldora to send Quincy up to help you back to bed."

Footsteps clattered down the stairs. Clayton blew out a breath and stared at the bed, which suddenly looked a mile away. Quincy had gone to help Zach Miller with a sick mare. And there was no telling when he would be home. He looked down at the cane in his hand and shook his head. "Looks as if it is you and me, Grandpa."

"Mr. Bainbridge."

Sarah. Clayton looked up, heart pounding. She was standing in the doorway to the winder stairs landing.

"Quincy is away, I have come to help you back to bed."

He stared, drinking in the sight of her—her slender form, her beautiful face, her light-brown hair piled high on the crown of her head. His mouth went taut, the knuckles on his hand gripping the cane went white. He was starved for her presence, and a man had only so much strength. He had already proven he was weak, and if he put his arm around her… He breathed deep, shook his head. "You are too slight, Miss Randolph. Your strength is insufficient."

She stared at him. His heart thudded, his pulse roared through his veins. He forced himself to look away, focused on her hand gripping the door latch. Remembered the soft warmth of it in his.

"We do not know when Quincy will return."

He nodded, stared down at his hand on the cane. "Nonetheless, I will wait. You may return to Nora." He put dismissal in his voice.

"Very well."

Her skirts rustled softly. The sound drew nearer. The scalloped hem of her dark-blue gown brushed against his leg. He clenched his jaw, stared at the cane.

"Here is the bell." There was a clang as she placed it on the chest beneath the window beside him. "Should Quincy tarry, and you tire, I will be in the garden with Nora."

Her skirt billowed, disappeared from his view. He kept his gaze fixed on the cane until he heard her going down the stairs. When he heard the murmur of voices from the kitchen, he put his free hand on the chest, tightened his grip on the cane and pushed to his feet. His left leg quivered. He took his weight on his right leg, set his jaw and moved the cane forward. *Well, this is it. Sorry, Doc. I have no choice.* He let go of the chest, shifted his weight onto the cane, swung his left leg forward, and stepped forward with his right. He paused, stood there on his right leg, using the cane and his weak left leg for balance, and rested. One step accomplished—three to go.

"Diphtheria." James Randolph stopped pacing and looked at his parents. "I shall leave for Cincinnati immediately and bring Sarah home."

"No, James." Elizabeth smiled at the son, who was so like his father, but made her voice firm. "Your father and I agreed that we would trust Sarah to the Lord's care."

"So I did, Elizabeth, but diphtheria…" Justin Randolph scowled, clasped his hands behind his back and rocked forward on his toes. "I agree with James, I think we have to get Sarah out of that city."

Elizabeth shook her head, tapped the letter in her hand. "Sarah says the epidemic is on the wane. And time has already passed since she wrote the letter. By the time James arrived the epidemic would be over and all danger would have passed. And Sarah is needed to care for the little girl and, now, to nurse Mr. Bainbridge."

Justin's scowl darkened. "Common sense—most frustrating at a time like this. But, you are right, my love—" his scowl turned to a smile "—as usual."

"I could go to Cincinnati and care for the toddler." Mary cast a hopeful look at her father. "That will ease Sarah's burden. And I am good with children. Aunt Laina says so."

"No, Mary." Justin's voice was firm. "It is good of you to be concerned for your sister, but one daughter so far away is enough. You will stay here. Though your idea is a good one. I will send Ellen back."

Elizabeth looked at him.

Justin gave an exasperated growl. "You know how Sarah sickens at sight of the slightest injury, Elizabeth. Ellen can nurse the man and—"

"And destroy what the Lord may be doing, not only in Sarah's life, but in Mr. Bainbridge's and the child's, as well?" Elizabeth placed her hand on her husband's arm, looked at her children. "I know you all want to protect and help Sarah—as do I. But can you not see, bringing her home or easing her burden would be doing her a disservice."

"Mother, you always think the Lord is in everything that happens to one of us." Mary shrugged her shoulders. "Sometimes things simply happen."

Elizabeth eyed her daughter. "Mary, Sarah, our *Sarah*, is nursing Mr. Bainbridge. She has cleansed his wound, and cared for him day and night. And she is caring for the child, as well, because there is no other to assume the tasks. And she is praying for Mr. Bainbridge's recovery and asks us to pray for him. And to continue praying that God would unite father and daughter. You do not see the Lord's hand in all of that?"

Tears filled Elizabeth's eyes. "Sarah is *praying.* She is returning to her faith. And I believe the Lord—in His own mysterious way—is answering her prayers. And ours. And those of Mr. Bainbridge's housekeeper and her husband. '*Grant it, O Lord.*'" She laughed in sheer delight at the story Sarah had related in her letter, of Eldora's attitude and prayer. "Sarah is furious with the two of them. And, I believe, it is because she has growing feelings for Mr. Bainbridge and is frightened by them. But that will pass when the Lord has His way."

Elizabeth looked at her family, saw agreement in her husband's eyes, doubt in James's, and rebellion in Mary's. *If only you could deposit your own faith in your children.* She sighed and continued her explanation. "I see God's hand very clearly in this situation. I believe He has used the unfortunate circumstances of Sarah's grief over Aaron, Mr. Bainbridge's accident and the diphtheria epidemic to force them and the child into a…a *cocoon* of closeness that can bring about healing for them all." She looked up at her husband. "Would you send Ellen to free Sarah from her nursing duties and perchance destroy what the Lord is doing?"

Sarah grabbed her straw hat, plunked it on her head and hurried down the winder stairs. She had listened to Nora's chatter and Clayton's deep-voiced responses long enough. She would follow his suggestion and go for a walk.

She stepped out into the kitchen, redolent with the

scents of a meal in progress, and strode to the door. "I am going for a walk, Eldora. I shall return shortly."

"No need t' hurry." The housekeeper buried her hands in the ball of dough on the table and pushed. "Now that Lucy's back, she can answer the bell and take care of things."

Yes. So I have been told. Sarah nodded and stepped outside. Rays of golden light beamed down from a sun riding high in a cloud-dotted, bright-blue sky. A breeze whispered through the air to rustle treetops. It was a perfect summer day.

She walked out the gravel way, glanced at the town and turned to follow the road up the hill. She was in no mood for people. She wanted to throw stones across a pond and cause the smooth, serene surface to splash and ripple. What she *really* wanted was to cause a ripple on Mr. Clayton Bainbridge's serene countenance. The man had no emotions! Except when it came to Nora.

Sarah slowed her ground-eating pace. It was amazing how Clayton had changed about his daughter. He spent time with her every morning and afternoon. And Nora loved being with her papa. And she was happy for Nora. She truly was. She was thrilled the little girl had her father's love and attention. It was only… Only nothing!

She glanced at the road ahead and turned down the path to Clayton's private place. She settled her straw hat firmly on her head and stayed as far away from the thornapple trees as possible. Tears filmed her eyes. She hurried past the spot where she had become entangled—where Clayton had freed her—and broke out into the open glade. The pond glistened in the sunshine, peaceful and calm. She gathered a few stones, walked to the large boulder and sat down. All desire to throw a stone into the smooth surface disappeared. She turned the stones over in her hand, studying the coloring and veining that made each unique.

Why was she excluded from Clayton's time with Nora? Why did he now call on Lucy if he had a need? He had banished her from his life. What had she done to make him so repulsed by her presence? And why did it matter so much?

Sarah lifted her gaze and stared at the water. Perhaps it was time to think about going home. She had accomplished her goal. Not the one for herself—she had come to escape grief and now suffered a greater hurt—but she had accomplished the purpose she had found on her arrival. Clayton loved his daughter. Nora had her papa. Yes. Perhaps it was time to go home.

She sighed, rose and walked to the water's edge. As soon as Clayton was completely healed and his life had returned to normal she would tell him she wanted to go back to Philadelphia. She would wait until then. For even though he no longer had need of her care and did not desire her company, she could not bear to go until she knew he was all right.

Tears flowed down her cheeks. Sarah dropped the stones into the water, lifted her hands and wiped them away. But still they came, faster and faster as the hurt in her heart grew and spread like the ripples on the water. She was unable to stem the tears, unable to restrain the sobs that burst from her throat in broken gasps. What had happened to her? She did not want to go back home. Did not want to leave Stony Point—or Eldora and Quincy. And Nora. Oh, how could she endure to leave Nora? And—

Sarah caught her breath, refusing to think further, to

give words to the ache in her heart. She looked down and studied the stones at her feet, picked up a small, smooth gray one and clasped it tight in her hand. It was a fitting symbol of Stony Point. She would keep it with her always. And whenever she looked at it she would remember.

Chapter Twenty-Two

"Here is the thread you asked for, Eldora. And I have something else for you." Sarah handed the housekeeper a paper-wrapped parcel.

"A present?" Eldora frowned. "There ain't no reason for buying presents." She picked up a knife and cut the string.

Only that I will soon be leaving. "I know, but I saw it in Mrs. Avis's store window and—" Sarah stopped at the housekeeper's gasp. "I hope you like it. I thought it would look lovely with your gray church dress."

Eldora lifted the black knit shawl out of the paper, fingered the wide lace edging. "I ain't never had nothing so fine as this."

"Then it is time you did." Sarah smiled at Eldora's pleasure. It took some of the sadness away. "And here is something for Quincy." She handed her a penknife with a bone grip. "I know little of such things, but I am assured by Mr. Jackson that it is a knife of finest quality. I hope Quincy will find it useful." *And that you will both remember me when I am gone.*

"Oh, my." The housekeeper turned the knife over in her hands, looked up. "Sarah, what—"

"Me gots a puppy!"

Sarah looked toward the door as Nora burst into the kitchen. Her gaze met Clayton's. He stopped in the doorway. She jerked her gaze to Nora, knelt to catch the excited toddler in her arms. "What is this?"

The toddler threw her arms about her neck and squeezed. "Papa gots me a puppy!" She leaned back, grabbed her fingers in her small hand and tugged. "Come see!"

"I would like to, sweetie, but…" She looked toward the door. Clayton was gone. And Eldora was watching. She fixed her mouth in a smile and kept her eyes down so the housekeeper could not read the hurt in them. "All right. I will come see your puppy." She took Nora's hand and walked outside.

"Hurry, Nanny!"

Sarah's throat closed at the feel of Nora's small hand tugging at hers. Tomorrow it would end forever. She blinked back tears. Everything she did today was so hard, so…devastating…because it was for the last time. There was no more clanging bell to be answered. Clayton was fully recovered. He had returned to his work on the Miami Canal last week. She had waited until she was sure he would not do himself harm, but it was only an excuse to delay her departure. Clayton was fine. It was time for her to go. Leaving would be excruciating, but staying was unendurable.

Sarah focused on the business at hand, lifted the bar and opened the carriage-house door. A small black-and-white bundle of fur barked and came running, tail wagging, ears flopping up and down. Nora plopped to the floor, giggling and squealing as the puppy jumped up and down licking her face and tugging on her hair.

Sarah closed the door so the dog could not escape and

walked over to the horses. Pacer nickered a welcome, tossed his head and thrust it forward to be petted. She rubbed his silky muzzle and combed her fingers through his forelock. It was always tangled. He lowered his head and nudged her chest. She stepped back to keep her balance and something attacked her exposed ankle.

Sarah leaned down and scooped up the gray kitten who had flopped onto his back and was batting at her skirt hem. He was big enough to do damage now. She tucked him under her chin and scratched behind his ears. He purred his contentment. She reached out and patted Sassy's neck, then sat on the feed chest and stroked the kitten's fur. Wiggles was her favorite. Perhaps she would get a kitten when she went home.

Home. Not Randolph Court. Not anymore. Stony Point was her home. Her heart squeezed tears into her eyes. She wiped them away and held her breath to stop the flow. She would cry tomorrow. Today she must stay calm for Nora's sake. She fixed a smile on her face.

"What is your puppy's name, Nora?"

The toddler shrugged her shoulders.

"You have not named him? Well, that will not do. How will you call him to you if he has no name?" She put Wiggles down, walked over to Nora and lifted the puppy into the air to better see his face. He wiggled and twisted his body, trying to reach her cheek with his tongue. "What a rogue you are." She put him back in Nora's lap. "You could name him Scamper…or perhaps Trouble."

"Uh-uh." Nora shook her head, grinned up at her. "He be Rogue."

Sarah looked down at the toddler sitting on the dusty, straw-strewn barn floor, holding a wiggling puppy in her pudgy arms, and memorized the picture she made. Every detail, from the bits of straw in her golden curls, to her happy smile, to the smudge of dirt on the stockings covering the short little legs sticking out from under the yellow-checked cotton play dress. This was the image she would remember when she thought of Nora in the years to come.

Sarah straightened the books and rearranged the stuffed animals that sat neglected on the shelf. Nora had lost interest in them since she was now free of the confines of this room and could go outside and play with live animals.

She turned and glanced around. So much had changed since she first walked into this room and was greeted by a harried young maid and a squalling toddler. *She* had changed. And she could not go back to simply being a pampered daughter in her parents' house. When she returned to Philadelphia she would work full-time at the Twiggs Manor Orphanage. Her aunt Laina would be glad of the help. And there were always so many children in need, it would keep her too busy to dwell on memories. Her shoulders drooped. It seemed all she did was run from memories.

Sarah swallowed back a rush of tears and walked to the dressing room to check her appearance. It was time. Delaying the moment of truth only increased the agony. She brushed a few stray hairs into place, pinched some color into her pale cheeks and headed for the hallway door.

It seemed strange to use the main stairs. She had become accustomed to using the winder stairs that opened directly into the kitchen. They were much more convenient when Clayton was ill and she had carried food trays up and down at every meal.

A strip of golden lamplight gleamed under Clayton's study door. He was still working. Sarah stopped, gripped the railing and held her breath for a count of ten. It helped. She continued down the last few steps, lifted her hand and knocked on his door.

"Come in!"

Tears stung her eyes. She blinked them away and lifted her chin. *Almighty God, please help me not to cry. Please. I know pride is a sin, but right now it is the only weapon I have to keep my feelings from being revealed.* It was a prayer unlikely to be answered, but it still made her feel better. She squared her shoulders and opened the door.

"Put the—" Clayton glanced up, rose from his chair, snatched his jacket off the back and shoved his arm into the sleeve. "Sorry, I thought you were Eldora with my coffee." He shoved in his other arm and shrugged the jacket into place on his broad shoulders.

She did her best to ignore the frown furrowing his forehead. And his eyes. Though she need not have bothered. He seemed not to want to look at her. Well, she would be out of his life soon enough. "Forgive me for disturbing your work."

"Not at all. I was going to talk with you when my report was finished."

How ironic if he was about to dismiss her. Well, she would not do so! Sarah clenched her hands at her sides and dug her fingernails into her palms. "I have come to tell you I wish to return home to Philadelphia—immediately." She took a breath, dug her fingernails in deeper. "Lucy can care for Nora until you can hire another nanny." *Thank You, Lord. I said it without breaking down.* "I will leave tomorrow." She stared up at Clayton. His face had that stony look again.

"I am afraid that is impossible, Miss Randolph." He looked down, straightened his suit coat. "I believe I once mentioned to you that the fourth of this month is the tenth anniversary of the opening of the Miami Canal. And that as the engineer in charge of the repair work, I am to accompany the governor on a gala celebration trip up the canal to Dayton aboard a specially outfitted packet." He looked up. "If you remember, I told you, the governor has requested that all those accompanying him bring their families along, and that provision has been made for young children and their nannies."

So once again he was forced to accept her presence. "I thought Lucy—" She stopped, stared at the muscle twitching along his jaw.

"Lucy is not capable of this undertaking." He picked up a book from his desk, turned and placed it atop the pile on the mantel. "The journey will take two days. You will need to include bedclothes for Nora in your packing. Please have everything ready by tomorrow afternoon. Directly after supper tomorrow night, Quincy will transport everything to the packet. We will board at nine o'clock the following morning."

Sarah stood staring at his rigid back, torn by the conflicting needs of her heart. She should refuse. She should leave tomorrow as she had planned and end the torture of being where she was not wanted. But she could not go away knowing Nora was on a *boat*. A canal boat to be sure, but still a boat surrounded by water. She shuddered. "Very well. I will do as you ask. But I will have my possessions packed, and I will leave for Philadelphia as soon as we come back to Stony Point." She turned and left his study, the curt nod of agreement he gave her stuck like a sword in her heart.

* * *

Nora was beside herself, trying to see everything at once. It was her first ride in the buggy, her first trip away from Stony Point, and she peppered Sarah and her father with questions. Sarah welcomed them. The short ride seemed endless.

"Here we are." The buggy rolled to a stop. Clayton stepped down and held out his arms. "Come here, Nora." The toddler leaned into his arms, stared wide-eyed at the commotion at the boarding site, and stuck her thumb in her mouth. Clayton shifted Nora to one arm and offered his hand.

Sarah steeled herself and placed hers in it. It was as she remembered, broad and warm, with calluses on the pads of the long fingers—but strong. Not flaccid and weak now, but so very strong. *She should have worn gloves.* She looked away from their joined hands, stepped from the buggy and held her arms out for Nora.

Clayton yielded his daughter to her, placed his hand at the small of her back and guided her through the crowd of people milling around a bandstand where a man was holding forth on a topic that was lost in the din. He urged her toward a packet boat decked out in red, white and blue streamers, with a large yellow banner that read Miami Canal—Ten-Year Anniversary, stretched along the pristine white railing that enclosed the open deck. A broad boarding plank slanted upward from the ground, spanned the narrow space of water between the packet and the docking area and continued its climb to the packet's deck.

Sarah's steps faltered. Her stomach knotted. She stopped walking and stared down at the water, felt the blood draining from her face, the strength leaving her legs. "Take Nora." The words were a whisper, forced from her constricted throat.

"No. She is your charge, Miss Randolph. And 'you are not so selfish as to put your fear above her needs'—are you?"

The challenge in Clayton's voice firmed her will. "No. I am not." Sarah lifted her chin, flashed a look up at him and stepped onto the gangplank.

He lowered his head. "Close your eyes. I will guide you. I promise, I'll not let you fall. You are safe with me."

His whisper fell soft upon her ear. His hand pressed more firmly against the small of her back, drew her ever so slightly closer to his side. It was amazing the courage his touch gave her. She braced herself against her response to his touch, to his nearness and hurried up the gangplank.

The courage left the moment she stepped onboard and felt the slight movement of the deck beneath her feet. She closed her eyes. *Help me, O God. Take away—*

"Bainbridge! I have been watching for you."

Sarah snapped her eyes open at the hail. A short, stout man, wearing a gray suit with a brocaded, maroon vest, separated himself from a small group of men on the forward open deck area and hurried toward them.

"Good morning, Commissioner Thomas." Clayton smiled and shook the man's offered hand. "It looks as though we will have fine weather for our trip."

"Indeed. Yes."

The man skimmed his gaze over her, lingered for a moment on her face. Did her fear show? She lifted her chin. He flushed and focused his gaze on Nora.

"Is this your child, Bainbridge?"

Clayton nodded. "This is my daughter, Nora, yes. And—"

"Beautiful child." The man clapped Clayton on the shoulder. "We have to hurry, Bainbridge. The governor wants you with him when he speaks, and he is about to begin." He turned toward the front deck area, filled with people, then turned back. "Have your nanny get the child settled. Little ones get restless at these sort of ceremonies—and we will be on our way after the governor's speech." He gave her a cursory glance. "The children and nanny quarters are that way." He pointed toward the narrow deck that ran along the left side of the centered cabin area.

Sarah glanced over the side of the boat at the water, caught her breath.

Clayton stepped to the outside edge of the narrow deck. His broad shoulders blocked her view of the water.

"I wish to see my daughter settled, Commissioner. I will join you in a moment."

He thought she was too frightened to care for Nora. Sarah straightened, squared her shoulders. "Nora will be fine, Mr. Bainbridge. I will bring her to you after the governor's speech." She glanced at the short man waiting for him and dipped her head. "Commissioner Thomas." She lowered Nora to the deck, took hold of her small hand and, gripping the rail on her left and fastening her gaze firmly on the highly varnished deck, walked down the narrow passageway.

"But I want to go see Mama and Grandpapa, Nanny Alice."

Sarah paused at the sound of the young child's voice and glanced at the open door of a room on her right.

"If you are searching for the children's quarters, you have found them."

The voice was soft, kind.

Sarah led Nora into the room. The cabin was small, with white painted walls, dark-blue coverlets on narrow berths attached to the walls and matching curtains at the windows that marched in a row above the beds. A small table with two chairs and two high children's chairs constituted the furnishings. A plump, buxom young woman knelt beside an open door at the far end of the room straightening a little girl's dress.

"So you have been banished to the nether regions with your charge until the festivities are over, also." The woman motioned toward the wall beside her. "I have claimed these berths. Those on the side wall will be yours. And this—" she indicated the room behind her "—is a very small, but adequate, dressing room." A smile warmed her round face. "There will be only the two of us sharing these quarters. I am Alice Gardner, and this—" she rose and took the child by the hand "—is my charge, Miss Portia Holbrook. The governor's granddaughter."

Sarah smiled. "I am Sarah Randolph, and this is my charge, Miss Nora Bainbridge. Her father is the engineer in charge of the canal repairs." She glanced down at Nora, who had leaned back against her legs, then smiled at the other little girl. "We are pleased to make your acquaintance, Miss Portia."

Nora stirred, took her thumb from her mouth. "Me gots kitties an' a puppy."

"You have a *puppy?*" Portia tugged her hand from her nanny's grasp and ran across the room to Nora. "What is his name?"

"He be Rogue. An' the kitties be Happy an' Wiggles an' Fluffy an' Bun'le. An' we gots horsies, too."

"We have horses. And I have a pony." Portia leaped into the conversation, clearly not to be outdone in the pet department. "His name is Noodles. And he is gray with white spots…"

"It looks as if our charges are going to enjoy each other's company."

Sarah looked at Alice. She was peering out a window, looking up and down the narrow walkway outside. "Yes, it does." She stepped to the two berths on the side wall. Their trunks rested on the floor beneath them. She leaned down and patted the mattress of the small one with the rail around it. It was softer than it appeared to be. "How old is Portia?"

"Almost four years."

"Miss Gardner?" The voice was low and soft, somewhat urgent.

Alice's face lit. She spun away from the window and hurried toward the open door. "Did you wish to speak with me, Mr. Adams?"

A young, brown-haired man, of medium height, stepped into the room. "If you have a moment, I am free until after the governor's speech and I thought perhaps—" He stopped. His face flushed. "I see you are busy." He backed toward the door.

Sarah looked at Alice, noted the disappointment wiping the smile from her face. "Pardon me, Miss Gardner. I do not mean to intrude on your conversation, but, if you feel comfortable with the suggestion, I would be happy to care for Portia while you speak with your gentleman friend."

"Oh, I could not impose—"

"It is no imposition. I am sure Nora will be happy for the company."

"Well…" Alice glanced at Mr. Adams. "Let me fetch my hat." She hurried to a trunk, grabbed the hat resting on top and headed back for the door. "Thank you, Miss Randolph. I shan't be long."

* * *

There was a burst of cheering and applause. The boat moved. Sarah caught her breath, glanced at the children happily engrossed in picture books and stepped to a window. People on shore were milling about, calling and shouting to each other and those onboard. White handkerchiefs and small flags fluttered goodbye from the hands of old and young alike. Crew members shouted to one another. Young boys ran on the towpath, cheering and keeping pace as the packet began its slow-moving progress up the canal.

The excitement of the moment overwhelmed her apprehension. She bent down and snatched up the small sunbonnet resting on Nora's berth. The little girl should not miss this occasion. And she had told Clayton she would bring Nora to him when the governor's speech was finished. Sarah frowned and glanced toward the door. She could not leave Portia. Where was Miss Gardner?

The plump, young woman rushed through the door as if her thoughts had conjured her.

"Come, Portia. You are to join your mother and grandfather." Alice Gardner lifted a bonnet out of Portia's trunk, tied it on the child's head and hurried toward the door. "Thank you, Miss Randolph." The words floated over her shoulder as she disappeared in the flow of people walking by on the deck outside the cabin.

"You are most welcome." Sarah laughed and turned to Nora.

"Me go see kitties." Nora's lower lip trembled. She held her arms up.

Sarah scooped her up and hugged her close. Poor little tyke, she was no doubt feeling overwhelmed by all the noise and excitement, the strange place and new experiences. "No kitties today, sweetie." She infused her voice with excitement. "But I will take you out to your papa and perhaps he will let you watch the horses pull the boat. Would you like that?"

"Horsies?"

"Yes." Sarah kissed Nora's soft, silky cheek. "But first you need to visit the dressing room."

The slight breeze played with the strands of hair that had escaped the red cord. Sarah frowned and lifted her hands to tuck the locks back under their restraint, saw Clayton glance her way and lowered them again. Perhaps he would not notice she had forgotten her bonnet again if she did not call attention to the fact.

"Who him?" Nora pointed a pudgy little finger toward the man walking alongside the horses on the towpath.

"That is the man who makes the horses pull the boat." Clayton smiled at his daughter. "They call him a 'hoggee'—it is his special name."

Nora nodded, twisted round in her father's arms, looking at everything. "Who him?" She pointed.

"That is the man who pushes the boat away from the banks of the canal."

"What he special name?"

"He is called a 'tripper,' and, yes, he has a big stick. It is called a pole."

Clayton grinned and looked her way. "Is she always this inquisitive?"

Sarah met his gaze. Her stomach fluttered. "Yes, she is." She looked away, looked back. *His eyes!* Her heart stuttered, and her tongue followed its lead. "I…I must answer at least fifty questions a day."

"You are very patient."

"Mr. Bainbridge?"

Sarah started. The young man who had come to the cabin asking to speak to Alice Gardner stepped up beside them. "The governor requests you join him at his table, sir." He glanced at Nora. "He also suggests it would be too adult an occasion for your child."

"How opportune." Sarah stepped forward, avoided Clayton's gaze. It was too unsettling. "It is time for Nora to eat. And then she must have a nap. All of the excitement has tired her." She reached for Nora. "Tell your papa goodbye, sweetie."

"Bye, Papa."

Clayton leaned down, received Nora's kiss and gave her one in return. He lifted his head, looked at her. "Goodbye, Miss Randolph."

Her voice deserted her. Sarah dipped her head, turned and walked away. But when she reached the corner, she could not resist a backward glance—and immediately wished she had. Clayton was at the governor's table, smiling as he bowed over the offered hand of a very attractive young woman. She eyed the woman's gown of shimmering green silk trimmed with rows of lace-edged flounces, looked down at the serviceable material, the plain full skirt of her own gown and wished fervently she had brought along one of her own elegant, fashionable gowns.

Sarah pulled the coverlet up over Nora's arms, moved over to the other wall and did the same for Portia. Alice Gardner had disappeared the moment she put her charge to bed. Not that she minded. The children were both fast asleep, exhausted by the day's excitements. And it was little wonder. There had been so much enthusiasm and fervor when the boat stopped and the governor spoke briefly to the people who lived in the small settlements along the canal.

She had lost count of how many stops they had made. Or of how many cannons had boomed in respectful salute or wild celebration. But she remembered how handsome and distinguished Clayton had looked, standing with the commissioners during the speeches. And how the governor's daughter had hovered nearby. The pretty, stylish, *widowed,* newly out of mourning, governor's daughter. Alice said Portia's father had died a year ago last month.

Sarah frowned, walked to a window and looked out. The narrow walkway was empty of people. The constant hum of voices had ceased. It must be late. She should go to bed, but the berth was uninviting. She was too restless to sleep. Where was Clayton now? Was he abed? Or was he standing out there on the moonlit deck with the governor's daughter?

Soft whispers caught her attention. Sarah glanced toward the door. Alice Gardner walked into the room, the glow in her eyes and the flush on her face visible even in the dimmed lantern light. It made her own loneliness unbearable. "I feel the need of some air, Miss Gardner. Would you please watch over Nora while I step outside for a few minutes?"

"Of course. It is a lovely night, Miss Randolph."

It was. A warm, gentle breeze caressed her face, teased the tresses of hair at her nape and temples as Sarah walked along the narrow passage to the now-deserted open deck at the front of the boat. Moonlight streamed down from the ebony sky to light her way. The night was soft and still. So quiet she could hear the clop of the horses' hoofs against the dirt of the towpath, the rustle of the streamers overhead. Footsteps.

Sarah whirled about. Clayton Bainbridge crossed the deck to stand beside her. "Good evening, Miss Randolph. You are up late." Concern shadowed his face. "Are you unable to sleep? Is it your fear of the water?"

Sarah shook her head, brushed a strand of hair off her face. "No. The canal boat is very different from a ship. And I find the water does not frighten me if I stay on the side of the boat by the canal wall. And, of course, the boat being towed by horses is very reassuring." She was babbling! Why did the man make her so *nervous?* She took a step back, put some space between them. "I simply came out for some fresh air before I retire." She took a chance and glanced up at him. "And what of you? Why are—"

"Hey! Hey! Lock!"

Sarah started at the crewman's shout and turned back toward the front of the boat. Light illuminated the darkened canal ditch, glimmered on the water.

A bugle blew.

"This is why I came out. Watch." Clayton spoke softly, his deep voice little more than a whisper.

A crewman ran by them to the front of the boat—waved a red lantern.

She looked up at Clayton. He had closed the distance between them again. She edged forward. "What is he doing?"

"Telling the lock keeper we are here."

The boat slowed, stopped. Men came into view, running on top of the stone wall. A minute later there was a rushing, swishing sound.

"Hear that? They have opened the first set of gates."

He had stepped up beside her again! Sarah wiped the

palms of her hands against her long skirt and looked at the small space between her and the rail. She was running out of room to move away from him.

"As soon as the water level is even, they will unhitch the towrope, and we will enter the canal chamber. The captain will steer us through while our crew helps the lock crew."

The boat moved forward, floated between thick walls of stone so close crew members jumped to them and joined the other men already on the walls.

Sarah stared at the massive walls. Had Clayton built or repaired them? She looked up to ask, but the question died on her lips. Clayton was looking down at her, his blue eyes dark and smoky with tiny flames burning in their depths. Everything in her went as still as the night. He moved closer. Her knees quivered.

"Locking through!"

The shout ripped through the air. Sarah jerked, came back to sanity. Water rushed and surged. Crew members leaped back onboard and went about their tasks. She groped behind her for the railing before she fell in an embarrassing heap at Clayton's feet, and watched them hitch the towrope to a fresh team of horses, grab their poles and take up their positions. She fixed a polite smile on her face and looked up him. "That was very interesting. Thank you for sharing your expertise with me, Mr. Bainbridge. But it is late, and I need to check on Nora. Good evening."

He did not move. He just stood there, looking at her. Heat climbed into her cheeks. He was probably wondering why she was acting so strange. She straightened her spine, let go of the railing, inched by him and walked down the passageway to her room.

Everyone was sleeping. Sarah went to the dressing

room and changed into her nightgown and robe. She draped her gown over a chair, walked to the empty berth, slid beneath the covers and stared out the window at the dark night sky.

She loved him. She could not deny it any longer. With all her being she longed to be Clayton's wife. To have his children. But it was impossible. He still loved his wife. And he barely tolerated her presence.

Tears welled, flowed down her cheeks. What was she to do? How was she to get through tomorrow without giving her feelings away? *Oh, dear God, help me to stay calm tomorrow, to not reveal my love to Clayton.*

Sobs threatened. Sarah took a deep breath and wiped the tears from her cheeks. Tomorrow. One day. She could manage that. She would simply stay as far away from Clayton as possible for the rest of the journey.

Stony Point. It wrenched her heart to think of leaving, but the time had come. Sarah looked in the dressing-room mirror a last time. Lavender half circles stained the skin below her eyes, a testimony to the last two sleepless nights. But there was nothing to be done about them. At least they would not be so visible in the shade of her hat's deep brim. She settled the yellow, flower-bedecked bonnet in place and turned away. The deep ruffle around the bottom of her yellow silk gown whispered across the plank floor as she walked to the bedroom.

The bare space on the rag rug increased the lump in her throat. Her trunk was waiting in the carriage. Quincy had carried it down earlier, right after Clayton had been called away on business.

She would never see him again.

Sarah's steps faltered. She stopped, held her eyes wide

and took a deep breath to stop the tears pushing for release. *Do not cry! For Nora's sake, do not cry.* She hurried through the bedroom, refusing to think about the woman who would live here in her place, and started down the winder stairs to the kitchen.

Nora's voice floated up to her. She set her mind against the horrid ache in her heart, fixed a smile on her face and stepped into the kitchen.

Eldora looked her way, disappointment on her face, censure in her pose. "So, you are really going." It was not a question. It was an indictment.

Sarah steeled her heart and nodded. "I must, Eldora. I hope someday you will understand and not judge me too harshly." She swallowed, forced herself to go on. "I will always remember you with gratitude and affection."

"Me go bye-bye?" Nora stopped petting Rogue and scrambled to her feet. Her blond curls bounced as she ran across the slate floor.

Sarah closed her eyes, took a breath, then opened them and knelt to take Nora in her arms. The last time. *Dear heavenly Father, help me! For Nora's sake give me strength.* She leaned back and looked into Nora's blue eyes. "Not this time, sweetie. Nanny Sarah has to go away. Far away." She cleared the tears from her throat. "And you must stay here with your papa, and Eldora and Quincy. And Lucy."

Nora's lower lip pouted out. She shook her head. She leaned close and put her arms about her neck. "Me wants you. Me go, too."

Sarah blinked hard, hugged Nora as tight as she dared and rose to her feet. She smiled and forced a playful note into her voice. "Now, what would your papa do if you went away with me? And who would play with the kitties and

Rogue? Gracious! They would be very, very sad without you." She glanced at Eldora, sent a silent plea for help.

"And who would I have to make cookies for?" Eldora shook her head, walked over and held out her arms. "And you know what else? I have a job for you to do. I promised your papa I would make him some ginger cookies. But I am almighty busy. Would you help me?"

Nora nodded and leaned into the housekeeper's pudgy arms.

Sarah whirled and ran from the kitchen. Tears blinded her. She wiped them away, fumbled with the front door and stumbled to the carriage. Her chest ached with pressure. Sobs racked her body. She wrapped her arms around herself trying to stop the pain, and huddled in the corner of the carriage as they drove away.

Chapter Twenty-Three

"How are you feeling this morning, Sarah?"

"I am all right, Mother." Sarah put down her book and summoned a smile.

"You did not eat any breakfast." Her mother eyed her, as only a mother can. "And you ate very little last evening."

"I was not hungry."

"And you were pacing around in your room until the wee hours this morning because you were not tired? Sarah, dear, you are talking to your mother." Her mother reached down and touched her cheek. "Did you get any sleep at all?"

"A little." Sarah took a breath, rose from her chair and walked over to look out the French doors. "I did not mean to disturb your rest, Mother. I did not realize you could hear me."

"That is not my concern, Sarah. You are." Her mother came up beside her, put her arm around her shoulders. "Do you want to talk about Mr. Bainbridge, and why you suddenly decided to come home?"

Sarah bit down on her lower lip and shook her head.

"Sarah, the Lord…"

"I am not blaming God for anything, Mother. I know now I was wrong to blame Him for Aaron's death. It was not God that decided to sail home on the *Seadrift* that day. It was Aaron. And he did so against the advice of a sailor who was familiar with New England weather. He warned Aaron of a coming storm. But it was such a beautiful day when we set sail Aaron was certain the sailor was wrong."

She shuddered, walked to the mantel and stared up at a painting of a clipper ship under full sail, her rail almost plowing the water as she skimmed across the waves. Her father had painted it. He often painted his ships. She hated the painting that hung over the fireplace in his study. It showed a ship, mast broken, rigging fallen and trailing in a raging ocean. He had been aboard that ship during the hurricane that so damaged it. But he had survived. Just as she had survived the storm that swept down on the *Seadrift.*

"I did not realize how dangerous sailing upon the ocean can be." She sighed. "Since I can remember, all I wanted was to marry a ship's captain and sail with him around the world on our honeymoon. I…I never thought further than that."

Sarah turned, looked across the library. "Is it possible to get a man mixed up with a dream, Mother? I mean, to think you loved a man when it was what he stood for that you really loved?" Tears blurred her vision. She wiped them away. "I…I thought I loved Aaron—and I did. He was always so calm and kind and respectful. But now I do not believe I was *in* love with Aaron. I just wanted to be safe. And I always felt safe with him. Not…nervous."

She took a breath, plunged. "Mother, when Father… *looks*…at you, do you go all breathless and weak in the knees, as if you are going to fall?"

"No, dear." Her mother shook her head, smiled. "*I* always go all breathless and feel as if I am going to melt."

Sarah stared, gulped, ran across the room to the safe haven of her mother's arms. "Wh-what am I going t-to do, M-Mother?"

Her mother held her close, stroked her hair. "A very wise lady once gave me some excellent advice when I was in a similar situation, Sarah. The same advice I am going to give you—go to Mr. Bainbridge and tell him you love him."

Sarah lifted her head, drew back out of her mother's arms and shook her head. "No. No, I cannot do that, Mother. *Ever.* You see, Mr. Bainbridge has made it very clear that he does not want me in his life."

"Him a *big* kitty." Nora pointed at the picture on the right side of the page.

Clayton smiled at her sleepy tone and looked down. His daughter was losing her battle against sleep. "Yes, a *very* big kitty. He is called a lion."

"What him special name?" She snuggled closer against his chest. Yawned.

"He does not have a special name. Why don't you give him one?"

She nodded, closed her eyes. "Me likes…"

Clayton chuckled, set the book aside and rose from the rocker. "That is one lion who will never have a special name." He kissed Nora's warm, rosy cheek, laid her in her crib and pulled the coverlet over her. She would soon be too big for the crib. He should go into the attic and see if that small child's bed he had slept in was there.

His child. The fact still had the power to knock him slightly off-kilter when he thought about it. The guilt over causing her mother's death lingered, hovered in the background, when he looked at her, but no longer consumed him to the degree he would not even acknowledge his own daughter.

He frowned, brushed Nora's curls back off her face. Was he doing her a disservice by not hiring another nanny? They seemed to be managing all right without one. Eldora and Lucy, even Quincy, watched over her while he was working. And he had breakfast with Nora every morning, and tucked her into bed every night. He had been the only one that could calm her enough to go to sleep when Sarah had left.

Sarah.

Clayton turned from the crib and walked into the adjoining bedroom. Sarah was the real reason he did not seek another nanny. He missed her. Longed for her presence.

He stepped through her door onto the landing, glanced at his own door, both open now as they had been when she was caring for him, and his face tightened. No, he would not hire another nanny. They would continue on as they were. The idea of another woman across the landing, so close to his own room, was intolerable.

He checked to make sure the gate he had built for the top of the stairs was latched. The bedroom doors had to stay open all night so he could hear if Nora needed him, and he wanted no possibility of his little daughter taking a fall down the winder stairs. He glanced down the stairwell, sucked in his breath at the memory of Sarah descending the steps, light from the lamp in her hand illuminating the downward spiral, glinting on the silky mass of brown hair loosely restrained at the nape of her neck and spilling down the back of her quilted robe. The mere thought of her struck him breathless.

Clayton fisted his hands. *Men are not permitted that luxury, though we are allowed to punch a wall—or each other. Or fight Indians.* Another memory. The house, his mind, his heart was rife with them. They had been talking about her crying, because she was upset by memories of the man she loved. The man who had so captured her heart she wanted no other. He stared at the wall, quivered with the desire to punch his fist through it. But it would solve nothing. And it would only, once again, prove his weakness. His lack of self-control. And it would show that he had been right to let her return to Philadelphia.

Clayton strode into his bedroom, the muscle along his jaw twitching. Letting Sarah go was the hardest thing he had ever done, but she deserved a man of honor and moral strength. A man like her fiancé, who had died in that storm at sea. A man who betrayed a deathbed promise to his best friend did not qualify.

"What is it, Eldora?" Clayton looked up from the cost estimations he was figuring for the northern canal extension.

"You have a visitor. She's waitin' in the drawing room. I'll bring tea." The housekeeper threw him a look and trudged off down the hall toward the kitchen.

She? Clayton frowned, rose and shrugged into his suit coat. Whoever it was, he would get rid of her quickly. He had work to do. Three long strides took him across the hall to the drawing-room doorway. A slender, dark-haired woman sat in an upholstered chair, facing away from him. He fixed a polite smile on his face and strode into the room. "Good afternoon. I am Clayton Bainbridge, may I help you?"

The woman rose, turned and held out her arms.

"Victoria! My dear friend." Clayton rushed forward and gave the older woman a hug. "I am astounded by your visit. I had no idea you were back home. When did you return?"

"Charles resigned his post in England two months ago. But we only arrived in Cincinnati last week. I would have come sooner, but my mother is ill. Let me look at you." She drew back and studied his face. "You are handsome as ever, Clayton."

"And you are just as lovely as I remember."

"Flatterer!" She laughed and took hold of his hand. "Now that the polite niceties are out of the way—" She pulled him toward the settee. "Come and talk to me. I have not had a chance to catch up on all that has happened since we left, and there is so much for you to tell me. Do you realize I have been gone over three years?"

"Yes. I know."

She stopped arranging her skirts and looked up at him. "That sounded grim." She studied his face so intently he wanted to squirm. "Are you not over Deborah's death?"

"There are some things you do not get over, Victoria."

"Bosh. Deborah was beautiful, Clayton, but it has been almost three years since her passing. She would want you to marry again. Especially as your marriage was… well…*chaste*. Except for that one time."

He went rigid. "You know of that?"

"Now do not go all offended on me, Clayton. I am old enough to be your mother, and you know my reputation for boldness." She placed her hand on his arm. "Of course I know. I was the closest thing to a mother Deborah ever knew. She confided everything to me."

"I see." Clayton surged to his feet, stepped to the fireplace and looked up at his grandparents' portraits so he did not have to face Victoria. "I am surprised you treat me with such affection."

There was a small gasp behind him. "What an astonishing thing to say. There has always been fondness between our families. Why would I not?"

He turned to face her, the muscle along his jaw twitching. "Because if Deborah told you everything, you must know I am responsible for her death." It was the first time he had said the words aloud. The first time he had spoken with anyone about his wife's death. It was painful, but there was something freeing about it.

"I know no such thing!" She peered up at him, gave his face a close perusal. "I do not follow your reasoning, Clayton. Please explain."

"How can you not understand, Victoria? I am the one responsible for the baby that took her life."

"That is preposterous, Clayton. Many women die of childbirth. Do you hold that their husbands are responsible for their deaths?"

"Of course not. But that is different." The bitterness and self-loathing poured out of him with his words. "Deborah had a weak heart and I knew it. I knew having a child could kill her."

"And so did she."

"Yes. But Deborah was innocent of such things. *I* knew that birth precautions often fail." There, he had admitted it all. Victoria looked stunned. He braced himself for her disgust.

"*What* birth precautions?" The words were quiet, reflective.

"The ones Deborah got from Dr. Anderson."

Victoria drew in a breath, released it. "She never told you."

Clayton scowled down at her. "Never told me what?"

"Deborah lied to you, Clayton. She knew you would never agree to treat her as a real wife because you were afraid she would become with child. But that is what she *wanted*." Victoria rose and came to stand facing him. "When Dr. Anderson told Deborah she had only a year, perhaps a year and a few months left to live—"

"What?" Clayton stiffened. "I never—"

Victoria touched his arm. "Listen, and you will understand."

He stared at her, gave a curt nod.

"Dr. Anderson told Deborah she was soon to die, and she decided the only way she could live on was through a child. She had nothing to lose but a few months' time. Either way she was going to die. So she planned, and she lied." Victoria took a breath, exhaled. "She swore Dr. Anderson to secrecy about her limited time to live and tried to convince you to treat her as a wife. I know how long you withstood her pleas, Clayton. But Deborah was nothing if not inventive when it came to getting her own way. You know that better than anyone. So she lied to you. She begged you to treat her as a real wife for once—only once—because she knew if she said *once* you would be more likely to yield. And she told you Dr. Anderson had given her birth precautions and assured her it was perfectly safe. She won." Victoria's gaze locked on his eyes. "Deborah knew exactly what she was doing *and* the risk she was taking with her life in doing it. You are not guilty of Deborah's death, Clayton. *She* is. It is all in the letter she wrote me."

Victoria turned and walked back to the settee, opened her purse and pulled out a letter. She came back and held it out to him. "I saved the letter because I thought your daughter—when she is grown—would like to know her mother wanted her so much she was willing to give up her life for her."

Deborah's death was not his fault. Clayton shook his head, lit the lantern and walked to the door in the upstairs hall. He could not grasp it. He had blamed himself for so long. But it had been Deborah's choice. Dr. Anderson had said her frail heart was about to stop beating, even without her having a child. It was only amazing that she had lived long enough to give birth. But Victoria believed that God had granted Deborah the desire of her heart, and part of her lived on in Nora. And he agreed. For the first time he understood why Deborah had named her baby Nora *Blessing*.

The sadness that had been with him all evening swelled. A cleansing sorrow. For the first time he was able to grieve Deborah's passing without guilt and anger. He only wished she had not lied to him. But that, too, he understood. He had been so determined to honor his promise to Andrew to keep Deborah safe, he would not have agreed to shorten her life by even one day.

Clayton set aside his musings, held the lantern high and climbed the attic stairs. The child's bed he wanted for Nora had to be up here somewhere. He ducked beneath a half-log rafter and swung the lantern to his right. The circle of golden light flowed over dusty trunks and pieces of furniture. Old toys.

He stopped, shoved a large crate aside and moved the lantern closer to a bench with a broken armrest, stared at the toy that sat on the seat. *Noah's ark.* His father had made the ark and carved the animals for him. He had forgotten all about it. He set the lantern on the bench seat, squatted on his heels and picked up one of the animals that crowded the deck of the ark. A deer.

A smile tilted his lips. His fingers had remembered what he had forgotten. The deer had been his favorite—which probably explained the missing antler. He put it down and picked up the bear, the fox, the beaver and otter. He looked inside and found the buffalo and horse, squirrels and rabbits. Crows, turkey and grouse perched on the flat roof, a cat and dog nearby. He grinned, blew off the loose dust and carried the ark over to the top of the stairs. Nora would love it.

Nora. He had Deborah to thank for Nora. It had been her choice to have a child. And if she had not lied to him about the birth precautions, Nora would not exist. The truth settled deep in his soul. He was not *guilty*. And all the torment he had suffered over the past three years had been self-inflicted. It had come from him—not God.

Clayton's heart almost stopped. Sarah was not some sort of punishing test from God, as he had believed. He frowned, brushed the dust from his hands and walked back to get the lantern. Even at his most angry moments, he still believed in God. Still believed in His sovereign power. And that He controlled the things that happened to those who accepted Him as their Lord. That truth had been in-grained in him by his grandparents from the time he could walk and talk. So what was God's purpose in bringing Sarah to Stony Point? To care for Nora because he had turned his back on his own flesh and blood?

Clayton reached for the lantern, glanced at the small chest the ark had sat on and opened it instead. Small balls of multicolored fine wool rested on a folded piece of fabric. He touched them, tears filming his eyes at a sudden flash of his mother, sitting in a chair by the hearth working needlepoint. He lifted out the fabric, stiff and yellowed with age, unfolded it and smoothed it out across his knee. A green vine with purple flowers formed a border around a needlepoint verse.

> For thou wilt light my
> candle: the Lord my God
> will enlighten my
> darkness. Psalm 18:28
> Joann Bainbr

A length of black wool trailed from the *r* in his mother's name. She had never finished the sampler. Clayton blew out a breath to release the pressure in his chest and read it again. And again. A sureness grew in him. Sarah had not been a test from God, she had been a gift sent to enlighten the darkness he carried in his heart. A darkness of his own creation. And in his hurt and anger and pride, he had sent her away.

Clayton's chest and throat ached. How many mistakes he had made. He closed his eyes and cleared the lump from his throat. "Forgive me, Lord. Forgive my arrogance…my pride…my anger. Forgive me for blaming You, instead of seeking Your wisdom. For holding control over my life, instead of yielding to You. I made a mess of things, Lord. And I thank You for Your mercy in waking me up before it was too late and I lost my daughter forever. Please help me not to make those mistakes again. Amen."

Clayton opened his eyes. Lamplight glowed on the sampler. He stared at it, smiled, then folded it and put it back in the small chest. A quick search discovered a small trunk that would hold all his treasures sitting on the floor beside the bed he was seeking. He placed the chest and the

Noah's ark inside, tucked the trunk under his arm and picked up the lantern. Light flowed around him, soft and golden, as he walked down the stairs.

Chapter Twenty-Four

She missed Nora. So much. Sarah tugged a leaf off a boxwood and pulled it apart strip by tiny strip as she walked down the brick path to the pavilion. She had not realized how deeply it would hurt to leave the toddler. But Nora had conquered her heart so completely it felt as if a part of her was gone. It was.

Sarah sighed, threw away the bit of stem that remained of the leaf and tugged off another. Her heart was back in Cincinnati, at Stony Point. She missed Eldora and Quincy. And the house. It was not grand like Randolph Court, but it was…home. She blinked, swallowed and thought of something else. The carriage house. How she longed for the carriage house, and Pacer with his welcoming nickers and head nudges. And Sassy. And Wiggles and Happy, Fluffy and Bundle. Tears overflowed. A sob caught in her throat. Who ever heard of naming a kitten Bundle? It was an absurd name for a cat.

Sarah threw away the leaf and wiped the tears from her cheeks. Crying did no good. She simply had to wait for time to take away the horrible hollowness inside. That empty place that only—she jerked her mind from the name it wanted to utter and searched for an acceptable substitution—that only Stony Point and all it stood for could fill.

She rounded the curve in the path and paused, looking at the garden bench that sat in its own little nook, created by the brick paving and the hedges that surrounded it. It was there, right there on that bench that Elizabeth had broken through all the hurt and fear harbored in her little girl's heart and become her mother. She had been only a little older than Nora at the time. And Elizabeth had been showing her how to make a tea set for her dolls from clay. And then that woman with the cane had come around this very curve and frightened her. Elizabeth had taken her in her arms and she had felt loved for the first time. What had the woman called them? *Urchins.* Yes, that was the word she had used. *Urchins.*

Sarah smiled and walked on to the pavilion. That woman had been her father's good friend, Abigail Twiggs. And she had grown to love her—after she had discovered the warm heart beneath the stern exterior. Aunty Abigail. She would have loved Nora.

Sarah gripped the railing, lifted her long skirts with her free hand and climbed the steps into the pavilion. This is where Justin Randolph had become her father, not her guardian. He had brought her a puppy—in a wicker basket with a lid. And he had hugged her close and kissed her cheek and she had felt safe at last. That was the day she had spoken for the first time since her mother had died. She had named the puppy *Mr. Buffy.* He was a wonderful dog that had been her constant companion from that day on. And now Nora had a puppy—Rogue. And she would not get to see Nora grow up with him. And she would never know the sort of love that existed between her mother and father because the man she loved cared nothing for her. He did not want her.

Tears spilled from her eyes. The pressure in her chest broke into sobs that clawed their way up her throat and gained freedom in painful gasps. She covered her face with her hands and rocked to and fro, giving vent to the pain she had been holding inside until she could be alone where no one would see her cry.

"I have found you."

Sarah turned and smiled at her younger sister. "I did not know I was lost." She sobered. "Did Mother send you after me? I fear I have caused her great concern since I arrived home."

Mary's lips curved in a wry smile. "You should have seen her and Father while you were away." She climbed the steps and sat on the bench.

"Oh, dear." Sarah let out a long sigh and leaned back against the railing that enclosed the pavilion. "Was it very bad for them? I tried to ease any concern they may have felt in my letters."

"Well, let me see… Father *and* James wanted to rescue you from Cincinnati and bring you home where they could make sure you were safe and well cared for. And Mother, though she talked them out of doing so, has spent hours praying for your safety and well-being, and that you would return to your faith in God."

Sarah exchanged a look of sisterly understanding with Mary. "I feared as much. Well, it seems Father and James have gotten their wishes. And Mother's prayers have been answered—as always."

"Truly? Is that why your eyes are all red and puffy? Because of your well-being?"

Sarah stared at her sister, shook her head. "You are circumspect as always, I see."

Mary smiled. "You have not been gone long enough for me to change. I fear that would take a lifetime." Her brown eyes darkened. "I am still as bold and forthright as ever, and it is very off-putting to young men. Especially since I have little physical beauty to overcome my character flaw."

"Mary!"

"I am only speaking the truth, Sarah. It is a fact of life you have never had to be concerned about, as men fall willing victims to your beauty and charms."

The words stung like salt in her wound. "Not all men." She spun around and gripped the railing, stared out at the garden, willing back tears. She had cried enough.

"Forgive my blunt and hurtful words, Sarah. I did not—" Mary sighed. "I thought you were sad over the child."

"And so I am." Sarah pasted a smile on her face and turned to face her sister again. "Nora is absolutely adorable and I miss her dreadfully. Now, shall we go in and find Mother and have some tea? It has been a long while since I have talked about fashion and the latest styles."

Clayton sat in the chair in front of Justin Randolph's desk and waited for his answer.

"And why should I grant your request to court my daughter and seek her hand in marriage, Mr. Bainbridge?"

"Because I love Sarah, and I want to care for her and share the rest of my life with her." Clayton met Justin Randolph's gaze squarely. "And while I am not as financially prosperous as you obviously are, Mr. Randolph, I do quite well. I own a farm, in addition to my home. And

I have invested in several growing businesses in Cincinnati which are prospering. I am well-respected and on the rise in my field of endeavor, and have recently accepted the position of head engineer for the northern Miami Canal extension to Lake Erie."

Clayton watched Sarah's father's face, tried to gauge his reaction to his litany of assets. There was not so much as a flicker of an eye to betray what the man was thinking. *Please, God, grant me favor in this man's eyes.*

"On the personal side, my home is solid and comfortable, not large but of adequate size with property enough for any additions we would choose to make in the future. I have a housekeeper, who is also my cook, and a maid to keep things tidy, so Sarah would not be overburdened in running our home.

"I also have a toddler daughter, Nora, who loves Sarah, and whom Sarah loves in return. I want only the best for Sarah, sir, and I believe I can make her happy." *Nothing. No reaction.* Clayton took a breath. "*And* last, because, though I want to do this right, *want* your blessing and that of Sarah's mother—if you withhold that blessing and refuse me the right to court her, I will defy you and climb the very *walls* of this brick mansion to see her and beg my case before her."

"I see." A smile broke across Justin Randolph's face. "*That* is the reason I was waiting to hear, Mr. Randolph. I wish you well in presenting your petition to Sarah." He rose and extended his hand.

Clayton grasped and shook it. "If I may ask a favor, sir?"

"Already?" Justin's eyes narrowed. "You are not in the family yet, son. My daughters will choose their own mates."

"I ask nothing more than that, sir. It is only—" Clayton cleared his throat. "I have some explaining to do to Sarah, and if you could arrange our meeting without mentioning my name it might be helpful."

Justin stared at him. A grin slanted across his mouth. His eyes crinkled at the corners. "Got yourself in trouble with her, did you, son? Well, that's easy to do with women. Do it myself on a regular basis." He chuckled and clapped him on the shoulder. "You stay here, Mr. Bainbridge, and I will arrange the meeting."

Clayton waited until Sarah's father left the room, then walked over and stared out the French doors that opened onto a porch, and from there to formal gardens as far as he could see. Could he make Sarah happy? Was what he had to offer her enough? Stony Point was certainly no Randolph Court. He turned back to the spacious room, glanced at the furnishings and thought about the tomahawk gashes on his front door and the bullet holes in his mantel at home. What right had he to ask her to give up all this elegance? What made him think he could compete with her dead fiancé? She had said she wanted no other.

His stomach knotted. His palms turned moist. What if she said no? How would he ever live the rest of his life without her? He glanced at the floor beside the chair where he had been sitting, swallowed and closed his eyes. "I have made enough mistakes, Lord. Thy will be done."

The library door opened, closed.

"You wished to see me, Father?"

Clayton turned. His heart, his very life stood in front of him.

Sarah gaped. Stared at him. A flood of emotions washed over her face so rapidly he couldn't identify them. And then there was only one. Fear. Her hand went to the base of her throat. The blood drained from her face. Her mouth worked, but nothing came out. He started toward her. She tried again, and one word came out on a breathless gasp.

"Nora?"

It stopped him. He had not considered— "Nora is fine."

"Oh." Sarah's shoulders sagged. "Oh, thank goodness." She closed her eyes, sighed. "I thought—" Her eyes opened, widened. She averted her gaze and glanced around the room, looked back at him. "What are you doing here, Mr. Bainbridge? And where is Father? I was told he wanted to see me here in the library."

"I am the one who wanted to see you."

Her gaze touched on him, confused, disquieted, then skittered away. "I do not think that is wise. If you will excuse me—"

"Sarah—"

Her gaze jerked back to him. She took a breath. Her hand went to the base of her throat again.

"I have come all the way from Cincinnati to speak with you. Will you please listen—without interruption?"

She stared at him a minute, then gave a polite nod. "Very well." She moved to the front of a leather chair, sat, rested her hands in her lap and lifted her chin.

His heart thudded. She was so beautiful. Proud, defiant and beautiful. *Lord, please give me the words to say to make her understand.* He looked down at the floor and gathered his thoughts. "Do you remember the night we talked about our childhood dreams? I told you about my mentor and best friend. What I did not tell you was that Andrew was an older man who had an only child he adored. A daughter who was sickly from birth and unable to do the things other children did. Andrew gave her every thing within his power. But he could not give her a healthy heart. And so he centered his life around making his daughter safe. And then he became seriously ill."

Clayton glanced Sarah's way. She gave a polite nod, but remained silent, as she had promised. "Andrew did not fear dying. But he feared leaving his frail daughter unprotected. So he called me to his bedside and asked me to marry his daughter, Deborah, and keep her safe always. I promised to do so."

Sarah stiffened. "I am sorry, Mr. Bainbridge, I know I said I would listen, but I do not see—"

"Please. Let me finish. It will not take long. And I promise I have a purpose." That caught her interest. Clayton went back to his story. "Deborah and I were married at Andrew's bedside. He died two days later." He paused, uncertain how to go on. "Some of what I must say is…indelicate. I will be as circumspect as possible." He turned toward the windows to spare her embarrassment. "The doctor informed us that, due to Deborah's frail condition, having a child would probably take her life. I was determined that should not happen and so we occupied separate bedchambers. In spite of visiting many doctors and employing every effort known, Deborah's health continued to decline."

He heard movement behind him and glanced in the window. Sarah had risen and walked around to stand behind the chair. At least she was still listening. He braced himself for what was to come. "We continued on as before. But Deborah changed. She became insistent that she did not want to die without knowing the…intimacies…of marriage. I was not willing to risk her life with a child and refused. But one night—"

"I have heard enough, Mr. Bainbridge!" Sarah whirled and swept toward the door.

Clayton hurried around the desk and blocked her way. "Let me pass."

"Not until you have heard what I have to say." He tried to hold her gaze but she refused to look at him. "Sarah, I realize you are a maiden and this is difficult for you to hear. But I promise you, if you do not feel what I have to say is important to you—to your life—when I am finished, I will allow your father to have me horsewhipped!"

Her lips quivered. She spun away and walked back to stand behind the chair. "Very well. If you will not let me pass, say what you must and say it quickly. Or I will have Father do as you suggest!" She looked the other direction.

Clayton clenched his hands and cleared his throat. "That night Deborah told me the doctor had given her precautions, and I yielded. Her wish was granted. Though she grew weaker daily she lived to give birth to the baby conceived that night. Her heart stopped beating a few minutes later.

"To my shame, I could not look at the child. She was, to me, a living symbol of my guilt, my failure to uphold the deathbed vow I had made to my friend. I was consumed with that guilt. I lost sight of anything good and saw only the shame of my weakness. I blamed God for everything and turned away from him. My heart, my life, was full of darkness."

Sarah had turned back to face him. The anger was gone, her eyes shimmered with tears.

"And then you came to Stony Point."

She did not move, her expression did not change, but he could feel a sudden tension emanate from her.

He took a step closer. "I did not understand, Sarah. I was so consumed with my own ugliness I thought you were a punishment from God. A test of my will. I was drawn to you from the start, but I was determined that this time I would not fail—I would not give in to my feelings for you though they grew stronger every day. And then you told me you still loved your dead fiancé and wanted no other. I determined then my only course was to avoid you. And when you asked to go home, I let you go. It was the hardest thing I have ever done."

She raised her hand, pressed the tips of her fingers against her lips.

To still an outcry? To protest his mention of her beloved? Clayton took another step toward the chair. "I have made so many mistakes, Sarah. But God in His mercy has forgiven me and set them right. All but the last. That is for me to do."

He bent down and picked up the small chest he had polished until the wood gleamed, sat it on the chair cushion, opened it, unfolded the unfinished sampler and handed it to her. "God showed me the answer to why He sent you to Stony Point, Sarah. You hold it in your hand." He took the last step that separated them as she read it. "You are my gift from God, Sarah. The light that brightened my darkness. I love you, Sarah, with all my heart and soul. Please forgive my foolishness, marry me and come home."

Sarah blinked away tears, looked up. Flames burned in the dark-blue depths of Clayton's eyes. Her knees buckled. She gave a little cry, dropped the sampler and grabbed for the chair back.

Clayton caught her. He lifted her up, drew her close against him and lowered his head. "I told you I would not let you fall." His warm breath whispered across her skin. He brushed his mouth against hers. "I told you you are safe with me."

Safe? Calm, comfortable, serene safe?

Clayton's arms tightened, his hand slid up and cupped the back of her head. His mouth claimed hers.

Sarah sighed, slipped her arms around his neck and answered his kiss, quite certain she would never be safe again.

Epilogue

The carriage climbed over the break of the hill and there it was, Stony Point. Her home. Every nerve in Sarah's stomach fluttered to life. She leaned out and drank in the sight of the rectangular stone house, with its set-back kitchen ell, sitting square in the middle of the point of land that forced the road to curve. It was not large. And there was nothing ornate or fancy about it. Its solid wood-plank front door had deep gashes in it from Indian tomahawks. But it was her home, and she loved every inch of it.

Clayton squeezed her hand, smiled when she looked back at him. He reached up and cupped her cheek, leaned down and kissed her lips. "Welcome home, Mrs. Bainbridge."

Sarah's heart overflowed into her eyes and blurred her husband's handsome face. He kissed the tip of her nose, then climbed from the carriage and offered her his hand. She placed hers in his, reveling in his touch, and stepped out of the carriage. He placed his arm about her shoulder, leaned down and opened the gate sandwiched between the two lamp-topped stone pillars that anchored the low stone walls enclosing the front yard.

Maaaa.

One of the sheep grazing on the lawn lifted its head and followed their progress up the slate walk. Sarah's pulse quickened. Her new life was starting.

The front door opened. Sarah caught sight of a smiling Eldora standing in the opening, and then a small figure darted out of the dim interior onto the stoop.

"Nanny!" Nora held up her pudgy little arms and bounced up and down, beaming a smile that rivaled the sun overhead.

Sarah laughed through her tears, scooped the toddler into her arms and hugged and kissed her until Nora squealed.

"I misseded you, Nanny!"

"She is not your nanny, Nora." Clayton wrapped his arms about them both and kissed Nora's rosy cheek. "She is your mama."

Mama. How wonderful that sounded. Sarah smiled up at her husband. He looked down at her, blue flames flickering in the depths of his dark-blue eyes, and her knees turned to water. Clayton's strong arms stopped her from tumbling backward off the stoop. He lowered his head, covered her lips with his, and her heart melted. No. She would never be safe again.

* * * * *

Dear Reader,

My dad passed away shortly before I began writing *Family of the Heart*. He was elderly and had led a full life, so I did not suffer the jarring sense of "young life interrupted" that Sarah and Clayton experience upon the tragic deaths of their respective fiancé and wife. However, with every loved one's passing, there is a sense of loss and of help-lessness in the face of that loss. And, inevitably, regrets arise in your heart, either for things done you wish undone, or for things that never were and now never will be.

In the story, Sarah and Clayton deal with the pain of their loved ones' passing by trying to run from their hurt, grief and regrets—or to ignore and bury them. They grow angry with God, blame Him and turn their backs on Him. And they allow their grief and anger to keep them from going on with their lives. Yet God, in His mercy, uses the circumstances of their lives to open their hearts to the truth, restore their faith, heal their hurt and bring peace to their troubled souls. He mends their shattered lives and blesses them with an everlasting love. God is like that. Therefore, it is my sincere hope that, should you someday find yourself facing circumstances that bring pain and sorrow to your heart, you will not make the mistakes Sarah and Clayton made but will instead run to the Lord, open your heart and receive the wondrous healing of His perfect love.

Sarah's younger sister, Mary, is a lot too skeptical and a little too stubborn to run to God, no matter what her problem. But God is patient and faithful and loving, and methinks Mary will be learning that lesson soon.

Thank you for choosing to read *Family of the Heart*. I would like to hear from you. I can be reached at dorothyjclark@hotmail.com

Until next time,
Dorothy Clark

QUESTIONS FOR DISCUSSION

1. Sarah Randolph, beloved daughter of wealthy parents, member of Philadelphia's socially elite, takes a position as a nanny. What drove her to do such a thing? Do you think God had a hand in her decision?

2. Grief comes to everyone in this life. How did Sarah handle her grief? How do you feel about her decisions?

3. Elizabeth sees God's hand in Sarah's decision to become a nanny. And in the results of that decision. Do you agree or disagree with her views? Why?

4. Clayton Bainbridge also suffers from grief. What complicates his grief? Do you think it keeps him from healing? In what way? Do you feel the complication to his grief is a common one? How can people get beyond this complication?

5. Are there similarities in the ways Sarah and Clayton deal with their grief? What are they? Do you feel these are common reactions to the loss of loved ones? What common trait(s) of human failing do you see in Sarah and Clayton? How does this trait(s) affect their personal relationship with the Lord?

6. Sarah and Clayton are both blinded to the Lord's goodness and love for them because of how they reacted to the things they suffered. How did the Lord open their eyes and hearts to the truth of His love?

7. What circumstances forced Clayton, Sarah and little Nora together? Do you believe God *created* those circumstances? Why? Or why not?

8. What had to happen in both Sarah's and Clayton's hearts before they could receive the blessings of healing and love God had for them?

9. Do you think Nora played a large part in the healing of both Clayton and Sarah? Do you think that was orchestrated by God? And if so, why is He able to use children?

10. Sarah and Clayton both got angry with God and stopped praying. What were the results?

11. Prayer, or the lack of prayer, plays an important role in the story. Do you believe the same is true in real life? What Scriptures can you think of to illustrate your belief?

12. Another aspect of Sarah's and Clayton's reluctance to enter into a relationship was the subject of loyalty to their departed loved ones. Do you believe, as they did, that it is betrayal of a departed fiancé or spouse to open your heart to another? Why? Or why not?

13. Harsh, hurtful things happen in this world, as they did in this story. Do you believe God uses such real-life events to draw people closer to Himself? Can you give an example?

Love Inspired.
HISTORICAL
INSPIRATIONAL HISTORICAL ROMANCE

Years after being wrenched from Alice Shepard's life due to his lowborn status, Nicholas Tennant returns to London. Now wealthy and influential, he seeks revenge on Alice and her family. Alice is now a beautiful, grown woman and a loving single mother, and Nicholas cannot deny his feelings for her. Can he abandon his thirst for revenge and become the man most worthy of her love?

Look for

A Man Most Worthy

by

RUTH AXTELL MORREN

Available October
wherever books are sold.

www.SteepleHill.com

Steeple
Hill®

LIH82797

Love Inspired.
HISTORICAL

INSPIRATIONAL HISTORICAL ROMANCE

Overnight, Delia Keller went from penniless preacher's granddaughter to rich young heiress. Determined to use the money to give herself the security she'd never had, building a house by Christmas is her first priority. That is until former Civil War chaplain Jude Tucker starts challenging her plans—and her heart.

Look for

Hill Country Christmas
by
LAURIE KINGERY

*Available October
wherever books are sold.*

Steeple
Hill®

www.SteepleHill.com

LIH82798

Love Inspired®

Operating on a sick little boy is Dr. Nora Blake's responsibility—but answering a reporter's questions about it is not. Especially because Robert Dale is delving into her life, too, and Nora won't allow a newspaper to profit from the child's story—*or* her own.

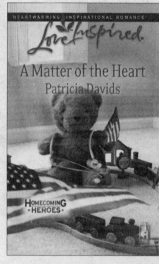

HOMECOMING ★HEROES★

Saving children and finding love deep in the heart of Texas

Look for

A Matter of the Heart

by

Patricia Davids

Available October wherever books are sold.

www.SteepleHill.com

Steeple Hill®

LI87500

Love Inspired
SUSPENSE
RIVETING INSPIRATIONAL ROMANCE

Seeking ancient ruins in
Desolation Canyon,
Kit Sinclair finds her
plans going awry when
tribal police officer
Hawke Lonechief threatens
to arrest her if she enters
the dangerous gorge. When
she risks his wrath by going
alone, he finally agrees to
lead her. Yet someone else
is watching them, and they
grow closer to danger with
every step....

Look for

Forsaken
Canyon

by MARGARET DALEY

Steeple
Hill®

*Available October
wherever books are sold.*

www.SteepleHill.com   LIS44309

AN UPLIFTING ROMANCE SET DURING THE 1860s
LAND RUSH ABOUT THE POWER OF FORGIVENESS...

ROSANNE BITTNER

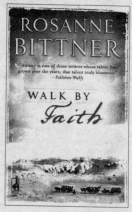

To provide a better life for her young daughter,
Clarissa Graham joins a wagon train headed west. But as the
trail turns increasingly dangerous, Clarissa fears her decision
could cost them their lives. Help comes in the unlikely form
of a jaded ex-soldier, Dawson Clements, who knows nothing
of grace, forgiveness or even love. Now Clarissa is about to
face an even greater challenge. Can she convince Dawson to
remain by her side for a journey that will last a lifetime?

WALK BY *Faith*

Steeple
Hill®

"Bittner is one of those writers whose talent has
grown over the years; that talent truly blossoms."
—*Publishers Weekly*

Available wherever paperbacks are sold!

www.SteepleHill.com

SHRB634

REQUEST YOUR FREE BOOKS!

2 FREE INSPIRATIONAL NOVELS
PLUS 2
FREE
MYSTERY GIFTS

Love Inspired
HISTORICAL
INSPIRATIONAL HISTORICAL ROMANCE

YES! Please send me 2 FREE Love Inspired® Historical novels and my 2 FREE mystery gifts (gifts are worth about $10). After receiving them, if I don't wish to receive any more books, I can return the shipping statement marked "cancel". If I don't cancel, I will receive 4 brand-new novels every other month and be billed just $4.24 per book in the U.S. or $4.74 per book in Canada, plus 25¢ shipping and handling per book and applicable taxes, if any*. That's a savings of over 20% off the cover price! I understand that accepting the 2 free books and gifts places me under no obligation to buy anything. I can always return a shipment and cancel at any time. Even if I never buy another book, the two free books and gifts are mine to keep forever. 102 IDN ERYA 302 IDN ERYM

Name	(PLEASE PRINT)	
Address		Apt. #
City	State/Prov.	Zip/Postal Code

Signature (if under 18, a parent or guardian must sign)

Mail to Steeple Hill Reader Service:
IN U.S.A.: P.O. Box 1867, Buffalo, NY 14240-1867
IN CANADA: P.O. Box 609, Fort Erie, Ontario L2A 5X3

Not valid to current subscribers of Love Inspired Historical books.

Want to try two free books from another series?
Call 1-800-873-8635 or visit www.morefreebooks.com

* Terms and prices subject to change without notice. N.Y. residents add applicable sales tax. Canadian residents will be charged applicable provincial taxes and GST. Offer not valid in Quebec. This offer is limited to one order per household. All orders subject to approval. Credit or debit balances in a customer's account(s) may be offset by any other outstanding balance owed by or to the customer. Please allow 4 to 6 weeks for delivery. Offer available while quantities last.

Your Privacy: Steeple Hill Books is committed to protecting your privacy. Our Privacy Policy is available online at www.SteepleHill.com or upon request from the Reader Service. From time to time we make our lists of customers available to reputable third parties who may have a product or service of interest to you. If you would prefer we not share your name and address, please check here. □

LIH08R

Love Inspired®

Playing Santa was not
workaholic Dora Hoag's
idea of a good Christmas.
But how could she refuse
Burke Burdett's request
for help in fulfilling his
mother's dying wish?
Especially when all Dora
wants for Christmas is a
second chance with Burke.

Look for

Somebody's Santa
by
Annie Jones

Steeple
Hill®

*Available October
wherever books are sold.*

www.SteepleHill.com

LI87499

Love Inspired.

HISTORICAL

TITLES AVAILABLE NEXT MONTH

Don't miss these two stories in October

A MAN MOST WORTHY by Ruth Axtell Morren
Though they were worlds apart, lowly bank clerk
Nicholas Tennant fell for his boss's lovely daughter.
Now a wealthy man, Nicholas is determined to get
revenge on Alice Shepard and her family. But Alice
isn't the spoiled girl he remembers; she's now a strong
woman of faith. Can Nicholas put the past aside and
become a man worthy of her love?

HILL COUNTRY CHRISTMAS by Laurie Kingery
A new house is Delia Keller's first priority when she goes
from rags to riches overnight. But the handsome former
Civil War chaplain Jude Tucker might just change her plans.
In the rugged Texas hills, he'll reach for a Christmas miracle
to restore his faith, and maybe win Delia, as well.

LIHCNM0908